Sub Rosa

SUB ROSA

Dara Lebrun

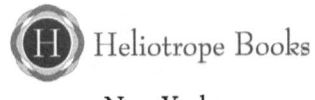 Heliotrope Books

New York

Designed and Typeset by Heliotrope Books

Cover by Naomi Rosenblatt with Dara Lebrun

For

A

Always,
though not
all ways

"She murmured this want.
Love may be toil, waste, death
Yet come pour love deep into me…"
      —*Carl Sandburg*

SAUL

Hotel

It could have been a room made of ice cream: this ceiling that fluttered with light, a hazelnut-beige door, a chair heaped with impossibly clean, white towels. Around her crept puffy duvets and pillows, two tanned arms flanking a chest that breathed easily with sleep, a leg with its knobby knee poking out from the blankets. Their bottom sheet had slipped off a corner to expose the pink mattress, like skin beneath skin.

He twitched suddenly, as though dreaming of a lunge. His eyes opened and she watched him too remember where he was. Lazily, she combed his small cloud of chest hair to find the Star of David from his grandmother. "This stays," he'd told her once, "no matter what else comes off." She traced the gold chain with her finger, venturing to his collarbone and up his neck to the smoothly shaved chin. Smiling, he whispered something too sleepy for her to hear.

She leaned over for an afternoon kiss with morning's flavor, their tongues nimble, warm, and mouths scrunched against each other's to the breaking point. Then she pulled away, brushing strands of black hair from her face.

"You'll be late," he whispered, glancing at the clock on the bedside table. "You know how your parents will be if you're late." Although he'd seen them only in photographs, he knew her parents. "And you'll carry the baby on the pillow, right?"

"No. They finally decided on Molly since my father will be the *sandek*. Spread joy between the two branches of family."

"I guess that means your papa's holding up?"

"The stroke was minor. He seems okay."

"And your crazy brother-in-law—still converting to the tribe?"

"That's the rumor."

"Why would anyone...?" he began, and stopped.

"Tamara never dated Jewish guys, and now she'll find herself married to one."

At the word "married," Saul sat up with a sigh, and Dahlia knew that her time with the man she loved was wending its way back to Earth. Soon she would leave the hotel room to attend a *bris* at her sister's home. She would have to shower without dampening her hair and show up at Tamara's with her bags, pretending to have come in straight from LaGuardia.

"Tamara guessed I'm with you," Dahlia said, brushing more black hair from her face. "Though I told her I was flying this morning."

"Have we been so obvious?"

His pale blue eyes blinked rapidly, trying to capture their wakeful focus. She reached for him again. He held her back.

"Let's get you showered," he said. "So your sister won't smell my cologne on your skin."

"It may not help—sisters read each other's minds."

"I thought my girls did that since they're twins."

"It happens with many sisters."

"Does Tamara still go to that Buddhist temple?"

Saul got out of bed, turning from Dahlia to find underwear and pants in his suitcase. Once on, the blue briefs clung snugly to his angular butt. As he shifted into profile view his fingers managed the intricacies of zipping his fly and buckling his belt as though he was playing flute. Seeming to feel her eyes on him, he continued to ask about her sister. "They've snagged her, right?"

"She goes to chant there every week—to find time for herself, and get away from Matthew and the kids. That's what I think."

"Why not take a walk in the park?" Saul asked, all zipped and buckled now, raking hands through his curly dark hair. Dahlia surveyed the abs and broad chest that were still bare, noting with satisfaction how buff he was for a man pushing fifty. He was, of course, always careful to remind her that he was forty-eight, but they were both beginning to think of him as fifty, and her as forty. When they'd met she had been "early thirties" to his "early forties."

"No one requires you to walk in the park," she said. "But people force Tamara to the shrine. That's where a cult comes in handy, I suppose."

"She's not in a cult," he stated, as though he could explain her sister. "More like a phase."

Dahlia began to protest that she knew more than he—after all, Saul had never met Tamara—and Dahlia had worried for her sister. Two years ago Tamara had nearly "gone off the deep end," weeping copiously over the phone, and shipping her a box of diaries. "If Matthew ever sees these," she'd declared, "our marriage is over." Dahlia had never opened the package or read a sentence of her sister's secret notebooks. She'd stored the box on a high shelf of her closet, assessing passivity as her prime strength. Rarely the source of family drama, she could be counted on to not interfere with those who were.

"Does Tamara tell anyone about us?" Saul asked.

"Not our parents. I think Matthew knows. But he's got enough else on his mind..."

Saul slid on an undershirt, bright against his tanned skin.

"Are Matthew and his sister getting along now?"

"Not really. But *my* sister worships Molly."

"I would think so, after all the cash Molly slipped her through the years."

"We probably don't know the half of it."

"Wish I had a sister-in-law like that."

"But you don't need one."

Saul mumbled that she was right—he didn't really wish he had a sister-in-law like that. He'd read about Molly Douglas and her philanthropic feminism and microfinancing in *Crain's* or *Fortune 500*. How someone like that, a creative techie type who once wrote ad copy, had ingratiated herself to fund managers was anyone's guess, he always said. And he "had some guesses."

Not knowing Molly well enough to defend her, Dahlia sat on the edge of the bed with a pillow folded on her lap and a scoop of shiny black hair dangling from her lowered head.

"Hey beautiful," Saul reproved softly. "I'm going to round up some coffee for us. You gonna get yourself into a shower? Or you gonna be a no-show for your first nephew?"

Bris

As the cab pulled up to her sister's apartment building, Dahlia noticed Molly and several others assembled beneath the canopy. She handed the cab driver a twenty dollar bill Saul had given her and watched change land in her palm.

Molly wore a black trench coat with a vintage scarf and European-looking leather shoes. She was chic in an unassuming way—an accomplishment in itself since she hailed from a family whose taste she'd proclaimed "unassailable but tired." She was the kind of daughter who should have made them proud. According to Tamara, Molly had won awards for her ad campaigns, collected exotic furniture, traded stock options, and co-owned a cool Cajun restaurant in the city. But there had been a seismic family upheaval years back, and only recently had amends been made. Tamara had never told Dahlia why any of it had happened. "Sworn to secrecy," she insisted.

On this cloudy April day a pair of sunglasses was perched in Molly's wavy, dark hair as though she had just lifted them to read the paper and had forgotten they were there. The two men with her wore designer suits and white shirts, unbuttoned to their collarbones with no ties. One of them had the dandyish, frisky hair and lantern jaw of a model—though he was probably in his forties.

The woman with them was tall, lanky and blonde enough to freeze Dahlia's blood. She was the type that Saul raved about, claiming, "Daya, if you ever haul me over I'll just have to find the ultimate *shiksa* dream." Dahlia reminded him that most of them were more generic than pretty. But the woman standing here was a natural beauty with high cheekbones, singing blue eyes, and shapely lips. Clearly not dyed blonde, her hair swirled easily to her shoulders in a '40s Hollywood way.

Dahlia felt like an interloper, crashing some kind of huddle among these four. But Molly nodded genially at her.

"So, can I hide my eyes when they raise the scalpel?" the man with frisky hair was saying. "Is that allowed?"

"Just close 'em discreetly," said the gorgeous, natural blonde whom Dahlia prayed Saul would never meet.

"Well," said the other man, who wore glasses, "we're really here for Molly."

"I don't want to force you to do anything," Molly emphasized.

"He'll get over himself," said the man with glasses.

"Hi Dahlia!" Molly stepped over with a friendly, if not formal, hug. "Can we help with your bags?"

"Please," said the man with short hair and glasses. Obligingly he picked up her suitcase, and they all headed indoors.

"Did you ever meet Larry, my partner?" Molly asked.

Larry, my partner.

Dahlia had assumed that Molly was as terminally single as she herself. But here was her escort—evidently Larry, the one in glasses, who shook her hand as they waited for the elevator.

Dahlia quickly sized him up: a bit older than Molly, not tall or hunky but stylish, and intelligent-looking. He was certainly more interesting than Tom, the guy Molly had been dating when Matthew and Tamara got married, and long before Molly had made her mysterious fortune.

"This is Eugenia; this is Steve," Molly continued, "and this lovely woman is Dahlia Szabó—Tamara's sister. My 'fellow aunt,' if such a thing can be said."

"Oh," said Steve, shaking her hand. "Good to meet you, 'fellow aunt.'"

Eugenia also extended her hand, then told Molly: "I'll walk upstairs."

"Nine flights." Molly raised her brow, and Eugenia smiled back, undaunted. Dahlia imagined Saul shaking hands with this tall blonde and looking her up and down as she smiled in that alluring way.

Eugenia wore white pants with suspenders that fell to her thighs (why keep them upright when you can let them fashionably dangle?), a simple black shirt and white blazer with the cuffs rolled up to reveal a striped silk lining. Dahlia felt suddenly short and 'square,' in the cotton polyester skirt suit Saul had bought on sale for her at Saks.

"I'll walk up with you," said Steve, who was hopefully Eugenia's boyfriend. And the two of them started up the marble staircase with its wrought iron rail.

A coat rack and umbrella bucket had been placed outside Matthew and Tamara's apartment door, and guests were taking off their spring coats and slipping them onto hangers as they stepped out of the elevator. Dahlia decided to keep on the jacket that went with her skirt suit. Molly looked elegant, once she removed her coat, in a black velvet dress and silver necklace edged with sea pearls. She removed the sunglasses from her head and snapped them into her purse.

It was fitting that she bear the baby on his pillow—the least her brother could do, to include her in this ceremony. Though of course, Matthew seemed to have no idea how much Molly had helped his family when he'd been out of work.

Their living room was crowded, and Dahlia watched Molly's cadre of guests—Steve, Eugenia, and Larry—contract into a circle of their own, while she herself was absorbed into a crowing clan of great aunts from Brooklyn: Renie, Chava, Sadie, Millie, all of them dressed like Cossacks' wives.

"How *byou-tee-ful* you are," they chorused, marveling as though Dahlia were a mahogany cabinet. "But still no boyfriend?"

"Boyfriend *schmoyfriend*. This one needs a husband."

"I'm dating," Dahlia said. She always said that at these kinds of occasions, to those kinds of relatives. It wasn't false.

Then her mother overtook her like a gust of wind.

"Daya, for heaven's sake, you had us so worried—I almost called the airline."

Dahlia glanced at her watch and said nothing. She was absolutely on time, arriving when others were arriving. But she had learned long ago that her parents' sense of time and, for that matter, space was governed by its own laws. Her older sister, Nurit, was even more disoriented. She had sent Tamara a bouquet from Israel before the child was born.

"Look Daya, I'm not sure Daddy's going to make it—you know, holding the baby. He might faint. How would you feel about doing it?"

The question was typically phrased like a demand.

"I—I mean, I could—though I'm not great with the sight of blood—"

In the background, a skinny fiddler and a bearded mandolin player treated the room to Yiddish tunes.

> *"To my little one's cradle in the night*
> *Comes a new little goat, snowy white.*
> *The goat will go to the market,*
> *While Mother her watch will keep*
> *To bring you back raisins and almonds,*
> *Sleep, my little one, sleep!"*

Matthew had apparently wanted the music. Tamara said it was "over the top." They seemed to disagree about everything. Already, Dahlia noticed them squabbling as they came in from a back room, Tamara holding a tiny bundle in a blue crocheted blanket.

"But he's *hungry*," she was saying.

"He can't eat now," Matthew countered her.

Before she could greet her sister and see the new baby, Dahlia was grabbed by Mama and marched across the room. Her father was slumped in an armchair, his ears half as long as his face. He had aged ten years after the stroke.

"Daddy," Dahlia said. His eyes looked warm and cloudy as they clasped hands.

"Mama was worried about you." Dahlia nodded.

"They're cutting his *schmeckle*," said her father, gripping her hand tighter.

"Fritz, listen. Daya can hold the baby."

He waved his wife away. "Don't be silly. I can do it. I want to do it."

"I'll do it if you need me to," Dahlia assured them.

"Relax," said her father. "I'm weak, but I'm above ground."

Mama had already fluttered off to the group of aunts and uncles that surrounded Tamara. Dahlia followed, eager to finally see the baby. As Mama lifted him from Tamara's arms, she explained that his crocheted cap and lace gown were among the few items that Fritz's mother had taken when they fled Budapest in the spring of 1944. This was the first time they'd be worn in the United States.

More people entered the room—several Asians, whom Dahlia figured were from Tamara's Buddhist temple, neighbors, mothers Tamara might know from the park, maybe some colleagues.

And the *mohel*, carrying a little black bag.

"I *hate* him."

Dahlia turned around. Her sister stood close beside her.

"I hate everything he stands for," Tamara continued to whisper.

"He looks beady-eyed," Dahlia agreed.

"And too pleased to be doing this."

The *mohel* put down his bag, shook Matthew's and Fritz's hands, and began arranging gauze pads and towels on the table. Dahlia was thinking about how Tamara had dreaded injections at the pediatrician's. Not that she herself had liked those needles. But Tamara had been particularly squeamish.

"He's a control freak," Tamara continued.

Dahlia giggled and asked, "Hey, where are the girls?"

"We've officially put the *goyim* on Grandparent Duty."

Matthew and Molly's parents—who were known as "the *goyim*" or "the gentiles" among the Szabós—were indeed tending to their granddaughters. Much discussion had ensued as to whether these two little girls should witness their baby brother's circumcision. It had finally been decided that "the *goys*" would stand in the back of the room with them so the girls could technically be present but "wouldn't get orchestra seats," as Matthew's father put it.

When the baby boy was back in Tamara's arms, Dahlia inspected his surprisingly sober little eyes that stared from beneath the brim of his blue crocheted cap.

"He knows something's up," she told her sister.

"Well," said Tamara, "he's just a week old. He's never seen so many people."

"And all here for him."

Tamara held his head, which—even with the cap—was shorter than her hand: an imponderably tiny head. Then Dahlia's phone vibrated with a text message from Saul, and she pardoned herself to run to the bathroom.

miss u already, he had written.

me 2, she replied.

She would probably see him that week, once they were both home—if he could steal away from his wife and family. But she loved taking trips with him and spending full days and nights together. They had looked forward to this occasion in New York for so long. She would miss looking forward to it.

A knock at the bathroom door made her jump as she sent her message to him. An elderly aunt called, "Is someone in there?"

"Yes, but I'm all done," Dahlia replied, exiting swiftly. Everyone was shuffling into the living room for the big event. As she brushed by, Dahlia overheard Molly's mother scolding Molly in a nasty tone: "...Making every other woman here feel underdressed, including *me*. This is a circumcision, not the Oscars."

Molly turned away from her mother and approached the two chairs—one where Dahlia's father sat—as *sandek* he would hold the baby on his knees—and the other for Elijah, where the baby would be placed afterward. Dahlia's great aunts began to fan themselves.

The *mohel* had put on a white coat and plastic surgical gloves. He began by asking everyone, "Please turn off all electronic and hand-held devices, or any appliance that could make a startling sound."

"And no cameras!" added Mama, from behind Daddy's seat.

Dahlia shut her phone, thinking: "Now for the brigade of sirens outside."

The *mohel* sang his opening prayer in Hebrew. Molly brought the infant solemnly over on a pillow, just a simple bedroom pillow with a light green case.

The *mohel* lifted the baby's lace gown and out popped two pink legs. Already he was crying. Matthew held a bottle in his mouth, and Tamara stood, shaking, by Matthew's side. As the *mohel* rooted around with an instrument that resembled a small set of pliers, the baby wailed more and Tamara shook more, her mouth contorting.

"Sit down," Mama commanded.

Tamara didn't.

Some of the guests turned away, not wanting to see the shiny, red dab of blood on the *mohel*'s glove.

Dahlia hoped her father knew what was happening—he seemed to waver in and out of focus. He seemed to hold and lose his breath. The father of three daughters and two granddaughters, he had almost not lived to see his first male descendant, Oren Jonathan Douglas, or "Obadiah," the *mohel* pronounced him, as the little one shrieked with pain. The name meant pine or ash tree in Hebrew, but also came from the Celtic name Oran. It represented both of his lineages.

The *mohel* had prepared a napkin soaked in wine that he now wadded in the infant's mouth for consolation. But Tamara, looking pale, pushed through the crowd and out of the living room. Dahlia noticed their mother following frantically, and relatives starting to murmur.

Matthew and Molly remained with the baby, Grandfather Fritz, and the *mohel*, who continued to recite prayers. As everyone sang "mazel tov!" and Dahlia's father was handed a glass of red wine, she tried not to hear the muffled sounds of her sister retching.

Deli

Daddy had rented the back room of a nearby deli so Matthew and Tamara wouldn't have to feed everyone at their apartment. A platter piled high with club sandwiches on rye and pumpernickel sat upon a buffet table with a white cloth, surrounded by cans of soda and V8 juice. Against the wall was a long shelf with a coffee machine and tins of tea bags, butter cookies, and cupcakes.

Whenever Daddy made a gesture like this he couldn't help but remind everyone, even in a nice-natured way, of how much he was doing. It annoyed Dahlia, yet she noticed the trait in herself. Whenever she treated a friend to even a small dinner or cocktail, she caught herself seeming similarly florid. She wished that she wouldn't; she found the behavior tacky, but had no other role model. Mama had never earned money or been in a position to treat others. And even if she had, she might not have behaved too differently from Daddy, since they were so much alike.

Her mother now wandered around the tables—clapping hands, laughing, nodding, her voice carrying across the room—as if to compensate for Tamara's absence. Daddy, though subdued from the stroke, still managed to charm booths of jovial relatives drinking root beer and eating pastrami. All of his and Mother's families clucked over his extravagance, his thoughtfulness, while the Douglas family kept to themselves and said little—as WASPs tended to.

But Matthew, in his yarmulke, toggled between the two families amiably with his new baby son.

At a small table some distance from the others, the two little girls sat with Molly and her annoyingly tall, blonde, pretty *shiksa* friend, whose name Dahlia had already forgotten. They all seemed so familiar with each other that Dahlia felt regretful. She lived in Chicago and came to New York too seldom to know these baby girls who weren't babies any longer: Kayla was a toddler and Mira was five, with large, clear eyes and long lashes. Mira and Aunt Molly scribbled with crayons on a paper placemat. The gorgeous blonde bounced little Kayla on her knee.

Molly's escort, Larry, had left with the other guy. Dahlia recognized that men of a certain age had no patience for family functions. Saul certainly didn't. He carried on like a martyr about them for weeks but always prevailed with patriarchal aplomb when the time came around.

"Your family's tame," Dahlia had pointed out to him. "We're the ones with strife and melodrama."

"Yes," Saul agreed. "And you would therefore know nothing about how dull and drawn-out tame occasions can be. Even with people you love. I just want to walk into a back room, think of you, and masturbate."

When Tamara finally arrived at the deli she seemed worn and exhausted, expending her last reserves of energy to assure various relatives that she was "just fine," but the circumcision had been "surprisingly emotional." Dahlia felt like ambassador of the family as she walked beside her sister, greeting everyone cordially, fielding questions about Matthew's new job, the little girls, their own father's recovery from his stroke.

She could never have pulled this off without Saul. Even if he wasn't right there, she could feel his affection from miles away. Before they met, Dahlia had been glum and standoffish with people, and Tamara had been the family ambassador. They had now switched roles.

Beyond earshot of the other tables, as they procured coffee and cookies, Tamara asked: "Did Saul take you to the Marriott or the Waldorf this time?"

"Ugh!" Dahlia waved her away. "Your breath stinks like vomit."

"Does not."

"You smell like Aunt Sadie."

"You smell like sex."

Sometimes the sisters reverted to acting not much older than Tamara's two little girls. The rare times they saw their other sister, Nurit, all three of them degenerated into the squeakiest baby talk and endless snitty fights.

"So now you have three children, just like we were," Dahlia reflected.

"Fancy that. So—was it the Sheraton? Or one of Trump's latest monstrosities?"

"Not your business."

"Oh come on—where'd you get your Saul fix this time?"

Dahlia's laughter cut into their words, dissipating the topic. "Your in-laws are being cornered."

Even when she was younger and less hunchbacked, their mother's aunt Sadie had a slow, hovering way about her, and she exuded a scent of talcum powder mingled with dank breath. But she was so sweet and well-meaning that it was impossible to cut her short. Now her head moved from side to side, from one of the *goyim* to the other, "like an old electric fan," Tamara whispered to Dahlia.

The sisters shared a wicked, intimate laughter, grasping each other's arms, falling back against the shelf with the coffee machine and cookies. No matter how many adult forms they would assume, from teenagers to senior citizens, they would giggle like girls, finding their own arcane humor in unremarkable occurrences.

Matthew intercepted their mirth, still holding the baby.

"Hi Daya," he said as he kissed his sister-in-law briefly on the cheek. "Thanks so much for coming." Then he turned to Tamara. "You seem better."

"I'm great."

"Well, you sounded dreadful upstairs."

"You did," Dahlia agreed.

"Thanks for listening to me puke."

Now they were grown-ups again.

Tamara carefully took the baby from Matthew and held him to her breast.

"Oh my poor, poor sweetie. Poor sweetie. He's had a big day." And more quietly: "His life will never be the same."

She rocked him in her arms.

"Congratulations," Dahlia said to Matthew.

"Thanks," he replied bashfully.

"You look like you've taken off weight?"

"I try," he said with an uncertain smile. "I wear long sweaters."

Dahlia liked her brother-in-law, despite her sister's many grievances about him. Matthew, more fragile and boyish than Saul, had a baby face with rounded cheeks, an upturned nose, and the beautiful sea-green eyes that both he and Molly had inherited from their mother. He could wax formidably stubborn on certain counts, but Dahlia knew that her brother-in-law was not a liar or cheater and would always stand by Tamara.

Agreement over two matters in particular had bonded Dahlia to Matthew: that Tamara's temple was a hoax, if not a cult ("Pseudo Buddho," he called it), and that Tamara should not favor their older daughter, Mira, over the younger Kayla.

Tamara insisted that no one could tell, that she paid equal attention to both girls. But she had to be honest with her closest confidantes—her sister and her husband: Unfortunately, the little one exasperated her.

Across the room, as if to remind them of her admission, came Kayla's screeches.

"Right in poor Eugenia's ear," muttered Tamara. "God bless her and Molly for taking care of them. Kayla's been driving me mad. She's so clingy."

"Maybe she's jealous of the new baby," Dahlia suggested.

"Whatever. She's on me all the time. And shrill like an alarm clock that never goes off even if you hit 'snooze.'"

"She's three years old," Dahlia reminded her sister.

Tamara glanced down at her new baby boy, stroking his delicate head.

"He's more quiet and independent, like Mira. Kay was jarring from day one, and a relentless klutz. She spilled milk on my cell phone last week."

"Mira must have done things like that too," Dahlia challenged her.

Tamara shook her head, closing her eyes reverently.

"She was always graceful. People are born with their temperaments. Anyway, I think Kayla's a bit autistic."

"She isn't," Matthew argued. "We've had her tested. You know that."

Tamara kissed the baby's head and continued rocking him.

"Kayla's just excitable," Matthew continued, more to Dahlia now than to his wife. "I was, at that age."

"I still am," said Dahlia. "In the right company."

"We know who that is," jeered her sister.

"Will you let up on me?"

Matthew shuffled away, leaving the sisters to grind their axes.

"So who's Larry?" Dahlia immediately whispered as he left. She hoped to keep distracting her sister from Saul. Gossip about Molly was in order—something about Larry didn't seem quite right for her. Molly should be with some Italian fashion model in skin-tight jeans, pointy shoes, who needed a shave. "What's with him and Molly?"

"Waddaya mean? Larry's gay as a goose."

"She said he's her 'partner'..."

"Business partner, dopehead! They own Mot Juste, the ad agency, together. Molly is as unattached and eligible as you."

"Maybe she has a Saul of her own stashed away somewhere," Dahlia mused.

"My impression is that men from every corner of the Earth dote at her doorstep." Tamara, still gently cradling the baby, moved closer and confided, "Once, I found a love letter at Molly's place—she was using it as a bookmark, can you believe that? It was from some guy named David who wrote something like he couldn't forget her, 'any more than a swimmer could forget water.'"

"Very romantic."

Saul didn't say such things to Dahlia. But he often repeated, "I think of you all the time, all the time"—as though he were continually surprised.

Tamara continued, "Just after Kayla was born and we were all estranged from Molly, I ran into her around the 86th Street station. She was talking with this amazingly cute guy. His name wasn't David—I remember *his* name well. Jordan."

Then Dahlia looked over at the girl's table and saw it happen.

Kayla slammed her pudgy little hand into the topping of a cupcake and tugged at Eugenia's white blazer, streaking it with chocolate.

Bravo! was Dahlia's first, and not noble, thought.

"Oh, Kayla!" whined Tamara, who had also noticed. "See what I mean?"

She entrusted the fragile, warm bundle of nephew to Dahlia, then sped across the room screaming, "Look what you did!" at Kayla.

Dahlia followed her sister to the little girl's table, her new nephew snug in her arms. Three-year-old Kayla bawled and Tamara scolded her, while Eugenia reassured them that it didn't matter.

"I own a restaurant and live with food spills. I'll get it to the dry cleaner—"

Dahlia could now hear Eugenia's slight Southern accent: "drah cleaner."

Then of course Mama jumped into the action. "Quinine water, sir!" she shrieked to a waiter in a mustard-colored jacket. "We need quinine water here!"

"Make that club soda, please!" called Molly.

Five-year-old Mira watched Molly intently, her head cocked. Aunt Molly's sea pearls were now strung around her neck. She about-faced to Kayla and shook her index finger, repeating their mother's words: "Look what you did!"

The waiter came along with a bottle of club soda, and Dahlia's phone vibrated; Saul was texting her again. She asked the waiter where the ladies room was.

When she handed the baby back to Tamara explaining, "Call of nature," her sister nodded astutely and rolled her eyes.

Ladies Room

Ravenous for Saul's message, Dahlia shut herself into a stall and locked it.

He was meeting college friends in Brooklyn at a Turkish restaurant on Coney Island Avenue. Mitch and Benny had been bugging Saul to reunite with them for years, only to be snubbed by him with such ceremony that they never took the hint. But this week they provided Saul with the perfect excuse to travel to New York City.

He'd texted Dahlia about delectable grape leaves, *but fluorescent lites, not 4 u!*

Dahlia refused to dine in bright restaurants that felt like medical offices or hair salons. He always asked her, "What are you eating—the food or the atmosphere?" It was one of their running jokes. But of course, he too preferred restaurants with low lighting so he wouldn't be seen with her.

She wrote back now: *chocolate on guest. Tam and Mama in hysterics.*

He wrote back: *slurp.*

She put her hand to her lips and giggled, even though she was alone in the ladies room. Would this be such fun, she often wondered, if they were married and always together?

She wrote back: *lick.*

He wrote: *me.*

She wrote: *me first.*

He wrote: *heads me tails you.*

Flustered by his wit, she fired off: *bite!*

A second later he replied: *ouch!*

She was going to laugh again when the bathroom door flew open. Through a crack in her stall door Dahlia saw Molly clamber in with the soiled white jacket and Eugenia at her heels.

"Won't have you decorated with chocolate," Molly was saying.

"But it's all gone."

"Let me be my compulsive self and soak it in hot water."

A faucet was swiftly cranked on.

"I just don't want Tamara to come down so hard on the kid," Eugenia commented as the water ran.

"Tamara is pickled in postpartum brine," said Molly. "You remember how I was after giving birth."

"'Remember' is one way to put that."

They both laughed.

Gluing herself against the tiled wall, Dahlia froze, phone in her fist. She felt like a spy who had just overheard a most revealing nugget: Molly had given birth. That must be the secret Tamara had sworn to, the reason Molly had been banished by her family.

Dahlia hoped she would learn more, but when the ladies room door flew open again a familiar voice sounded off.

"We'll take it to the dry cleaner!"

Mama's leather shoe appeared just below her stall door. Dahlia could see a run in her stocking the size of a dime.

"That's okay, Mrs. Szabó," Eugenia said obligingly, "Molly's handled it."

"No, give it to me. Tamara is beside herself."

"About a little chocolate?"

Apparently, Eugenia didn't know the Szabó family.

"Please don't worry," Molly entreated.

"Tamara says there's a good dry cleaner up the street…"

"Please don't worry, Mrs. Szabó," Eugenia repeated.

Dahlia didn't want to admit it, but that tall, blonde Eugenia seemed to know how put others at ease; she was probably a great maître d'. The door to the ladies room creaked shut as Eugenia escorted Mama out by the arm.

Peering through the gap in her stall door, Dahlia watched Molly lean over the sink. She thought of how Matthew had lost his job three years back—what a bizarre story, about his preferring to urinate privately, in the stall, not out in the open at a urinal. "Real men use the urinals," Saul had explained to her. "And even realer men don't wash their hands. But fear not, Daya—I'm not that 'real.'"

When Molly turned the water off, Dahlia decided to do something legitimate, like pee, just in case she was discovered. She quickly sat on the toilet, hiked up her skirt, and checked her phone as she forced her bladder to tinkle something.

u still there? Saul had written.

Always 4 u.

But she didn't text that—she just thought it.

When Dahlia emerged from the stall, Molly seemed so engrossed with drying Eugenia's white jacket that she seemed oblivious to Dahlia's having been there all along.

"Oh, hey," she murmured, holding the jacket beneath the noisy hand-dryer.

"You did a great job with that stain," Dahlia said as she washed her hands.

"I don't know if the darkness I'm seeing now is moisture or chocolate."

"I don't see *any* darkness!"

"I've spent too many years in print production," said Molly. "I can spot a point five percent tint, if one's there. Ask my designers." She smiled, her ginger-green eyes glowing. "Though I strive to be gentle with them."

"I'm sure you are."

Now Molly stood back with the jacket as Dahlia put her own hands beneath the hot air jet.

"Are you still at that gallery?" Molly asked.

"Oh yes." Dahlia wouldn't leave a job that allowed her Mondays and Tuesdays off or she'd never see Saul. She made herself indispensable to the Michelle Wiley Gallery, even though it meant working on weekends.

"I don't know if Tamara mentioned that I've done some interior decorating in the last years," Molly continued.

"Um, yeah—she said something about you going out to the Hamptons to do a restaurant."

"Quite unexpected. I did one here in the city before that—actually, Eugenia's Cajun place. These people from Easthampton came in and liked it so much that they hired me. Now I'm getting residences."

"Nice," said Dahlia, turning her hands over beneath the warm air and wondering if the father of Molly's child was a married man. Why else would there be so much shame and secrecy about it?

"Decorating is a side business," Molly explained. "But I enjoy it more than advertising these days. Maybe I'm ripe for a change. I've been working with artists. I design rooms around paintings or prints rather than finding artworks that fit a room."

"I'll bet artists love that concept."

Now they were leaving the ladies room, heading back upstairs.

"People drop ten grand on a sofa and don't think twice," Molly was saying. "But they wouldn't pay that much for a painting. The sofa gets used by the kids and dog, and no one even sees it at a dinner party. But everyone looks at artwork on the wall."

"What kind of work are you seeking—figurative, abstract?"

Molly stopped on the stairs, Eugenia's clean white jacket draped over her arm.

"No category. Anything good. A lot of what passes as art in New York bores me. Then you suddenly happen upon a treasure."

"Much like the Chicago art world," said Dahlia.

"Well, as Brecht said: 'Better a gem in manure than a stone in a mountain stream.' Do you like the work your gallery represents?"

"Fortunately, yes. It would be hell to publicize it otherwise."

"I have upcoming projects that will require new talent, as they say."

Dahlia opened her purse, looking for her business card. She almost felt that she and Molly were purposely delaying each other on the stairs, anticipating chaos. Baby Oren was screeching, and Kayla was crying now, or laughing, and someone—at first Dahlia suspected Mama, then she realized it was Tamara—was yapping at the girl.

"If you like our website and want to meet any of the artists, I'd be glad to introduce you," offered Dahlia, handing Molly her card. "Really. If you want to check out the Chicago art scene, stay with me anytime."

Except on a Monday or Tuesday.

Home

After an overdose of parents, babies, and whining children, Dahlia was thrilled by the silence of her home. She enjoyed living by herself, with two spayed male cats she'd adopted from the shelter—Phoenix and Ashes—her art books and paperbacks, her collection of Royal Doulton tableware, and lace curtains from the Old Country that had belonged to her father's parents.

It was the second story of a frame house on a tree-lined boulevard near DePaul University. The landlord couple lived below her, while one other tenant, a retired widow, rented the apartment adjacent to hers. Mrs. Johnston was often away and asked Dahlia to take in her mail. In exchange, she looked after Dahlia's cats during the rare occasions that Dahlia left town.

Such cursory contact was perfect for Dahlia, just enough—a different lifestyle from her childhood, with parents shouting at each other, at her sisters, at someone or another. Perhaps this was why she'd never felt desperate to have a family.

Sometimes she felt lonely, especially if she hadn't "gotten her Saul fix" on a given week. They had their standing Monday and Tuesday dates, but now and then he cancelled at the last minute, when an emergency came up at his job or one of his kids got sick. Whatever it was, she hoped he told the truth.

"Don't be mad at me, Daya," he'd say, invoking her childhood nickname to soften the blow. "Please don't be mad."

He had mentioned in New York that he might not be able to see her until the Monday after their first week back. A frustrating text repartee from Sunday had lasted into Monday morning.

Can't do 2day, he finally wrote. Then, an hour later: *Condensed visit?*

Whatever that meant—a conversation without sex; sex without dinner; a cat without a grin?

She had written: *what time?*

He didn't reply. Then: *sorry, don't be mad.*

She didn't reply.

Finally he wrote: *c u in 1 hour.*

At times like that she was almost ready to show him the gate, to level ultimatums as she had over the past six years: "I can't do this anymore! I want someone who's available all the time and not hiding me from his life—I want an equal." But those brushes with losers on dating sites or the more frightful gargoyles with whom her friends set her up had propelled her back to Saul with open arms, and without conditions.

In the last year she had decided that she was through with "trying other men." It was as doomed as trying dopey hairstyles, when her natural hair was long and black, not even going gray yet.

Her resolve had stabilized her and Saul's understanding that she was his—his mistress, his girlfriend; it was settled. Anyone who told her, or even implied, that she "deserved better" had no idea how irrelevant most single men were.

Now she awaited him, gazing out the window. Right on time his cab pulled up at the curb—he always visited her by cab, did not want to even risk driving his own car to Lincoln Park. There were branches of Hadassah near Dahlia's street, and his wife chaired some committee at the Greater Chicago Chapter in Skokie. Any number of these "nonprofit gadflies," as Dahlia called them, could recognize him or his car. When he took Dahlia for sushi or when they strolled through the park after lovemaking, he wore disguises: sunglasses and a visor hat in warm weather, or a woolen sock hat and thick scarf in winter.

"Cheryl wouldn't give a damn," he claimed. "We haven't had sex since the twins were born. She's even told me, 'Find a girlfriend.' Not that I'd let her know I have—but her brother Richie, now he's got a gun, and that crackpot would shoot. He's never liked me."

Short of murder at the hands of his unstable brother-in-law, Saul told her that he worried about his relationship with his children and his image in the public eye. He managed the biggest mall in Evanston and was sometimes photographed in local papers or interviewed on TV. Dahlia had understood. She even humored him and purchased a platinum wig he could wear under his hats. "So you'll look like every Swedish boy from Minnesota who goes to DePaul. I'll call you Sven."

He now appeared at her door in sunglasses and a mackinaw, under which was a black polo shirt and pleated pants. She fell into his arms without a word. He rocked her back and forth, then into the apartment, shutting the door. She plucked the dark glasses off his face, letting them scuttle across her shiny oak floor.

Then she kissed him with the sudden release of spring rain. His coat, shirt, her blouse and bra, both of their shoes slid off as though a breeze had caught them. The cats sat still and didn't claw each other. Half-clothed, she poured water for both of them. They kissed more, laughed, and cuddled. He lifted her up at one point and carried her to bed, her legs wrapped about his hips and arms around his neck, her bare breasts jiggling against his chest, his lips losing and finding hers, her long dark hair getting in the way as it always did.

A distracting five days had pulled them apart. She'd bid her family farewell in New York while he reunited with his back here. She'd returned to folders piled on her desk at the gallery and an inbox of unanswered emails; he'd met with security at the mall—apparently there had been an incident in the parking lot.

But now they found each other again as Time shut its vigilant eye and sunlight seeped through her scrim of curtains, flinging lacey shadows across the walls as trees swayed outside. Their bodies found new ways to slap gently against each other, like wind through sails or waves against the prow, a pulse beyond human will. It fed and sparked her until she gripped her feet around his legs, pulling downward, digging her heels into his calves. He moaned low against her ear so she knew he was feeling that naughty ecstasy shimmer between their legs, which made it all unbearably bright. His moans got louder, forming words like "Oh baby," and "I'm coming;" she stretched as her own belly seemed to whir, the heat in her groin exquisite, and she cried out so loud that the cats skittered away and hid.

"The *Kama Sutra*," he whispered after a couple of silent minutes, "should take lessons from us." Then he stroked her arm as she shut her eyes and her breathing became even. In her dream, she knew he caressed her.

"Don't go, Sasha," she whispered when she awoke. "Can't you stay a bit longer?"

He cleared his throat. "If we're going to walk in the park I must take my shower."

He kept a stash of Palmolive soap bars like the ones Cheryl had at home so that he could camouflage the scent of sex. Dahlia kept them in a small wicker box in her bathroom and never used "his soap;" its fragrance made her nauseous.

Saul rubbed his eyes. Phoenix, her white Angora, had come out of hiding to jump up on the bed beside them. She could see Saul grow tense, fearing the white Angora fur. Cheryl had noticed them once on his shirt and commented strangely that he was "starting to get white hairs."

"It's never easy for me to leave—you know that." As he said it, the sheets felt so warm and inviting—especially with the cat.

"Can't you tell Cheryl that something came up, with all you do for her and the kids? Would they really complain if you're home a little late?"

"Well, think of Tamara," he said. "Is she at liberty to come and go from her family?"

"Her babies *need* her. Your kids aren't even home all the time."

She suspected that he overestimated his impact on them—especially on his sixteen-year-old son, Alex, an avid hockey player who stayed up late finishing schoolwork and vanished on weekends. Girls called him up, "but he doesn't go steady with anyone," Saul had reported. "Not yet." Or maybe he didn't tell Saul everything he did with girls any more than Saul confided in him.

The twin daughters, Wendy and Lisa, were fourteen and forbidden to date "those good-for-nothing crumbs," Saul called them. "At least not good enough for my little beauties. But that's probably how every dad feels."

They were little beauties, with Saul's dark ringlets and bright blue eyes. He had shown Dahlia many photographs of them—so many that she was learning how to tell these young identical twins apart. In fact, the only photo that Saul let her keep of himself included Wendy clutching him around the waist.

If Dahlia had to guess which child was his favorite, it would be Wendy.

That must be hard for Lisa, the quieter one. Somehow, Dahlia knew how Lisa felt as the quiet child, who was often taken for granted and overlooked.

She remembered being their ages, in another era and locale, sandwiched between her two sisters in the back seat of the Volvo, heading up the peninsula on the Bayshore Freeway. Nurit, in her Patti Smith craze, lugged a cassette player everywhere, and Mama would scream, "Don't listen to that junk in the car with us," and Nurit would scream back that it wasn't junk—it was poetry. Then Daddy would scream that he was driving, so he should choose what they listened to, and he wanted news, they should all listen more to the news—when he was young, he didn't have the luxury not to. "My life was the news."

And of course Nurit shot back: "Radio news is just a state-sponsored narrative!"

And on Dahlia's other side, usually the left, Tamara had taken to reading books like *The Narnia Chronicles*, *A Wrinkle in Time*, *The Hobbit*.

"You'll ruin your eyes reading in the car," Mama always snapped, and Tamara always ignored her.

Dahlia had pulled inward, dreaming about boys at school, the handsome devils who played lead guitar, drove Barracudas, and cut math class to cohort with sleek, long-haired girlfriends. She imagined being one of those girlfriends, even for a single occasion, like Cinderella, sneaking into their place. She studied how those couples walked with their arms around each other, and how they kissed sensuously with lips and tongue. Her fantasies shut out all the family screaming.

Saul's kids never fought over what music to hear in the car because they had iPods and their cars were so sprawling that each kid could have imported a TV to watch. A former real estate client kept giving Saul ludicrous SUVs, like little school buses. Dahlia had driven around once with him and felt queasy—realizing she was more than a fly on the wall—when she noticed the girls' tennis racket bags, Alex's hockey puck, somebody's fleece wool jacket tossed over a seat.

They were her phantom family.

Some people had in-laws. She had phantoms.

"I believe you'll be pleased to know," Saul announced as he wrenched himself out of Dahlia's warm bed to shower, "that Cheryl Finerman has booked tickets to visit her mother between July thirtieth and August eighth."

Dahlia gasped, leaped up, and threw her arms around him, squeezing her naked body against his. Phoenix gracefully jumped off the bed.

"Why didn't you tell me?"

"I wanted to save it for a surprise," he said, as her embrace knocked him off balance.

"So the Mitch-and-Benny college reunion story washed?"

"It sure did."

Dahlia embraced him tighter. Her birthday—her fortieth birthday—was August sixth.

"Thought you'd like to hear it," he whispered into her black hair.

As she nodded, her hair stroked his cheek.

He laughed again, clearly trying not to get aroused.

"You think I forget you when we're not together. But I think about you all the time."

And she chorused his inevitable refrain: "All the time."

Then she stood back and he studied her with a quizzical smile. "I don't forget you. Perhaps you forget me?"

"Fishing for compliments?"

"No. But I wonder what you think when I'm not around."

Dahlia found herself quoting Molly's suitor whose romantic letter Tamara had spied: "'I couldn't forget you, any more than a swimmer could forget water.'"

TAMARA

Diaries

She wished she could scream her joy to even one person.

"Think about where you'd like to go for your birthday trip," he'd offered when they walked in the park. Had she ever seen the Hagia Sofia, the Taj Mahal?

"Oh Sasha," she said, "I'd be happy in New York or Florida—wherever you told her the Mitch-and-Benny reunion was happening. Wouldn't that be easier for you?"

"Let's not think about my convenience, for once. It's your special birthday. Let's go somewhere you'd really enjoy, somewhere you're curious about."

If they left a day later than Cheryl and returned a day earlier, they would still have eight days—which was more time than they'd ever spent together.

Dahlia wanted to share this little thrill with someone.

But she knew that if she called Nurit overseas she'd get a lecture about her immorality and bad karma. Tamara was less ideological, but she too was harsh. She didn't believe in what Dahlia was doing—"Shamelessly *shtupping* someone else's husband," her younger sister often scolded.

Aside from her sisters, Dahlia had three kinds of friends: old friends who also shunned her relationship with Saul and had distanced themselves from her, old friends who didn't cast judgment but always wanted to "introduce her to someone," and new friends who didn't know about Saul and never would.

Then there was Molly—not an "old friend," or even a friend, yet Dahlia had known her for years. She was not a sister, yet she was family. And Molly knew, at least abstractly, about Saul. But she had never remarked upon it, never volunteered the slightest hint of aspersion or disapproval. Thankfully, she never suggested setting Dahlia up with anyone. Instead, they had spoken after the *bris* about artwork and interior design.

It had been refreshing to speak with a woman about something other than men.

When she wasn't preoccupied with her birthday plans, Dahlia found her mind skipping like a sparrow over the mysteries of Molly. Who was her baby, and what had happened to it? She must have gotten pregnant intentionally—Molly was too resourceful to have had "an accident." Dahlia herself had been on the pill for years. It wasn't hard to come by.

All of this was probably explained in Tamara's diaries from two years ago. Dahlia felt overcome by a desire to read them now. She had never been asked not to. She had been asked only to make sure that Matthew never saw them or heard about them.

Tamara went through cycles of intensive diary writing, usually when her life was stressful. She would convert everything into a meticulously written story. Apparently, this helped "mesmerize her out of a funk," as she put it. And it also helped her remember conversations while they were fresh in her mind. Back in high school she'd written up her arguments with Nurit and their parents in crisp detail.

Dahlia herself had never felt the faintest urge to write in diaries. She had secretly enjoyed Daddy scolding Tamara back then for "spending so much time on a project that no one will ever see." But when Tamara read back a conversation they'd had a year ago her father had changed his tune, declaring that she had talent and should become a writer.

"But I can't write fiction," Tamara had protested. "I don't make anything up. I just write exactly what I know and see."

"Be a journalist," Mama suggested.

"She'll need to write fiction for that," Daddy had rejoined.

Dahlia easily found the box of diaries on a shelf in her closet, beneath her plastic sweater bags—a simple brown UPS box sealed with packing tape, which contained several notebooks.

The first one she grabbed seemed like the most recent. There were notes about the Heart Sutra and forgiveness, and then various haikus:

> I pray to Buddha
> And keep on
> killing mosquitoes.
> —Issa

This was followed by a long, rather dull exegesis on *letting everything be as everything is*. Dahlia hoped Tamara's earlier notebooks, the ones in which she was losing her mind, were more interesting than this one in which the Pseudo Buddho temple was finding her mind for her. She reached for the one at the bottom of the pile with a soft leather cover and flipped to a middle page: *I wish I could be Jordan's friend. He knows this family too.*

That sounded more promising. So she started at the beginning, the earliest date, almost exactly three years ago:

4/27/03

I took Matt for better or worse. Now is one of those worse times. Everything's happening too fast to understand, and I'm getting whiplash. If I don't write it down somewhere I will go crazy.

Last week they axed him. They'd been beating around the bush for a while, but they leveled the blade on Tuesday.

Schmuckface suddenly showed up in his office with a security guard and said, "Okay Douglas, you're out of here. Pack it up and don't come back."

At first Matt thought it was a prank and just stood there.

"I said, start packing."

"What happened?" my poor husband asked. "What's going on?"

"Don't play dumb."

"Is this some kind of joke?"

All his books and files came home in a couple of shopping bags, which are still in the foyer. The goys don't know about it, and I haven't told Mama and Daddy either.

Dahlia remembered that worrisome gap between Matthew's jobs. She'd heard about it through her own haze of loving and fighting with Saul.

4/30/03

He hasn't gotten out of bed for days now. Hasn't showered and is beginning to smell waxy. Last night I slept in the girls' room and I told Mira, "Daddy has a cold."

5/2/03

These fuckers knew we had refinanced and are putting in a new kitchen. Matt said they never took him seriously. Oh, we know Sean and Lenny did, but the others didn't respect him. That's what's eating at him now. Years of being jousted then ousted.

They told him he had blurted out "confidential information about a client," which is a heap of horseshit. Matthew's so discreet that he verges on paranoid.

I feel terrible for him, but I wish he'd reassure me that he'll get another job. We're close to the bone with two little ones, and unemployment insurance is a pittance compared to his salary. We have to put the severance money into repaying our hefty refi. And of course we have my salary, but how far can it stretch before it snaps? Then there's this assessment the damn board keeps alluding to.

Yesterday Mama and Daddy offered "interest-free loans," which I may take them up on. Though I need another loan like I need another soiled diaper around here. Talked to Dahlia as well. She was shocked—thought Matt's position was so solid, that he'd make partner soon. Appearances!

Matt still has not told the goys. They called us yesterday to see how Baby Kayla is doing, but we were "not available for comment" and never called back.

5/6/03

Today feels like spring, some consolation after the April snowstorms.

But then I wonder, do I even want spring? So I can peel off my sweaters and reveal to the world the lump I've become, a lump that eats and suckles and now lives beside another lump that sleeps all day?

Will warm weather bring fights about using the air conditioner? Light evenings that will make me feel claustrophobic staying inside? Jealousy of other women's great legs?

O have mercy and stay chilly, World!

"Jealousy of other women's great legs?" Dahlia muttered, remembering her sister in bikinis, making fun of Dahlia in her one-piece.

5/12/03

Matt's birthday is tomorrow. I asked him what he'd like to do, and he said he didn't care.

"Well that's great," I said. "Of course, we could do something fun and different— like you staying in bed and eating corn bread and pop tarts and watching American Idol, *and me changing Kayla's diapers and reading* Barbar King of the Elephants *to Mira. How does that sound?"*

He didn't answer, just looked out the window.

5/15/03

So I ran into Molly today. It was like seeing a ghost who's more alive than the living.

She popped out of the 86th Street station with some preposterously sleek young dude, and they were talking so intensely that they walked right passed me. I considered not saying a word to her, because Kayla was in the carriage…the niece she's never been allowed to meet.

But something made me turn and follow them down Broadway.

When I called "Molly!" they both whipped around. Hell, was he cute. So thin his pants hung off his hips, crazy black hair, like he'd just gotten out of bed, big brown eyes, and raggy, unshaven cheeks that you want to run your tongue over. And I haven't thought about running my tongue over anyone, including my husband, for a while. His shirt was open. He wore silver chains and beads, even cowrie shells, and held a funny-looking instrument case in one hand.

If I knew I was going to meet him today I would have dressed like a human being, not a rag doll.

Molly could see what I was thinking.

"Fancy meeting you here, Tamara," she said. "Well, it's both of our neighborhoods. This is Jordan."

I touched him. I shook his hand. I couldn't say anything when he looked at me the way men used to look at me.

"I know you," he said. "Heard you on Molly's voice mail, seen photos of you for years."

"I'm sure I looked better twenty pounds ago."

Jordan shook his head with the sweetest hint of protest.

"Is that Kayla?" Molly was peering into the carriage.

"Sleeping," I said. "Of course that means she'll be up later, and I won't sleep tonight. Can't get her on a schedule, like Mira."

"How is Mira?" Molly asked wistfully.

"Using the potty now," I said. "And starting to speak in sentences."

Molly hung her head, and I felt like shit.

"We should meet in the park so you can see her again. It's time," I told her.

"You'd break my brother's injunction?"

"Do you know that he lost his job?"

She asked what happened.

"Matt won't say much. In fact, he's been in pajamas for two weeks, since he filed for unemployment insurance. Frankly, everything stinks. We're paying for a new kitchen that the contractors didn't even finish…"

Jordan said something like contractors make musicians look dependable.

"And you'd know." Molly's smile told me they'd had more than sex. They'd had trouble. Then she said to me: "Call me anytime, or come by. We should talk. If I can help you I will."

We all said goodbye, and I told Molly it was great to see her, I'd missed her and she said, "Likewise." I was pushing Kayla's carriage uptown on Broadway when suddenly Jordan bounded up beside me like a rangy puppy.

"Tamara, I want you to have my CD."

He handed me one that was still wrapped in cellophane.

"Oh, thank you," I said.

I could hardly look at him. The word Ladino flew into my mind. I'm not even sure what that means—I think it's the Sephardic equivalent of Yiddish. I just thought of wailing songs and flamenco guitar and Jordan's dreamy dark eyes.

"Call Molly," he said. "Really. Call her."

"I'm going to."

"It's easy to take her for granted," he confessed to me. "I'm the expert. I didn't realize she could be hurt. You forget that a strong person hurts too. Don't make my mistake."

Then he kissed my hand. HE KISSED MY HAND.

I looked back and saw them walking, his arm around Molly's shoulder. She wasn't touching him.

As I headed to the park a pigeon landed before me on the sidewalk and spread its wings, like an angel—a common slob pigeon. Somehow that broke my heart. I parked the carriage, sat on a bench outside Riverside Park, and lost it.

What beautiful man solaces me when I'm hurting? Matthew and I used to care for each other that way.

Jordan pulled me back to that more vulnerable and romantic time in my life.

Those great-looking guys Dahlia and I used to meet who'd buy us drinks in cafés, in New York, in Ireland or Paris. Even that crazy one who wanted us both at once, who called us Sweet Hungarian Paprika and Spicy Hungarian Paprika—I forget which of us was "sweet" and which was "spicy."

And Brendan, with his long dark bangs and Dublin accent singing "The Town I Loved so Well." That part of my life is over forever. It's not like every second of it was great while it was happening. There was a lot of faking, a lot of boring tripe.

But it's gone now.

Not for Dahlia. Once those good-looking guys had started buying her drinks she'd never stopped to get married. And as for that guy who'd wanted them both, she'd driven around with him in a 1930s MG convertible, and she had been Sweet Paprika. He had pegged Tamara as Spicy. She thought to remind her sister, but remembered that she was spying on her diaries.

5/17/03

"When was the last time you put on a new pair of underwear?"

I was hurling underwear at my husband, one pair after the other.

Then I called him a mushroom on a log.

He looked shocked—well, wake up and smell the laundry!

"Tamara, quit it!" he barked at me.

But no, I didn't want him to lie around one more night, laughing over one more fucking stupid TV show while I bathed the girls and read to the girls and tried to clean the living room and organize our bills, and answered phone calls from his fucking mother and made up excuses like, "He's working late!" (Yeah, right.)

"I'm not quitting anything!" I screamed at him, and with some effort I yanked the whole underwear drawer out, and it crashed to the floor. "I'm the one who gets up early every morning and deals with whatever contractors do or don't show up; I'm the one who meets with Veronica and gives her bottles and food and cash for the kids and then goes to work all day, and deposits your unemployment check in the bank at lunch hour. All you do is sleep and watch TV and sleep more, and maybe eat some processed carbohydrates, then sleep again, then watch TV, maybe take a shit if you're lucky, then sleep again..."

"Well, figure it this way," he said. "I'm resting up. Because I know we can't afford Veronica anymore, and sooner or later I'll be doing her work."

"Can't afford Veronica? We NEED Veronica."

"You think your dad had a Veronica when they were hiding in the Swedish embassy in Budapest? We're not the gentry class these days, Tamara."

"I don't understand this. Why are you thinking about Veronica's job? You should be looking for your own!"

"With what recommendations? With what connections? You don't get it."

He threw his arms up.

Then I suddenly did get that all these weeks he'd been lying around here reeking of b.o. and eating chips and laughing at silly TV shows, he was burying the coffin of his career.

I said something like: "If that's how you're thinking, why haven't we talked?"

He said something like: "Why don't you ever ask me? You're so busy taking charge and worrying over everything—you look at me with pity. Do you realize you sometimes cringe when you see me?"

Then he told me what had gone on in the men's room with him and Schmuck-face, as we sat in a mountain of underwear on our bed.

I'm not convinced that it's why they fired Matt. Everyone in that office knows what gets Schmuck-o through an afternoon. I hate afternoons myself, especially be-tween two and four. Can barely keep my eyes open; you could gag me with a spoon. But some of us get by on coffee, nothing stronger. And Matthew had seen...

At that point Tamara's black pen lost its ink. Lists that she had titled "Painful Math"—expenses, loans, bank account balances—followed in blue ink.

Dahlia put down the notebook for a moment. Her sister had been paying more in mortgage alone than Dahlia earned each month.

She looked across the room at her empty Royal Doulton sugar jar, decorated with a filigree of orange and yellow roses.

Four years ago, when she had first moved into this apartment in Lincoln Park with its oak floors and high ceilings, Saul had offered to help her with rent. "When I'm here," he said, "I make myself quite at home."

But she'd refused to accept a cent, though she earned thimbles to his gallons.

"It's a matter of principle," she'd told him.

One morning last year she opened the sugar jar to store some wrapped can-dies left over from a gallery opening. To her surprise she'd found a pile of tightly rolled bills with thin rubber bands around them.

When she deposited them into the bank, the amount equaled half of her rent for three years.

After his visits she still found rolls of bills jammed in with the candies. He must slip them in when she went to the bathroom or checked the weather online or something.

They never spoke about it.

5/21/03

Jordan's band is called Black and White, *and piano keys slant across the CD cover—which of course was "designed by Molly Douglas, produced by Molly Doug-*

las, Dedicated to with loving gratitude to Molly and all she's made possible."

I just remember his aphrodisiac lips saying, "Call Molly."

5/22/03

Today Lenny Kaplan called us.

"How's Matt doing?" he asked when I answered.

"Not well."

"Is he around?"

"No, he's out."

Out of sorts. Not out of the home. I doubt he's been outside for days.

"Tamara, you know my hands were tied."

"Yes, we understand."

"But if he ever needs a referral from me or a heads-up..."

"That's kind of you to offer, Lenny."

"He did fine work—beyond technically competent. Clients have already asked about him."

Lenny always mumbles, like he's chewing gum or yawning.

"I appreciate hearing that. I'll let him know you called."

I felt that Lenny had one more thing to tell me, but didn't.

5/23/03

Today Mariko at work left everyone pamphlets about her Buddhist temple.

I got off the train at 72nd Street and wandered to Riverside Park. I must have sat for hours as the sun set, listening to cars rush by on the highway. I read about Mariko's temple and was struck by a quote from an old Japanese proverb: "If you seek shelter then rest your wings beneath the largest tree."

That's when I decided to go to Molly's.

I called Veronica instead of Matt. Just told her I would be home late and asked her to stick around. I was ready to pay extra. Luckily she could stay.

When Veronica left, I figured Matt could look after our girls. For once. If it was going to be his new career he'd better get used to it.

5/24/03

Molly and I went through our finances, and she proposed a way to help. I felt incredibly close to her. It was like having a real older sister, not a basket case to feel sorry for, like Dahlia or Nurit.

Dahlia slammed the notebook on her lap.

"Thanks a lot," she muttered. "And fuck you."

She had wanted to get to know Molly better. Now she felt only resentful.

Still, after a wounded moment Dahlia reopened her sister's diary and read on, as though she were gobbling chocolates, knowing that she was headed somewhere risky.

Maybe Molly's "no longer Matt's sister," as he put it—but she is mine.

"Suppose I whack that refi down by three quarters? So you'll still get the envelope from the bank, and he'll see you writing the checks."

"And he won't know the difference."

I said that with surprising derision.

"Come by next week with your mortgage statement," Molly said. "We'll take care of it. I'll also give you a credit card from one of my companies. For the extra things you may need—a cute sweater for Kayla, a doll for Mira, a pedicure or massage for yourself. And whatever you tell my brother, or don't tell him, is up to you."

"But this is too good to be true."

"It's nothing. Tamara, if you want three hundred grand, you've got it. But if you want a good relationship with my brother"—she shrugged—"I don't have that myself."

5/26/03

Went to the Cajun place with Molly. When I called to tell Matt I was "out with friends" he sounded nonplussed, not mad at me. Veronica was still there, bless her, just ready to leave.

"I'll be back in an hour," I promised him.

He said it was good for me to get out of the apartment. I was pleasantly sur-prised by his empathy—the old Matt, the man I'd loved and married. Still around sometimes.

Molly and I headed downtown in a cab to a restaurant she now co-owned with this person Eugenia, she was saying. I didn't understand how; the story was too com-plicated and the Scotch she served when we were talking over my finances too potent. It didn't matter. I was figuring that my visit to her had saved us two or three frigging grand a month. I could sit back and quit worrying; no crisis on my shoulders now.

"We have live music in the evening—jazz and Cajun, to complement the cui-sine. But tonight we have a bluegrass band called The Hot Flashes. All women over forty-five..."

I asked if Jordan's band ever played there, and here's what she said:

"Er, well—that's touchy. Hypothetically, yes. Actually no. Jordan and Eugenia in one room is not my idea of a fun night...any more than mixing plum wine and cognac."

I made a drunken note of it: find out who Eugenia is, exactly, and why she and Jordan are "not fun" to mix. And while I'm at it, here are some reasons why my crush on Jordan is more fucked than a wood bin of matches:

I'm married.

He's Molly's ex.

I'm married to Molly's brother.

Anything else? Let's see. I have two babies, and I look like shit. Oh, and let's not forget that Molly just bailed our asses out of debt.

So it was good I wouldn't see him there, or anywhere.

It was just a feeling that swept over me like a sun-shower that day we met at the 86th Street station.

Dahlia now flipped forward, avoiding more pages of frantically scribbled math. She wanted to know whether her sister had an affair with Jordan—if that was why she carped about Saul. Scanning for the name *Jordan*, she stopped at the sight of her own.

"They think she has no interest in dating anyone and no social life. That's why they wonder if she's agoraphobic or something, like an adult Asperger's case."

"Not our Dahlia," Matt said.

Across the room Dahlia's two cats batted each other with their front paws and scrambled on the oak floor. Dahlia dropped the open diary on her knees. Her parents declared her "asocial" because they didn't know how she spent every second, and Tamara pronounced Kayla autistic at age three because she spilled milk on her mom's cell phone and bawled. Who were *they* to cast aspersion—Tamara chanting in her Buddhist cult, and her parents more high-frequency than a cage of canaries?

Dahlia remembered, with a brief smile, her college boyfriend's reaction to Mama and Daddy: "Too bad their compulsive energy can't be harnessed for the good of humanity."

She glanced back at her sister's diary again.

"Dahlia's 'given all to love,'" he said.

"Can we be more Emersonian? Please, Matt?"

"Dahlia's in a dream world. But it's more innocent than anything we can say about Molly."

I could've smacked him, or at least screamed. But we kept the decibels low, in deference to our sleeping baby, so I trailed him around, hissing: "My sister is fucking another woman's husband, behind her back, hoping that one day he might leave her! You find that innocent?"

Husband said, "Not my style. But it comes from love, and love can be weak."

"Oh, kudos for your heartwarming compassion. Meanwhile, Molly helped her best friend have a child. That's all she did, Matt. She kept up her end of an agreement."

He gave me an eerie look, with his golden-green eyes and unshaven cheeks, before uttering the cliché of all times. "Behind every great fortune is a great crime."

Then we both looked at the bedroom door, and there was Mira. I had no idea

how long she'd been standing there flexing her skinny little body, or what she'd un-
derstood of our exchange. Veronica must have brought her home from the Davises
without our even noticing.

There it was: Molly helped her best friend have a child. But what about Molly's
birthing a child herself? It slowly occurred to Dahlia that some mixture of this had
happened.

6/9/03

Matthew resents that Molly knows how to win the game.

He's a pussy, at home in a bathrobe.

He doesn't get that people have different strengths. Not all of us can marry and
have families. Not all of us can win the game. That's why we need each other.

"Once we pay your mortgage," Molly told me in the cab, "we'll pop some cham-
pagne."

Oh, I'll drink to this favor...and to not telling Matthew about it.

Not that Molly asked me to keep it secret; she said that what I do or don't tell him
is my choice. And she's giving me a credit card, to buy all the skin lotion and perfume
he doesn't allow me. I'll have to stash it all at work, but who cares? I'll have it.

So it was fine for Tamara to keep secrets from her spouse but not for Saul to
do so. Dahlia flipped through more pages, getting paper cuts on her sister's gripes
about a co-worker, shopping lists, and another call from Lenny Kaplan.

But Dahlia wanted to find out if her sister had cheated on Matthew.

WASPy Boys Named Colin

6/16/03

I thought about Colin, alone at his table with a paperback—broad shoulders in a plaid shirt the colors of peanut butter and jelly, thick brown hair dangling over his face. What the fuck is going on with me?

I've been in love with Matthew so long that other men became wallpaper.

Haven't looked at them in years.

Now can't stop.

Wished I knew how the conversation had gone with Colin and Eugenia. Not that it mattered. And it didn't matter what Jordan said to Molly either...but it did.

I have fans again.

Even if my husband isn't one of them.

7/17/03

The irony, that Dahlia and I had labeled a whole genus of males "WASPy Boys Named Colin." Even if their names were Eric or Curtis or Gregory, they were all "WASPy Boys Named Colin."

"He'd like to meet you."

The mythic Eugenia migrated my way, rolling her hips.

"You guys...if you're trying to make fun of me..."

"We're not!" Molly contended.

"Promise," said Eugenia. "He really asked who you are."

"Should I invite him to the table?" Molly coaxed. "He's all alone."

"Really nice guy," added Eugenia. "NYU student—from Ohio, I think."

"Oh, Jeez" I told them, "I've had so much wine that I can't think, much less talk, to someone I don't know."

"Best time to do both," said Eugenia.

"Heed her—she was a bartender for fifteen years."

"Well, maybe it's the best time for singles. But I'm a married mother with two young children."

"So is Leah of The Hot Flashes," said Molly. "And she talks to Colin. In fact, it was Leah who detected the eye contact between you and him."

"Eye contact! You mean me trying not to stare."

"And him pretending he didn't notice, and wasn't elated."

"Molly!"

I stood up, grabbed my purse, and marched out.

Could not be there one more second.

But hadn't had so much fun in years.

Dahlia slammed the notebook shut and stared out her lace curtains at the flickering green leaves that blurred with her tears.

After years of calling Saul "a creep," her sister wasn't even as loyal as he. Dahlia knew that she was Saul's only girlfriend. Even if he wanted a whole harem—and she was fairly certain that he didn't—he was too fretful about being caught to do anything about it. And he didn't have the time.

But there seemed no end to the men who orbited her sister's galaxy, according to this diary. She was even recycling her Brendan fantasy, after all that heartbreak. And Molly's ex, Jordan, and now the Ultimate WASPy Boy Named Colin.

But had she gone so far as to cheat on her husband?

7/21/03

I must be crazy. I must be losing it. I am losing it. Today at lunch I went downtown, to Washington Square Park...looking for Colin.

I knew I could probably find him again at Eugenia's Cajun some evening. But that would be too obvious. It must look like I just ran into him: "Oh, weren't you at my sister-in-law's Cajun hoedown a couple of weeks ago?"

But even that sounds contrived.

I must design this as cleverly as Saul and Dahlia do their thing.

If I had less pride, I'd ask her for tips.

7/22/03

For a while things were getting better with Matt. He was actually out of bed and dressed in the morning, taking walks, reading the paper and looking at online job ads. Things were starting to feel normal.

"And then he talked to our parents," Molly guessed before I could tell her. "Our wonderful, supportive parents. Always there to lend a hand when the chips are down."

Even if they didn't lend a helping hand, they didn't have to knock the chips even lower. Well it's really just Glynnis—harpie/sadist/bitch-witch!

No matter how whack my parents are, they don't cut us down like that.

We were on our way to her bank for the money order when I told Molly about Jill's offer. "My friend at work has a house by the Jersey shore. Thought it might be good for Matt and me to get away from home, be out by the sea, and just talk. We need to talk. He's agreed to go on the second weekend in August. We'll take the baby with us, but I was thinking of leaving Mira somewhere else so we don't get distracted with her. How would you like to have her for that weekend?"

Molly said, "Tamara, I'd love nothing more."

I told her, Matt doesn't have to know.

Molly said she didn't want to put me in that position.

I held up the mortgage envelope.

I'm in it already, to my elbows. Look, what can I say? "He's not making good decisions now. In his own way, he's out of control. We've done things his way for a long time, and we've hurt you and hurt ourselves. Before we hurt our daughters, it's time to try my way."

7/28/03

"Do you remember Aunt Molly?" I whispered to Mira as I lifted her into the Maclaren stroller beneath our canopy. "We're going to see Aunt Molly now. She's Daddy's sister, just like Kayla is your sister. Of course, she's a grown-up."

"I know," said my disarmingly precocious daughter.

We won't leave town for another two weeks. But I figure I'll get Mira accus-

tomed to Molly before she stays with her for the weekend.

It will be the first time she's away from us.

I know this is the right thing to do. I told Mira that we're playing a game, and if she doesn't tell Daddy, I will take her to the water park downtown. We even shook on it!

Matthew, of course, is asleep upstairs. The more the goys slam him about not looking for work, the more he sleeps.

It's a lovely day and I'm in a shirt I rarely wear because I thought it looked slutty. Someone gave it to me as a present. Some friend I lost touch with. It's the kind of thing I almost threw out a million times but kept, for some reason.

People look at me pleasantly as I walk past them. Maybe they're looking at me pleasantly because Mira is so cute. I don't know. All I do know is that Colin told Eugenia that I'm "very pretty," and Molly's money order was accepted by the bank—I sent it Registered Mail with a cover letter, like the loan officer told me to.

So life is better because at least we can afford it, and at least I still make an impression on men and haven't become an extraneous and invisible married mom.

All thanks to Molly.

She deserves to know Mira.

Dahlia agreed.

In fact, she even agreed with Tamara's assessment that her affair with Saul was reprehensible, and that Molly's surrogate motherhood for her friend—clearly the source of all the family *tsuris*—was not. She appreciated Matthew's defense of her sincerity but knew that his sentiment was ill-founded.

Adultery was something she had grown up knowing was immoral, something the Ten Commandments condemned.

And she was helping the person she loved to do it.

Phil

To Dahlia's disappointment, there was no description of Molly meeting Mira.

For all the distress of reading her sister's diary, Dahlia would have enjoyed that scene between Molly and Mira.

And there was not much more about Colin.

But WASPy boys Named Colin could evidently be named Phil.

8/6/03

Like a stalker, heading down to Washington Square every day—at lunch or after work. Keep hoping I'll just run into him, but of course I won't. There are thousands of NYU students, and who knows where Colin lives and when he takes classes?

But I just can't swallow my pride and go back to Eugenia's or even go to one of Jordan's gigs that I see listed online…that would be even less cool.

Everyone would see through me like an X-ray.

I have to find some guy that nobody knows.

And it's Dahlia's birthday. In honor of her, I'll start my adulterous quest!

8/10/03

Now I really must hide this notebook. Maybe I'll throw it in the Hudson River, or send it to Dahlia or Nurit. Just keeping it at home makes me feel like I've taken in a stray cat with lice and other vermin that will hurt my family.

Okay—I'll just write it, write it, write it. Matt doesn't know I do this. He thinks I work on something for the office when I'm scrawling in here.

And who am I writing to anyway?

My future self?

My present subconscious?

My daughters, when they get old enough to understand this?

My grandchildren or great-grandchildren?

God?

Everyone, no one?

I'm doing this almost as a physical act, like shaking out my hands or running in place.

Today I met a young man on line at the deli on University Place, hoping to "run into" Colin. I took one look at him paying for his turkey club sandwich, slipped the rings off my left finger, and tucked them into my purse. He wasn't as tall as Colin but cut and hunky with curls of blond hair, a cutely squashed snub nose, wearing an NYU T-shirt and khaki shorts.

I asked if he had change for a five, and that's how it all began.

We ate our sandwiches out in Washington Square Park together—couldn't believe myself. I still had half an eye open for Colin! My new friend is Phil, and he's from upstate New York. I was letting my slutty blouse slip over my shoulders and practically shoving my boobs in his face...but oh so nonchalantly. He took the bait, let us just say.

Told him my name was Dahlia.

I used the credit card Molly gave me to check us into a room at a hotel on Waverly. She'll never find out. I was telling her how guilty I felt last month, running up nearly six hundred bucks on clothes and toys for the girls and a couple of spa treatments for me—that, after all she did for our mortgage.

She waved me away. "My assistant handles it. I don't look at bills."

I told her she should give me a monthly cap so I don't go hog wild.

She said, my "wild hog was a Wall Street wife's appetizer." Apparently some friend of Alessandra's spent seven fucking grand on a fucking purse. Not even an attractive purse, Molly claimed, adding: "Not that it would matter."

I insisted on a monthly cap, and she finally said, "Two grand. How's that?"

"It's really hard for me to accept money I don't earn," I admitted. And we resolved that I'd do some freelance proofreading for her agency, Mot Juste, once I'm back from the Jersey shore—an arrangement that's boosted my morale.

But Phil was impressed when I whipped out the platinum card. He tried to look at my name and I hid it, telling him it was "my sister's credit card. And she'd kill me if she knew what I was using it for."

He lifted his eyebrow, set fire 'down there.'

Another expenditure from the platinum card awaited him: black silk bikini briefs with a matching bra. I almost went thong, but Jill told me that hers got stuck inside on her honeymoon—and it had plastic baubles on it. Don't know what she was thinking.

Before we walked into the room Phil grabbed me and we started making out. He doesn't kiss as well as Matthew, which, I guess, is a good thing. Or is it? What's the point of an illicit lover if he doesn't kiss as well as your husband?

But the compliments he whispered sure irrigated my parched ego. I felt treasured, like I used to feel with Matt. He swept his hand over my bare boob and told me I was "just perfect."

What should I do first, I wondered as we teetered by our bedside—married vixen that I've become, overworked publishing employee on a lunch break, worried mom abusing the privileges of her sister-in-law's credit card? To what tasty transgression could I treat this flattering undergraduate who thinks I'm named Dahlia?

I imagined one scenario, rejected because I knew he'd come too fast, and I revised the blueprint—old pro that I am at anticipating the arc of male desire. Just running my fingernails lightly down his abs and thighs, thinking to myself, 'This may be the last time in your life you ever touch such a firm body.'

Guilt welled up about Molly. Shit, what would she think if she saw me now?

Even though she and Matt aren't even speaking...well look, she can touch guys like this all the time. She's free. She's single. This is my one indiscretion. I'm not going to make it a habit. Anyway, she had teased me about Colin. That must be her way of granting me permission...

Phil was a "Silent Wonder," as Dahlia and I used to say.

Climax without a sound!

I kind of missed those arousing little grunts and moans of Matt's...by the time I came, the man on my mind wasn't Phil or Colin. I was thinking of my infuriating husband.

Kind of ridiculous to go out of my way to cuckold him, to even spend his own sister's money doing it, and to end up thinking about him anyway.

Does it mean I'm ultimately loyal—or an even worse traitor?

8/11/03

Before we parted, Phil insisted that we see each other again.

Like a total bitch, I said, "Listen, I live in Chicago. I'm involved with someone, and I don't want you getting hooked on me."

"I am already, Dahlia."

I told him to meet me at the deli at half past noon on Thursday.

But this is it.

Matt and I are leaving town this weekend, and we're going to work everything out.

I'm just cracking my knuckles with Phil.

Dahlia hurled the diary across the floor, sending both cats in a terrified frenzy into the closet.

The Ten Commandments Redux

"What I don't understand," said Saul after he'd heard Dahlia's rehash of her sister's tawdry secrets later that afternoon, "is how Molly had three hundred big ones to fork over to an estranged brother and sister-in-law. Who has such funds at their fingertips, not tied up in investment?"

Dahlia remained on her bed, gazing at the ceiling.

"How do we know it wasn't tied up?" she finally replied. "There was a gap of some weeks...between their first meeting and Tamara paying the bank. I mean," Dahlia grumbled, "if you would just read it for yourself..."

But Saul refused, shaking his head from side to side.

"I'm not reading your sister's diary. It was juvenile enough that you did."

She buried her face in the pillow, furious that he was dwelling on Molly's assets and not Tamara's infidelity.

They hadn't had sex that afternoon, and they weren't going to.

"Molly was setting your sister up to leave Matt," Saul insisted. "In an understated way. Telegraphing to Tamara that she'd have plenty of financial support. No matter what."

Dahlia sighed angrily and rolled back onto her side.

"Jesus, Sasha! Matt lost his job, he was too depressed to get out of bed, and they had two babies. Tamara's world was going to shit. And no one else—not the *goys*, who have money, not our crazy parents, or me, or Nurit—did a damn thing to help her. No one did, except Molly." Dahlia raised her torso, supporting herself on her right arm. "And now you ascribe evil motives to the one person in that diary who doesn't come off like a weasel?" She swallowed and added, "Including you and me."

Saul closed his eyes for a full second.

"It was like reading a cheap novel," she continued, "but everyone you know and care about is a character."

"I'm sorry your sister's diary upset you."

"You don't sound sorry."

"Look, if you'd just called me I would have talked you out of reading it. What good has come of this? You've changed your relationship with Tamara forever."

Dahlia sat up beside him, their thighs barely touching, her head down with long, dark hair conveniently masking her face.

He took her hand and rubbed his thumb on hers.

"Shall we get something to eat?"

"I was so caught up in my own stuff," she mumbled, "that it didn't occur to me to ask how my sister was getting by with Matt out of work."

Saul dropped her hand and began to stroke her back.

"You should never have nosed into all this, Daya."

"But she's right. Socially, I am kind of a basket case."

"Is that what she called you?"

"Among other things."

"The danger of reading words written in the heat of the moment."

She liked the heat of his hand on her back.

"It wasn't a heated moment. It was many reflective moments…" She felt a tear choke out of her. "My sister's so…I could never write the way she does. Can't believe she introduced herself to this guy as *Dahlia*…as me." She let tears come, almost like hiccups now. Saul sat quietly beside her and continued to caress her shoulders and back.

In Lincoln Park they chose a shady bench near the lagoon. He always preferred shade and low-lit restaurants when he was with her. As usual, she found his angst overblown and paranoid, but complied with his wishes. One day, it would be nice to live naturally with him, to introduce him to her family and friends, to sleep beside him and awaken together whenever they chose. But this couldn't happen for years, until his kids were on their own. He'd been clear about that.

For now, their alibi for being spotted together was his discussing another possible purchase from the gallery. He had, after all, bought a painting six years ago. After she'd initially rebuffed him for being married and avoided him, he'd popped up with a deposit on a huge oil painting for the reception area of his office. He'd been determined not to fizzle out of her life.

"Tamara didn't audition her boyfriend well," he remarked as they unfolded the wax paper from their hero sandwiches.

"She was at her wit's end."

"The reason everything's worked so long and well with us is because we're not insane," Saul continued. "You didn't even want me at first. Remember?"

Dahlia nibbled her salami and cheese and barely swallowed it.

"That's how I knew I could trust you," he said.

He had told her this before. She laid the sandwich upon the paper bag on her lap and looked out at a team of kayakers in the distance, their oars skimming the lagoon like a huge dragonfly wing.

"So does Tamara still see this young kid?"

Dahlia shook her head no.

"It was a mess, Sasha. From what I read in the diary, he followed her to the subway the last time they met. So she hailed a cab. But she had the driver follow him—and she saw him return to the hotel where they'd been."

"Trying to trace her credit card."

"Bribing one of the desk managers for her name, apparently. When Tamara called the hotel from her office, they said he'd offered them a hundred bucks for the name on her card. No one had given it out, but they couldn't vouch for every employee's honor if he were to come back another time.

"So she was in a little dilemma. If anyone did leak the credit card info, he might try to find her at Molly's agency. Of course, she'd introduced herself as 'Dahlia' and said it was 'her sister's card.' But Molly still might figure it out."

"Oh you Szabó sisters…" Saul slid his eyes toward her. "Such trouble you make for men."

"Such trouble we make for ourselves," Dahlia corrected him.

"You're not eating."

She shrugged.

"You want some ginger ale?"

"Sure."

He handed her a can from the bag.

"So don't tell me. He called the agency and got Molly on the phone and blurted out everything to her."

Dahlia pulled off the tin can lid, careful to entrust it to the paper bag and not litter in the park she loved.

"Honestly, Sasha. You can be so naïve sometimes." He often bewailed her naïvety, so she felt no compunction about reminding him of his own. "Molly doesn't answer phones any more than you do. She's the boss, remember? He couldn't get to her. This crazy Phil just started posting in the *Village Voice* and the 'Missed Encounters' personals in Craigslist. 'DESPERATELY SEEKING DAHLIA AT THE DELI.'"

"Cute," said Saul, as he wolfed his sandwich down.

"For two months he wrote in the *Village Voice: Dahlia, meet me at the deli half past noon on Thursday.* In Craigslist, he got more explicit."

"Examples?" asked Saul, his mouth filled with bread, mayonnaise, and lettuce.

Dahlia sipped her ginger ale, wondering if she should say it.

"*Phil wants to fill your secret gap.*"

Saul turned to face her, swallowing sharply.

"A little creepy, no?"

"A lot creepy."

"She didn't audition him well," he repeated. "A married person must choose a companion with great care, especially when children's lives hang in the balance. Ironically, you have to be even more choosey than when you were single."

Dahlia didn't comment.

"What was that movie with Glenn Close and the dead bunny? Grotesque something…?"

"*Fatal Attraction.*"

"I was thirty when it came out. Just dating Cheryl and considering marriage. Had a hunch I could end up like that husband if I didn't watch out."

"Imagine Tamara, every Thursday at noon knowing that he was at the deli. Waiting for her."

"Waiting for Dahlia."

"That's what drove her to the Buddhist cult temple. Roiling guilt and angst. *Repentance by hair shirt*, she wrote."

"Of course," Saul mused, "I held out for beyond 'pretty and available.' I needed compassion and maturity too—a gorgeous, secretive woman with long, black hair." He stopped eating to turn and face her with a smile. "Jewish Girls Named Dahlia. There she was, on that obscenely freezing night in March, on the shuttle bus from O'Hare."

They often reviewed their beginning, their shared mythology: how she'd noticed his strong nose in profile, the dark curls peeking out from his wool hat, his piercing blue eyes, and cheeks tanned from a visit to his mother in Florida. When they'd faced each other, a startling energy. Still, neither of them said a word for ten minutes.

Dahlia had thought: *Lord, You work in strange ways. You send me on a fruitless Club Med vacation where I didn't meet anyone worth a glance. But now, on my way home from the airport I behold the most splendid man...who introduced himself as Saul, and is probably Jewish.*

Since he'd worn gloves she hadn't seen his wedding band.

They'd agreed to meet for dinner that next week.

It was the only week in her life that she'd actually subscribed to dreams coming true, not just for characters in films and books—but for her.

Then there was dinner, the ring on his finger, and the disclaimer: "I'm not looking to leave her. We get along well and have kids at home. My wife's not the possessive type, but I don't want to throw anything hurtful in her face."

Dahlia said, "Though I'm very attracted to you, this isn't what I'm looking for."

He begged for a chance, she declined, and he showed up a month later to buy that painting. *The Lord giveth, the Lord taketh away, and then...trick or treat.*

"So that young fool still searches the city for Dahlia?" Saul asked as he finished his sandwich.

Dahlia had packed hers in the paper bag, to eat alone later.

The sky was growing pale, and soon Saul would be driving home to his family.

"Did he find out where she lived and show up with a strangled pet?"

"He stopped posting in Craigslist and the *Voice*. That was it." Dahlia shrugged. "Tamara figured someone may have shown up at the deli and just said, 'I may not be Dahlia, but I wouldn't mind a little filling...'"

"Ah, but the Szabó sisters are a hard act to follow."

"Would you please stop making us sound like some vaudeville routine?"

"I'm bestowing a high compliment."

Saul folded his paper bag, neatly scoring it with his long fingers.

"I'd wager Matt would agree. You're sure he doesn't know Molly paid off their mortgage? Because I can tell you—if my sister conspired with Cheryl to do that behind my back, I'd feel like a burnt weenie on a stick. But that may have been her intention."

"You've got Molly wrong, Sasha. She didn't run after my sister with offers. Tamara came crawling to her. Have you ever been out of money?" she suddenly asked.

"No," he said. "Maybe I wasn't born with a silver spoon. But at least a stainless steel one."

"So you don't know how God-awful that is."

"I can imagine."

"No you can't. You have no idea what horror my sister faced every day."

"Middle-class professionals in Manhattan don't face 'horrors,' Daya."

"With babies and dwindling incomes and a demoralized husband…"

She wanted to say: "Don't even try to understand." She wanted to throw her empty ginger ale can at him and march away. But she also, and just as fervently, didn't want him to leave her and go home to Cheryl. She suddenly felt incensed with Cheryl, sick and tired of sucking it all in.

For a moment, she understood Phil's crusade.

MOLLY

If Not Now, When?

Over the next week she and Saul focused on nothing more freighted than their travel plans for her birthday. They were mulling over Edinburgh, Crete, or Nova Scotia—someplace beautiful and new for both of them.

After making love they took her laptop into bed and poured through glossy photos of gorges with waterfalls, alpine views, stone castles, the Edinburgh Festival, Greek coastal villages.

Sometimes he taunted her about Phil: "that lost soul waiting for Dahlia in the deli," "waving at you from Waverly Place," or "looking to fill your caverns of desire." She found it ridiculously funny. A new devil-may-care intimacy had gushed between them after the awkward day she'd read Tamara's diaries. He even started showing up at unexpected times—Saturday morning before she left for work, or a Thursday evening when she was watching TV.

In ur hood, he'd text. *Can I cum by?*

Then one day, to her absolute shock, he emailed her a photo of his cock poking out of his pants. And so began their foray into "sexting."

That same week she decided to pack up Tamara's diaries and try to forget that she'd read them. Just as she was taping up the UPS box again, her parents called to say they were planning to give her "a little money" for her fortieth birthday, as they'd given Nurit. Of course, "a little money" could be anywhere between two hundred and fifty and a thousand dollars, depending upon mysterious factors, and she wouldn't know the upshot until she opened the envelope.

But she told them how much she appreciated it.

"Anyone special in your life?" they inevitably asked.

"Everyone in my life is special."

"You know what we mean."

"I don't want to drag you through the warp and weft of every date…I'll tell you if anything gets serious."

Daddy cleared his throat formally: "Daya," he said. "You're going to be forty. If you're not going to get serious now—when will you? Need I phrase it so classically as 'if not now, when?'"

Dahlia didn't know what to say.

"You know," her father went on, and she was suddenly aware that he'd retained his Hungarian accent simply because he was stubborn, "at the *bris* we were talking with the *goys* about you and Molly Picon."

Daddy's name for Molly was "Molly Picon," after a Yiddish film star from his boyhood.

"Glynnis feels that Molly's expectations of men are too high," her mother piped in. "And I said, 'You know, I think that's the problem with Dahlia too.'"

"No one's Prince Charming," her father reminded her. "Especially once you marry him. Just ask your mother."

"I'm not *kvetching* anymore, Fritz."

"There was a time you wouldn't stop."

"Well, we both have big mouths."

(*No!* thought Dahlia.)

"Molly's going to be in touch with you," her mother mentioned.

"Yeah, Tamara told me that a while ago."

"Why don't the two of you go out on the town and find yourselves some nice bachelors?" her father coaxed. "Someone to show you a good time on your birthday, and maybe even for the rest of your life."

Mama added, "Honey, you know we're always here for you."

A few days later Molly contacted Dahlia about Haley Thames, a young print-maker who was going to show that month at the Wiley gallery. Molly would try to get to the opening reception. She wrote that *Thames' work may be perfect for my client* and alluded to a conference room in a *high-profile production studio in the city*. But Molly would have to see the scale and texture of the prints in person, not only online, in order to make the decision.

This sale could be a coup for the young artist, and Dahlia would be happy to help it along. *Please feel free to stay with me*, she'd written to Molly.

Thanks, Molly wrote back. *If I'm traveling solo I will take you up on your kind offer. But I'll probably come with a friend and we'll stay at a hotel near your gallery.*

"Come with a friend," Saul repeated as he read over Dahlia's shoulder, one afternoon. "That's what we do, isn't it?"

"I'd like to think I'm more than your friend at those moments."

"Of course. But friend first. And always."

What was up with that? she wondered.

"Saul," she then said, not looking at him and not calling him by her pet name, Sasha. "You know, we have less than two months before our trip. We should book reservations."

"I'm waiting for you to choose the itinerary."

"Thought I told you, northern Michigan and Toronto, like you said."

He'd take her through Bloomfield Hills, Michigan, to show her the house where he'd grown up, the temple of his bar mitzvah, and his high school. Then they'd go on to the Upper Peninsula, then maybe drive through Canada to Toronto.

"You're sure that's what you want?"

"Yeah. It's hot in August, and Crete will be crowded. I don't feel like leaving this hemisphere and speaking another language. Just not in the mood."

"Okay," he said. "Gosh, I wish we had Molly's credit card...I am a bit concerned about these charges being traced."

"Should I ask my sister?"

"Oh, no, no, no. I was kidding."

"Well, let's use my credit card," said Dahlia.

This was such a novel concept that he didn't reply at first.

"I have a Mastercard."

"I'll certainly reimburse you," he promised.

"No need."

Dahlia pranced across the room to the porcelain sugar bowl. She grandly opened the lid to his rolled bundles of bills.

"Sasha—you're blushing!"

"I never understand why you don't at least put it in the bank," he said, his face noticeably pink. "Maybe Molly will give you a lesson in trading stock options when she gets here."

"I never wanted you to do this," she emphasized. "It's all well and good, because now we can use it for our road trip. But I have a job—and family."

"You have a job." He scowled. "Your job doesn't give you medical or dental, to say the least for a 401K. Suppose you had an emergency?"

"So you're my emergency fund?"

She placed the porcelain lid on the table.

"You're turning forty, sweetheart," he said. "Time to start planning for more than next Friday."

"As you and my parents seem hell-bent on reminding me."

"We who care deeply want you to make prudent decisions about your future."

Your future—not our future?

Who'da Thunkit?

Two weeks later, Dahlia threw her windows open and burned patchouli incense. Molly was due any second, but her apartment exuded another unexpected visit from Saul—preceded by a fuzzy, emailed snapshot of his fingers twined around his cock, thumb against the head as though presenting her with ripe fruit. He'd been given a Blackberry that wasn't on the market yet by a colleague, and it boasted a megapixel camera—which he was putting to creative use.

She'd called him frantically and asked for a rain check, but he'd shown up anyway, looking irresistible. "A quickie before Molly shows up?"

"I have my period."

"Oh," he crooned, low and smoky, "suck me, baby…"

It started with her mouth sliding over him, frothy with saliva. But she couldn't resist throwing off her skirt and straddling him, hot and wet with menses, closing her eyes and imagining the photo of his dick, both of them moaning, gasping, fucking like mad.

"A woman is extra-sensitive with her period," he whispered when they stopped, shivering in an embrace. He made her nerves rejoice where she didn't even know she had them. And the room reeked of their joy.

Molly's plans had changed several times, and she hadn't been able to attend the opening reception. She was on her own, not "with a friend," so Dahlia had welcomed her. Now she was sorry she hadn't told Molly to stay at a hotel.

The intimate, saline essence of the room blended outrageously with patchouli; Dahlia ran to the sink and squeezed lemon dish detergent all over the glasses in which she'd served water to Saul and herself. Maybe introducing a third scent would make everything else unrecognizable. She even considered cat food.

Before she knew it her buzzer rang, and in another instant Molly was standing before her with an overnight bag, her nose twitching like a bunny's.

"Sorry about the—incense. Sometimes this kitty litter gets pungent."

"No problem at all," said Molly lightly. But her eyes flashed, and Dahlia could see that she knew everything.

"Let's get your bag into this room."

The previous tenant had walled off a small "study" area where Dahlia kept a futon and a narrow desk for her laptop. The last guest who'd stayed there had been Mama, three years ago. Dahlia hadn't used the futon since and didn't know if she even remembered how.

The odor was less pronounced in there. But Dahlia, feeling descended upon and exposed, glanced nervously at Molly's compact suitcase and the shopping bag she carried. "You travel light," Dahlia remarked.

"And lighter yet."

Molly handed Dahlia the shopping bag, which, beneath a flourish of colorful, curled gift ribbons, contained a hardcover art book of Bonnard paintings that looked heavier than Molly's suitcase, and several sepia coffee cans that said Café du Monde.

"For me?"

Dahlia remembered Tamara describing Molly as "ultra-generous."

"How do you know I love Pierre Bonnard?"

Molly shrugged pleasantly, her green eyes almost golden. Tamara always described Matthew's and Molly's eyes as "changing color, like sea water."

"What I appreciate about him and Matisse—they paint women from the inside. Know what I mean?"

"They paint us as we feel ourselves," said Molly.

"You wonder how they knew."

"Have you ever had chicory coffee?" Molly asked her, cocking her head.

"I don't think so."

"We were just down in New Orleans a week ago, savoring it by the banks of the Mississippi and getting confection from beignets all over the place."

Then Molly's cell phone piped some phrase from Vivaldi's Four Seasons. She smiled cryptically and pardoned herself.

Dahlia stepped outside, overhearing Molly gush to someone: "Flying without you sucked. I sat beside a stranger who didn't stop downing gimlets and belching. Made me feel single again in the worst way."

Her voice grew softer, and Dahlia darted over to shove a fan into the open window, covering her mouth to keep from laughing about Molly's belching stranger and the general absurdity of her own situation. But as she turned on the fan she felt annoyed. People assumed that women like Molly were alone, but clearly, Molly was speaking to someone in the kind of affectionate tones she herself spoke to Saul. Still, that incriminating word echoed in the fan's whir: *single, single, single.*

Molly came into the room again, looking intently at lithographs on the walls, the lace curtains from Budapest that fluttered in the fan's breeze, china plates on Dahlia's table, and the felines, who had gingerly emerged from under Dahlia's bed.

"Phoenix and Ashes," Dahlia introduced them.

"Which came first?"

"They're a team."

"With my moods they sure are," Molly said bent over to stroke Ashes behind the ears. He was a shade dustier than the perfect white of Phoenix.

"*Ashes of love, cold as ice—you make the debt and I pay the price,*" Molly sang softly to the cat. Then suddenly she asked, "That your phone?"

"Where?"

Molly pointed to the chair legs.

"Oh…shit."

Dahlia stooped down to grab Saul's heart-sized Blackberry from the floor. She held it in her hand, remembering that he'd thrown his jacket on that chair. It must have slipped out of his pocket and onto the floor.

"Actually it's my boyfriend's." She looked uneasily at Molly, who was still singing to Ashes and stroking his ears. "He's probably going nuts. It's some kind of beta model ... given to him by someone at RIM...got a megapixel camera. Can we keep this between ourselves?" Dahlia pleaded.

"Sure," said Molly, standing up to pay attention to her, not the cat.

"My boyfriend"—the words would be squeezed out like pulp in a juicer—"is married. I don't really know—see, I can't get in touch with him if he doesn't have this phone on him."

"Email?" asked Molly.

Dahlia shrugged, her face hot from the sudden confession.

"Let me see that."

Dahlia handed Molly his Pearl Blackberry, and she began fiddling with it.

"I don't have his work email," Dahlia explained. "And he won't get a text without this."

"Try emailing him at home," Molly advised. As Dahlia pondered whether she could get away with doing that, her phone rang.

"Sasha!" she cried when she heard his harried voice. "Yes, Molly just found it here under a chair."

"Look," he was saying, "Can you have Molly call my home number and say she found it on the street or something?"

"Hold on, I'll ask."

Dahlia briefly described the request to Molly, who was ogling his Blackberry, her eyes opening wide. She nodded her assent, still staring at the small screen.

"Let's pretend she's staying at the Marriott or something," Saul was saying when Dahlia got back on. "I'll tell her that I'll meet her in the bar there. The problem is that I gotta pick up Wendy from gymnastics because Cheryl's at a Hadassah fundraiser and Alex isn't around. So I may have to take Lisa and Wendy with me to the city."

"Why is that a problem?"

"I don't want you to be there," he said with surprising bluntness.

"Why not?"

"Because," he continued, clearly anguished, "I won't be able to hide anything from my girls. If I just meet up with Molly, who I've never seen before, I can probably pull it off. And I have to invite them along—it will look strange otherwise."

"Will it really?"

Dahlia thought back to being fourteen years old. If Daddy had told her that he'd had to meet some stranger in a hotel who'd found his lost briefcase, she couldn't imagine feeling suspicious if he wouldn't take her with him—and she said as much to Saul.

"I don't want to get into this now," he snapped. "Parenting is different these days. Look, could you put Molly on, please."

"He wants to speak to you," Dahlia grumbled.

Meanwhile, Molly's hand was over her mouth. She walked slowly over the polished wooden floorboards to where Dahlia sat speaking on the phone.

"Anyone you know?" she whispered, tossing Dahlia the Blackberry as she took the receiver.

There, on-screen was Saul's prick coming out of his pants.

Molly tipped her head and said coyly into the phone: "Hi there."

Then she was quiet for a while.

Dahlia looked down at the photo, which was not the same one he'd sent earlier. Perhaps he'd amassed some variations on a theme?

"We can do that," Molly finally said. "I was going to invite Dahlia out to dinner. We can meet you beforehand."

Molly stood beside Dahlia, pushing a couple of keys on the Blackberry over her shoulder. Other shots of Saul's manhood, caressed variously by his fingers, were rendered in quick succession—like an old-fashioned flipbook.

Over the receiver she heard his voice. "I've told Dahlia that I don't want her to be around because my daughters may be with me. I take it she's explained our situation."

"Well, I'll need her to show me around," Molly protested mildly, still perusing the explicit images on his Blackberry screen. "I don't know this town at all. I suppose she can wait for me in a coffee house."

To Dahlia's horror, the next image that flashed was of her own hand on her breasts. She remembered him taking it that morning, "as a memento."

"I'm putting her back on," Molly said crisply, pushing the Blackberry Dahlia's way. "You two work it out together. Anything is fine with me."

She then walked toward the window with the whirring fan.

"Am I crazy to be upset that he doesn't want me to be there?"

They sat at the teak table eating tangerines and cherries, and Molly regarded her for a studiously silent minute.

"How long have you been seeing him?"

"Six years."

"And you've never met his kids?"

"We're under wraps."

"Got it. I suppose I can understand his discomfort, being pulled between the two worlds he's created. But it seems thin-skinned, doesn't it? You just want to say, 'Grow up already.'"

"You really do," Dahlia whispered, picking at her tangerine but not breaking the rind. The man who'd come by to love her that afternoon, who'd emailed her intimate photos of himself, didn't want her to be in the same room as his daughters.

Molly effected a consoling expression. "Be flattered by your hold on him. Men are particularly susceptible to sacred and profane love, though none of us are as immune as we'd like to be when it comes to our families." She looked toward the window and its wavering lace curtains for a moment, then turned sharply back to Dahlia. "You should know better than to let him keep photos of you on his phone. They could end up anywhere."

"He told me he'd destroy it after today. He promised me."

Dahlia tried not to sound melodramatic as she punctured the rind of her fruit with her fingernail.

"Looks like he's got quite a collection of himself."

"I noticed. But Molly, don't you ever—sext?"

"What? You mean customize pixilated porn for my beloved? No thank you. I'm too modest."

That sounded right.

"Hey, is that his email inbox?" Dahlia asked, popping a tangerine section into her mouth.

"And it's conveniently open—no need to guess any passwords."

Molly showed her how to access the messages, and Dahlia combed through notices from the PTA—*Last Newsletter of the School Year! Ninth Grade Potluck Supper!*—spam from local restaurants—*Enjoy the Playoffs with $2 Beer & $1 Fries at the Bar!*—registration for Wendy's gymnastic camp, the schedule for Wendy's debate team, and an invoice from Lisa's flute teacher. There were several letters from a julie_herman, who Dahlia realized was his sister Julie—"married to the world's most boring man, Bob Herman," Saul had often described his sister and brother-in-law. Julie's emails were all about *scheduling Ma's dialysis treatments when she comes here*, and *Call Ma Sunday, she wants to hear your voice*. An email from Cheryl's hadassah.org account about the car transmission: *Fixed yet?* Apparently she was a woman of few words.

But then, as Dahlia sat unabashedly slurping tangerine sections and biting cherries off stems with Molly, she noticed a choice subject line that read *Re: Happy Anniversary*, from the same hadassah.org address. Saul had apparently initiated this one, and Dahlia stopped chewing her cherry and nearly swallowed the stone.

He had written to his wife, *Happy Anniversary, sweetheart. Delightful surprise this morning.*

And she'd replied: *Who'da thunkit?*

Dahlia read it over twice, then four times. She noticed that he'd kept the email, from two weeks ago.

"Can I ask you something?" she whimpered to Molly, showing her the email exchange between husband and wife. Molly read it and looked back at Dahlia as though she were sorry she'd have to comment. Dahlia didn't force it.

Cups of Tea

He called again, but Dahlia let Molly handle making arrangements. He suggested the Marriott. Then he said no, they should meet at a convenience store. He'd rush in and emerge again with his phone. But five minutes after they'd hung up he called Molly back to explain that Lisa had seen him go haywire when he hadn't found his Blackberry in any briefcase or coat pocket, so there would have to be more drama to his recovering it. They should go ahead with the hotel plan and perhaps even have a drink. Molly requested somewhere other than the Marriott, "which I can see anytime in New York. Can you suggest a one-of-a-kind historical hotel here?"

When she got off the phone she asked Dahlia, "How can you *steyand* his Midwestern *eyaccent*?"

"What accent?"

"You don't hear it?"

Dahlia looked at Molly blankly before shouting: "He doesn't even want me there! He doesn't want me to meet his girls!"

"Okay," said Molly, seeming accustomed to people erupting. "Let's choose one of three strategies—you can"—she held up her hand and tagged one finger for each point—"cooperate with him and not come along; you can defy him and show up anyway; or you can fool him and come in a disguise."

An hour and a half later, Dahlia sat in a bar at the Congress Plaza Hotel on

South Michigan Avenue in the platinum wig she had once purchased as Saul's own disguise. In the time it had taken him to pick up Wendy at after-school gymnastics and then drive from Highland Park to the city, Molly and she had bought a wide straw sunhat and an outfit that they agreed was like nothing Dahlia would ever wear: a shapeless, gray jersey dress and hand-knit wool shawl from a thrift shop in Lakeview.

Dahlia didn't recognize herself in the bar mirror.

"I'm better off brunette after all," she'd said earlier when Molly fixed the platinum wig on her head and they tucked her dark hair into it. "My skin turns green with this corn silk around it."

"Being blonde is an art," Molly had affirmed, and for some reason Dahlia remembered Molly's pretty blonde friend from the *bris*.

Saul was to meet Molly in the hotel lobby, and they anticipated that he would bring her into the lounge for a drink. Sure enough, Dahlia now noticed Molly emerging in her denim jacket and black pants with Saul following her in a white polo shirt and khakis, his gold bar mitzvah chain glinting on his neck, the chain that never came off, no matter what else did. Surrounding him like bulwarks, his twin daughters looked taller and thinner than Dahlia imagined. Of course, she'd seen pictures of them as eight-year-olds and now they were fourteen. As they drew closer she saw, with a pang in her breast, the enchantingly doll-like creatures with smooth cheeks, huge blue eyes like their father's, and locks of curly black hair.

The whole gaggle settled several seats down the bar from her.

Beneath her hat and wig, Dahlia's heart squeezed like a party balloon. She kept the shawl spread over her arms and sat still as she could, barely touching her cup of tea with its deteriorating lemon. Saul seemed not to notice, much less to recognize, her.

As she peered at them surreptitiously from under her hat, Dahlia could tell which girl was which: Wendy stood between Molly's and Saul's barstools while Lisa sat beside her father, long wires extending from both ears and culminating in an iPod. Dahlia quickly thought that the difference between herself and them and her at that age is that she'd be wearing a lanyard or some plastic beads around her neck, rather than an iPod.

In her strawberry-red plaid blouse, Lisa kept her eyes down as she nodded to music. Wendy's dark hair was swept up into a sweatband, and she still wore her gymnastics getup with a white sweater tied around her inconceivably meager waist. These girls were so thin that Dahlia wondered how their intestines actually fit inside them.

Wendy chewed gum harshly and eyed Molly as though trying to assess her intentions, maybe wondering *had she really just found Dad's phone on the street?*

"Won't you sit down and have some ginger ale or Coke, Cookie Puss?" Saul begged, and Wendy shook her head. "Water? You won't gain weight from that." He smiled at Molly, blushed, and asked her, "How do you have time to manage two businesses in New York?"

For the first time since she'd known him, Dahlia heard the Midwestern accent Molly referred to: "How do you have time to *meyan-age?*"

"It takes endless time to keep one business going."

Wendy leaned her head proudly on Saul's shoulder, staring Molly down. She clearly agreed with her astute, handsome father.

"I don't have children," Molly replied. "I have time."

Dahlia wished she could see Molly's expression but saw only her wavy, dark hair and a hint of profile.

"The human race will go to seed if intelligent people like you don't have children," Saul commented—taking an interest in her, Dahlia felt. Too much interest. "It's no longer survival of the fittest. It will become survival of the sickest—the Third World rat race, religious fanatics—"

"Well, fanatics of all stripes are right about one thing: a population tends to decrease when its women are educated and free to make choices."

"Great," Saul lamented. "By keeping women slaves to reproduction, backward jerks will rule the world."

"Don't worry," said Molly. "Artificial intelligence will get there first."

"But if there are no more good and smart people, then who will make the robots?" Wendy asked her earnestly.

Dahlia thought of Cheryl, mother of these two bright, bewitchingly lovely girls and wife of Saul. How proud she must feel, how validated as a woman in every way.

By contrast, what had she to show for herself at nearly forty? An illicit love affair with this doting father, inappropriate photos of herself on his phone, and a job that barely paid her.

She gazed at the soggy lemon in her teacup.

Then a big man wedged himself between Dahlia and the others. His pudgy face was red, and his tweed jacket too small. He half-perched on the barstool, half-stood up, dialing his mobile and then bellowing, "Hey, sorry our attorney was so hard on you…"

At first Dahlia was glad he'd sat there, shielding her from Saul and his minions, but she eventually grew annoyed.

"At the end of the balloon's term, as I understand it, you'd pay off any outstanding balance. Here, let's go over the monthly payments."

The man produced an Excel printout from a folder and plopped onto the seat, now almost entirely blocking her view of Molly, Saul, and Wendy. She could still see Lisa bobbing her head to the iPod music, sliding her eyes over to her father and identical twin sister as they spoke with the intriguing stranger from New York named Molly.

The bartender brought this animated party two beers for the adults and two Diet Cokes for the young ladies. Mr. Loudmouth beside her ordered a Scotch, and Dahlia assented, without enthusiasm, to the bartender's offer of "more hot water" for her sluggish tea and lemon.

The loudmouth roared on about balloon mortgages, listing payment rates, slowly and boisterously, sometimes repeating them. Perhaps the person on the other end was deaf.

Dahlia sipped her tea with even less enthusiasm than she'd ordered it, barely catching snippets of Saul's conversation with Molly, like: "But we interact with AI every day and increasingly expect it to run our lives. Look at your Blackberry..."

Wendy had spit her gum into a napkin and was sipping the long, cool glass of Diet Coke, watching Molly challenge her dad. Lisa tried not to seem interested. Saul gazed eagerly into Molly's face, just as he looked into Dahlia's when they made love. Dahlia remembered her breasts clapping against his cheek and forehead just that morning when he'd come by for "a quickie" and lost his phone beneath her table.

Then Mr. Loudmouth moved forward and raised the volume on his litany about interest rates. Dahlia felt like she was in a movie theater, trying to read subtitles around some impenetrably gross and ill-positioned head. It seemed that Saul shared her vexation.

"Excuse me, buddy," Saul said to him, "could you please keep it down?"

The man seemed unaware that he was being addressed and blabbed on.

Molly, Saul, and Wendy shared a laugh. None of them had noticed the odd platinum blonde in her big straw sunhat and ugly shawl beside him. She was blending with the scenery, just as she and Molly had planned.

Suddenly Dahlia's heart fired a neuron to her brain.

She remembered Tamara's words: "men from all corners of the world dote at her doorstep"; "Molly knows how to play the game and win"; "she's more of a sister to me than either of my two losers."

Dahlia lifted the teacup to her lips as Molly waved a paper napkin on which she'd scribbled *LOWER YOUR VOICE, PLEASE!* in front of the loudmouth's face. He nodded reluctantly and did so.

Now Saul and Wendy were completely impressed with Molly, and even Lisa had been drawn into her spell. Dahlia stood up and walked to the women's room. Her tampon was leaking.

For what seemed like a long time, she sat in the booth, head in her hands, pulling at platinum hairs from her wig.

She remembered devouring Saul's text messages in just such a toilet stall at the deli after the *bris*, but such levity seemed long ago. If not for the road trip they'd planned for her birthday, Dahlia would have felt inconsolable. At least they'd be alone together for a full week, hiking through mountains and swimming in lakes. It would be summer, and her birthday. They'd have time to talk about all of this.

Somewhat bolstered—and no longer leaking, with a fresh tampon—she came out again to pay for her tea. Saul and the girls were now gone, and the loudmouth had migrated to another corner of the lounge where he could hold court in his preferred boisterous fashion. Molly sat at the bar chattering on her own phone. They'd planned that Dahlia would leave the hotel first and wait for Molly at the Starbucks two blocks away. Then they'd go back to Dahlia's neighborhood for dinner.

Out on South Michigan Avenue, Dahlia looked this way and that for Saul and his twin girls, but saw no sign of them.

When Molly showed up at the crowded Starbucks, Dahlia barely grunted an acknowledgment.

"Well, we did it," Molly said.

"Hope you had fun."

Molly looked surprised, her golden-green eyes widening. How Saul must have enjoyed those pretty, romantic eyes.

"I'm sorry?"

Dahlia shoved her half-consumed paper cup of tea across the little round table and got up to leave. Molly followed her.

"Can we catch a cab easily or should we call a service?"

"New York isn't the only city with cabs," Dahlia huffed.

"Easy," said Molly pleasantly. "It's a fair question."

And it was all the more fair since Molly was paying for it.

"Where would you like to eat dinner?" Molly continued when they were settled in the back seat of a car, heading north to Lincoln Park.

Dahlia knew she wasn't behaving nicely but felt unable to stop herself.

"I don't know what you're thinking," Molly continued, "but we kind of couldn't stomach each other."

"Who?"

Dahlia eyed the blister of colored lights that throbbed along the lakeside. This cab was a luxury, something she'd never do alone.

"Your boyfriend and me."

"That's not my impression," said Dahlia.

"What impression could you have with that buffoon hollering interest rates?"

"It seemed to me you were charming them silly."

"Wendy and I hit it off," Molly reported. "She's a sharp kid. I liked her. But Saul and I are not each other's cup of tea."

"What do you mean?"

"He's a suburban libertarian with his head in the sand. Funny how Americans like that understand hoarding, but not sharing."

"He flirted with you," Dahlia protested.

Molly sat back, exhaling. Dahlia continued looking out the window.

"He was competing with me in front of his daughters."

Again, Dahlia said nothing.

"Besides," Molly continued, now clearly trying to appease, "not only would it be unthinkably gauche of me to come here and interfere with your love affair, it's hardly my style to fight through the mystique of a mistress and the fluff of a 'who'da thunkit' wife for the questionable reward of his attention. He's a good-looking man, I grant you that. Must spend hours on the bench press—"

"So you noticed?"

"But I'd throw him across a room before I'd jump his bones. That I can promise."

Silence was Dahlia's only weapon, and she wielded it well. Saul had given her plenty of occasions for practice.

"I'm not 'on the market' anyway," Molly stressed. "I'm crazy about someone."

She scrolled through her cell phone in the quasi darkness and produced a glowing photograph of herself and her blonde friend.

"That's the Mississippi in the background, with the *Steamship Natchez*. We were having our morning coffee and beignets. Have you ever been to New Orleans? Talk about a phoenix rising out of the ashes these days."

But all Dahlia saw was a photograph of two attractive, single women with vibrant smiles and wind blowing through their hair, and it made her miserable. She turned away. Molly seemed to want more of a response from her, but Dahlia saw through the tactic: since she was being such a brat, Molly wanted to change the topic. But she wouldn't swallow that bait and get either of them off the hook.

They stopped off in her apartment so Dahlia could shed her wig and costume before going to dinner. As she undressed in the bathroom Molly murmured on her cell phone to her object of affection: "You know how we spend eight hours apart and come back with full-blown melodramas? Just wait 'til you get a load of my evening."

Dahlia stepped out of the bathroom in her jeans and a blouse, brushing her long dark hair and feeling better, since she now recognized herself in mirrors. Still, Molly's loving banter irritated her. Something wasn't right, and it was more wrong than anything that had actually happened.

"Sorry I was a bitch," she apologized, once Molly was off the phone.

"Sorry if I gave you the impression that I was flirting with your guy."

Dahlia sat stiffly on her bed. "You were very gracious."

Without having made light of anything, Molly's touch had been gentle. She had not taken Dahlia personally. Now she settled near the bedside on one of Dahlia's teak chairs.

"My mother disowned me a while back," Molly began. "You must have heard."

"Tamara was pretty oblique about it."

"No big secret: Both Mom and Matthew didn't speak to me for three years. After enduring something so draconian, I'm not fazed by anyone's passing moods." She paused. "We all get into moods. I'm terribly moody."

"Molly, this wasn't a mood. I made ridiculous accusations." Dahlia held the hairbrush in her hand, stroking its bristles and clawing at her fingers with them.

"It's clear that you feel uncertain about this man's love."

She nodded slowly, stung by Molly's acumen. After reading the "Who'da thunkit?"exchange, and witnessing his warm attention to his daughters and even to Molly, she simply wondered what claim she had on Saul. What was irreplaceable between them? What couldn't he find with his family—or with a new woman?

"I'm having a hard time," she admitted. "We're so close and passionate one moment, and he's off bounds the next. I can't speak about it with anyone. My married friends get uncomfortable. Nobody wants to endorse it. Everyone wants to sanitize it. Even my sisters pick on me. People treat me like I'm carrying some kind of plague. But this is the person I love."

To Dahlia's surprise, Molly looked at her quizzically.

She had never seen Molly—who was always poised with a witty remark, an insight, or at least a credit card—at such a seeming loss. Phoenix and Ashes tumbled around on the wooden floor as if performing calisthenics for the two pensive women.

"You make these risk speculations," Molly finally said, "About who to possibly confide in, and who you'd better shut up around."

"Exactly."

"Dreading the disaster that might attend a heartfelt disclosure."

Dahlia watched her cats skirmish, their white and gray fur blending on the honey-brown oak floor.

"I have a friend who stopped hugging me goodbye after I told her about Saul and me. She didn't want to touch me, like I was contagious."

Molly replied with a brief laugh. "You don't want to *know* about that one."

"But you sound like you have a pretty cozy situation."

"Well, yes. But there's a moat around it."

My Sister's Sister-in-Law

They went to a neighborhood sushi place that Saul liked. The lighting, of course, was low, and the décor combined 1950s Americana with Japanese furniture. They chatted about meeting Haley Thames the next morning at the gallery and how museum glass was wonderful because it could subdue reflected light and allow people to actually see the artwork.

A young Asian waitress came along, and Molly welcomed Dahlia to get anything she wanted. So she ordered her usual sushi deluxe plate, while Molly ordered black cod with vegetables and: "shall we brave some light, dry sake?"

Now Dahlia felt calm again, her mind alive with something other than Saul. Though she was curious about Molly's love life, she felt relieved not to be discussing relationships—almost worried that she'd make an ass of herself again.

"I'm looking for artwork that will harmonize with the intergalactic blue and silver wall paint we've planned for these conference rooms," Molly went on, her eyes brightening.

"I think you'll like Haley's prints."

"It's a toss up between her and two other possibilities."

From the corner of her eye Dahlia noticed a party of three frumpy characters being seated at the next table by their young waitress. It was difficult to say whether they were men or women; their loose clothing and cropped hair gave them an air of being practitioners of Wicca, or members of a science fiction book club—all decidedly past their primes.

"This is a deal-breaking assignment," Molly explained. "If I succeed, it could foretell a new career. After eighteen years, I'm ready to leave advertising."

"You'll leave it with a strong background in design, I'd think."

"Two-dimensional design. This third dimension—space that people live in—fascinates me."

Sake arrived and the waitress poured it into their small, glazed cups. Molly lifted hers and Dahlia corresponded, appreciating Molly's flair. Her boyfriend was lucky, whoever he was. Molly was such a cheerful and energizing presence.

"To new dimensions."

"To spaces people live in," Dahlia echoed.

Discreet piano tones infiltrated the talk and laughter around them as warm sake singed her throat.

Then Molly said, "Hey—do we know what *his* place looks like?"

"Saul's? I've never been invited."

"But haven't you ever just driven by and looked?"

"I don't have a car."

"Surely you must be curious, as a visually sensitive person, about the style of his house?"

"Are you suggesting I stalk him?"

"I'll bet it's ugly!" Molly declared, placing her cup on the table for emphasis.

A bowl of warm edamame was served. Dahlia began eating, realizing she was famished. Too many platinum wigs and too much tea, with too little food and her period all afternoon.

"I'll bet it's an eyesore with aluminum siding—'practical, cost-effective.' Do we know what his wife looks like?"

"We've seen a photo or two online. She's…" Dahlia shrugged, popping edamame into her mouth and speaking with it half-full. "I mean, she's fine."

"Unremarkable," ventured Molly with a flip of her head. "Safe."

"Not homely, not beautiful. Just there."

"You're probably hotter with him. Do you have photographs of the two of you together? I mean, respectable photographs?"

"Well, no. Who would take them?"

She was starting to wish Molly hadn't raised this topic. Yet she'd never had the chance to discuss Saul in an exploratory way, even with her sisters.

"Would you say…" Molly seemed to think better of what she was going to ask.

"What?"

"Never mind."

"Mind!" Dahlia smiled and sipped a little more hot sake.

"Would you say you're with him pretty much for the sex?"

One of the frumpy people at the next table seemed to glare at them. But Molly was soft-spoken, and she'd posed the question in tones even lower than her usual.

Dahlia blushed through her bones.

"The sex is really good," she whispered. Molly leaned in to hear. "But it's more than that. He's seen me through so much—not that my life is terribly interesting."

"Of course it's interesting."

"Well, to me. But not much really happens."

"You're the mystery woman of your family," Molly said kindly.

"Mystery? They call it asocial. I 'stay in all the time and don't go out to play.'"

"Well, my mother thinks I'm abnormal."

"You? Why?"

Now Dahlia was sure people from the next table were trying to eavesdrop. They had stopped speaking among themselves and were watching Molly and her like a TV show.

"Because I bore my friend's baby, but not my own," Molly stated.

Dahlia regarded her, along with the captive audience from the next table, her fingers gripping the little cup of hot sake.

"I was a surrogate mother," Molly continued. "Gestational surrogacy, it's called. My friend's egg, her husband's sperm, my womb. Andy's five now, he plays checkers, and he's adorable. My godson."

Dahlia remembered the descriptions in Tamara's diary. And then she remembered to forget them, as Molly filled her in on the details she'd already read: "They wanted their own child and gave me a hedge fund account in exchange for my labors. Mother and Matt found the whole concept disgraceful and didn't talk to me for years. But it's helped me to make incredible things happen."

"Tamara always expresses gratitude—"

"We're helping women, here and abroad…at early stages that other investors don't touch." Molly smiled in a deflecting way and said, "But back to my question. Is sex the big draw here?"

"It's hard to separate it from other parts of being with him." She knew Molly would understand when she added, expressly *sotto voce*, "Even moments when nothing sexual is happening feel sexy with him."

"And with other people you can be fucking and not feel sexual."

"I hate that."

"He got on my nerves," admitted Molly. "And I question relationships that are based on deceiving someone else. But if you're close physically and emotionally, that's hard to come by. Would you continue to be so compatible, I wonder, if he left his wife and spent more time with you?"

"I'd like to think so."

Their salad was served, with simple lemon dressing and a sprinkle of sesame. The gnomes at the other table seemed to recede back into their own conversation.

"He's mentioned," said Dahlia, "that he has a hard time associating sex with a family situation. His wife feels like a sister or friend—'a close friend,' he's called her. He says they're platonic and that they get along well that way."

"Who'da thunkit?" muttered Molly.

Dahlia concentrated on gracefully eating her salad. Not surprisingly, Molly was skilled at navigating food with chopsticks and not making a mess of it.

"The problem is that you're skimming crème de la crème special time with him," she said. "You have no idea how he'd be as the 'normal milk' of your life."

"Sometimes I think he's better off with his wife," Dahlia confessed. "I'm not terribly domestic."

"Oh, I don't have a Suzy Homemaker bone in my body," chirped Molly.

"I know how to decorate a room more than I know how to live in one."

Molly grinned from over her salad and said, "That's the challenge—to make a life that's as beautiful as the rooms it's lived in. Is Saul on par with your lace curtains from Budapest and hand-painted porcelain?"

Dahlia didn't answer, but posed the question: "You barely know him and you barely know me. But you had a taste of each of us today. What do you think?"

"You're less arrogant than he is," said Molly quickly. "If you were together, I wager you'd have some good years and get tired of him. But then again, maybe not...just remember, he's at his zenith now, with those twin daughters fighting for his attention...and two adult women also vying for him. What dominion! But fast-forward five years, when his daughters are dating and in college."

"And he's in his mid-fifties."

"How empty will his nest be?"

Molly cocked her head cutely, chopsticks poised. The piano music swelled and gained momentum. Dahlia realized that in the best-case scenario she would inherit Saul in those empty-nest years.

As if Molly could read her mind, she leaned over the table and said, just above a whisper, "My criteria for 'til death do us part is someone who prevails in the worst times. Look, we both know it's easy to sit on someone's knee when the wine is flowing and the food is good. But what happens when things just suck? That's the litmus test."

"Does your boyfriend pass muster?"

"My boyfriend," repeated Molly, sitting back again.

"That pet you speak so fondly to in New York."

Molly shrieked with enough laughter to rekindle the attention of the frumpy people from the next table. "My boyfriend!" she cried, shaking her head.

She leaned in again and told Dahlia: "Let's just put it this way. Two years ago my 'pet' and I were walking after midnight—like the Patsy Cline song—to pick up milk for the next day's coffee. We were between Riverside and West End, heading toward Broadway, and I was blabbing away when my 'pet' suddenly lunged over to a bank of tin trash cans by a brownstone, removed a lid, started clanging it and screaming 'HELP!'

"Before I knew it, a light flicked on in the brownstone and a terrifying gang of thugs charged away from us, down the hill to Riverside Drive.

"Someone let us into the brownstone. We called the precinct, and we weren't the first to report those marauders. They'd been mugging people at gunpoint and raping women for weeks. The cops caught up with them on Riverside."

"Goodness," said Dahlia. "How did he know they were following you?"

"Tuned in. And smart enough to *not* say: 'Molly, run!' Because the scumbags would've caught up and outnumbered us. And they were armed."

Molly's eyes glowed in the low lights, and Dahlia nodded, impressed.

"If I'd been with any number of exes—at best, I would have been mugged. At worst, beaten up, raped, shot…who knows? Tom or Jordan would've shit in their pants and clung to me."

"I hear you," said Dahlia. She assumed that Saul would have shaken like a palm frond in a hurricane, given over his wallet, and begged the guys to leave them be.

"I've never known anyone with such quick reflexes as 'my pet.'"

"Is the sex good?"

"Celestial," said Molly. "Other-worldly."

"Then what's wrong?" Dahlia had a sudden intuition. "Is he black? Puerto Rican?"

"Do you remember," Molly asked, pouring more sake for each of them, "when we came of age, the clarion call in relationships was: 'I need my space'? Before myspace became an Internet sensation?" Molly threw her head back and crowed, "I need my space, man!"

The frump convention from the other table was gawking again.

Molly went on. "That pretty much lasted into the nineties. Then came the philandering husband's chestnut: 'I've met someone.'" Molly threw her arms out Romeo-style and recited with poise: 'Honey, I'm afraid…I've met someone.'"

Dahlia put her hand to her mouth and giggled.

"Now, in our postmodern, post–Ellen Degeneres era, women burn out of the woodwork with the wildfire proclamation, to boyfriends and media: 'I'm with a woman!'"

It was the look someone gave them from the next table that clued Dahlia in.

Her jaw dropped. She hoped there wasn't food in her mouth.

"You're with…what's her name? That tall, attractive blonde."

"I sure damn am."

Molly polished off the sake in her cup. "Classified information," she told Dahlia. "No one in the family knows. Not even Tamara."

Dahlia suppressed a sudden urge to cough.

"Not that they haven't been given ample hints," Molly continued.

It was the kind of revelation that tolerant people should accept, and on the surface would—feeling, nevertheless, privately unnerved.

"You look surprised."

"Shocked," Dahlia admitted, staring into her salad plate. And to fill the silence that followed, she stammered, "I had…the impression you were…a world-class connoisseur of men."

"Are you kidding?"

When Dahlia dared to look up, Molly appeared vulnerable, her head tilted and her large, ginger-green eyes fixed on her.

"I always found the most passive underachievers and oddball boyfriends. You remember Tom. What was so world-class about him? I mean…" Molly sighed, clenched her lips briefly. "My relationships with men became predictable. I was the engine and they took the ride. I felt resigned to being 'the strong one.' Dreamed of meeting an equal, but powerful men never cottoned to me."

"Did you cotton to them?"

"Successful men can't figure me out. They're of the 'what's in it for me?' school, and I am living defiance of it. Ask your Saul."

They ate in silence for a moment, and Dahlia felt the stares of people from the next table burning into her head.

"Most successful women resent me too, by the way," Molly finally said. "But Eugenia *gets* me. And she gets *to* me."

"I see. How long have you been together?"

"Five years. She helped me through the surrogate pregnancy. I would've been lost without her. I kind of veered into the shoulder of the road for a while there."

"And nobody in the family knows about you two?" Dahlia persisted. "Even though, at the *bris* and all…"

"Five years ago I made the mistake of telling them upfront that I was pregnant with Alessi and Pete's child. I've learned the hard way that honesty ain't the best policy with the Douglas clan."

"Still, five years…"

Dahlia's voice sank as she said it. She'd kept Saul secret even longer.

"My sisters know about Saul," she quickly added. "But not my parents."

"And let's both face it: that can raise the thermostat in a sexual relationship—the taboo, the secrecy of it. We've staked Our Space. We've Met Someone. And I'm With a Woman."

Their entrées were served, Molly's black cod in teriyaki sauce with asparagus and string beans, and Dahlia's sushi deluxe. She immediately wished she'd copied Molly's order for something warm and fragrant. To heighten the effect, Molly raved about how Eugenia cooked for her and how gay men they knew invited them over for scrumptious meals.

"Hetero guys can be great cooks—but not my exes," she qualified. "My typical morning with a guy was: wake up freezing because he hogged the blankets and then listen to him bitch if I hadn't put up coffee. With Genie I wake up to sweet biscuits and chicory coffee. I hear her sing to herself and feel so…unlonely. It's strange that we don't have a word in English that's the antonym to *lonely*."

Dahlia thought for a moment of what that might be—*connected, affiliated*? Nothing really came to mind. Nothing was equally visceral.

Molly sampled her cod and nodded with approval, while Dahlia surveyed her cubes of sticky rice and sliced fish tethered by seaweed.

"Saul's never cooked for me," she told Molly, "but he gets me coffee and bagels in the morning when we stay at hotels."

"How often do you do that?"

"Not often enough."

Dahlia dipped her first piece of sushi into ginger sauce and wasabi.

"But," she said, "we're going to spend a week together in August, to celebrate my fortieth birthday. His wife is visiting her mother with Lisa, his son is going on a bike trip, and Wendy will be in gymnastics camp."

"What'll you do with him?"

"Drive through northern Michigan and Canada. End up in Toronto, probably. We were thinking of Nova Scotia, but it's too far. We have only a week and just started booking rooms at inns and hotels in the Upper Peninsula."

Dahlia ate her white fish, wasabi burning her throat as the confession burned her face. Of course she'd been dying to tell someone all about the trip, to share it with one person other than Saul. But now that she'd revealed their plan, it seemed far-fetched—and, after seeing his daughters with him—downright devious.

"We'll have time to work out some important things," she reasoned.

"Like what?"

"The way we communicate."

Molly daintily cut her asparagus with chopsticks and lifted it to her lips. After swallowing she asked, "What about the way you communicate?"

Dahlia wondered how Eugenia took to this first-degree questioning. That hot blonde seemed to get some mileage out of mystery.

"It's…it's a power game," Dahlia found herself saying.

"In what way?"

"He calls the shots. He determines when we can and can't see each other and for how long. It all revolves around him and his family."

"Is that any surprise to you?"

"No…"

"Then how have you abdicated power?"

It was a simple question, but Dahlia couldn't answer it. She plucked a piece of tuna with her chopsticks and dropped it again like a klutz, then glanced over at the next table of gnomes being served bowls of soba noodles by the obliging young waitress.

"Want some more sake?"

Dahlia nodded. She noticed that with someone like Molly, who always offered to pour more sake or hail a cab, it was easy to become passive, and perhaps understandable that her boyfriends had been.

"So what kind of shots do you want to call?" Molly persisted.

"Of course I can't tell him how to arrange his time with his family. I'd never ask him to leave his wife. It's nothing radical. I just don't want to be taken for granted."

"Suppose you were to cultivate an alternative companion?" Molly suggested. "Give Saul a little competition. Even just a date or two."

"That wouldn't be fair. My heart wouldn't be with anyone else."

"Phil didn't seem to mind."

Dahlia looked dumbfounded. Molly poured her sake.

"You don't remember him, do you?"

Waiting for Dahlia at the deli, waving from Waverly Place…

"Er, uh, I certainly remember him. I'm just surprised that…you do."

"He traced me, through Tamara's credit card from my company. Which—look, it's okay. We know you had to borrow it."

"Well, wait a minute," Dahlia began, feeling that she'd become Tamara's moral dumping ground without any say in the matter.

"It's fine," said Molly with a friendly nod. "Tamara and I were happy you'd enjoyed some time with this funky whippersnapper. She even paid me back for your hotel visits."

Dahlia remained agape. All she could think was, good thing she had read those diaries. Good thing for Tamara's marriage. Dahlia gathered that Molly was actually closer to Tamara than to her own brother, but she knew that blood could run thicker than wine.

So she prepared for the sacrifice. Up until that minute, her rapport with Molly had been the most bracingly honest she'd had with anyone in a while. But she couldn't spill those particular beans to her sister's sister-in-law. She would have to lie now to save Tamara's face. She was annoyed enough with her sister to remotely consider blowing her cover, but she couldn't do it to Matthew.

"Did you ever actually meet Phil?" she asked Molly.

"Oh, he's waged quite the campaign to see you again," Molly replied with a brief laugh and another slice of black cod. "He was milling around outside my building one evening. Must have recognized me from our company website, because he followed me, singing 'Love Has No Pride.' I just thought he was a crank and kept walking. But then, to my astonishment, he said, 'Do you know Dahlia?' I remember that so clearly, even though it was years ago now."

"Three years since I've seen him," Dahlia mumbled, avoiding Molly's eyes.

"Did you tell Saul about him?"

"It wasn't that important."

"You may have missed an opportunity."

Dahlia shrugged, prodding a piece of ginger with her chopstick.

"I may have."

"Would you pardon me for a minute?" Molly suddenly asked, standing up and pushing her chair in. "I must fly to the powder room."

As she made her way through the crowded restaurant Dahlia whipped out her phone. Sure enough, Saul had texted her.

Phone back! Molly's quite a lady. Glad I met her.

Dahlia was about to reply, *Guess who's dying for Dahlia and waving from Waverly Place?* but didn't. Saul had popped up that morning, sent her salacious photos of himself, made love to her, lost his phone, left her apartment smelling like blood, sweat, come, and tears, and forbade her to meet his daughters. Now he was swooning over Molly.

Dahlia turned off her phone and put it away, resisting the tug to let him in on the latest wrinkle.

"Excuse me! Miss!"

The gnomes at the next table were flagging their waitress, calling out to her in sharp, abrasive tones. The young Asian woman appeared, and they whined to her in unison against the piano music. "I cannot do anything about the air condition-ing," Dahlia overheard her say in clipped English.

By the time Molly returned, they were all up in arms about their soba noodles being cold and the room being "close and clammy."

As she took her seat, Molly found the scrap paper from her chopsticks. She scrawled something with a pen from her bag and passed it to Dahlia, as though they were in school: *AGING QUEENS.*

Dahlia nodded, suddenly understanding.

"I didn't mean to embarrass you about Phil. It was the sake talking."

Molly smiled sympathetically, her tastefully scant makeup fresh on her face.

"Do you still hear from him?" Dahlia asked.

"Not anymore. For a while he kept emailing about his stand-up comedy routine and begging me to 'bring Dahlia along to the club if she's in town.'"

"Does Tamara know about this?" Dahlia asked again, barely enjoying her first taste of salmon, her favorite sushi.

"She says she tries to keep out of your business."

"Gallant of her. Did you ever make it to Phil's comedy show?"

"We actually did—Eugenia, me, and our friend David. Wasn't half-bad. Not that I follow stand-up comedy in New York."

Dahlia remembered that name, David. As Molly spoke about how stand-up comedy is sometimes hilarious and other times stupid, Dahlia recalled Tamara saying that David—or, at least, *a* David—had written that letter to Molly about "not forgetting you any more than a swimmer can forget water."

"Who's David?" she interrupted Molly.

Molly stopped speaking and looked slightly surprised.

"David was a weird situation. Now he's a friend."

"Excuse me!" someone said.

A large, lozenge-shaped face that was fringed with straight white hair suddenly appeared beside Molly's. Around his neck a shabby silk scarf was draped. His chest looked big for his stubby legs, as though he were in a perpetual state of being foreshortened—like a pug. Quasimodo had migrated from the next table and was crouching at theirs.

"Do you have any idea how loud the two of you are?"

Molly looked stunned.

"I beg your pardon, but I can hardly hear her."

He shook his head, repudiating her claim.

"We're leaning in together like a couple of wind-bent trees," Molly protested.

"This isn't open mic night!" he snapped.

"This isn't the public library!"

They stared at each other, Molly skeptical and faintly amused, the Hunchback of Notre Dame absolutely hostile.

"Stay home if you don't want to hear human voices," Dahlia added.

Quasimodo turned around, shaking his head in dismay, exchanging sighs and groans with his righteous comrades at the next table.

When the waitress came around with their check in a leather case, Molly glanced at it, folded a wad of bills in, and handed it back, saying, "All yours."

"Thank you," chimed the waitress, somewhat mechanically.

Dahlia had been so happily distracted by the last embers of sake, the cool, tangy green tea ice cream, and Molly's reports from New York that she'd forgotten to check her phone for texts. She'd learned, for example, that Matthew's plans to study Halachic law for his conversion were upsetting his parents and Tamara. She heard about her young nieces discovering shoes on "indulgent shopping trips" with Molly.

Their waitress trotted diligently back, her eyes sparkling.

"Are you sure you ladies don't want change?"

"Absolutely," said Molly. "I co-own a restaurant in New York, and I know that serving people is tough work."

The girl looked moved, leather binder clasped in her slender hand.

"Thank you so much!" she said. "Is there anything more I can get you?"

Molly deferred to Dahlia. They both shook their heads no.

"But one favor."

Molly beckoned and the waitress leaned in.

"Those folks"—Molly indicated their rankled neighbors—"have been terribly shrill. Would you please tell them to lower their voices so we can finish our ice cream in peace?"

The girl looked penitent.

"Yes, of course I will. I'm so sorry."

MATTHEW

A Jig and a Hornpipe

Haley's prints—with their lithographic grain, their pencil shavings, and coffee grinds mixed into the surfaces—captivated Molly more in person than they had online. Much to the delight of Dahlia's employers, Molly purchased one to take home and show her client.

Outside in the warm morning breeze, Molly held her bubble-wrapped print and barely existent suitcase as Dahlia impressed upon her, "I know you're busy in New York. But could I speak to you now and then about Saul? It really helped."

"Anytime. Now you know my secret too."

They embraced before Molly got into her cab to the airport.

That evening Dahlia's apartment felt morbidly still, even as her cats skittered over the wooden floor, bandying around colorful ribbons from Molly's gifts.

In the yard below, the landlords served barbecue and chattered with guests. Dahlia could smell roasting steak and hear a radio farther off playing Verdi, something woeful.

And Saul wasn't returning her texts.

He'd written prolifically the night before, when she'd been out having sushi with Molly: *Hey sweetheart. Where r u?* And *Everything ok?*

She'd responded in the morning: *All fine. When can I c u, Sasha?*

But no answer had come. She'd shut and rebooted her phone in case there was a technical problem. But there wasn't, nor was he too busy to speak. This was punishment. *Oh, you didn't reply to me immediately last night. Fine. See how you like it.*

Their game was absurd, something third grade girls would come up with—holding each other hostage to silence. But it gnawed on her, and Dahlia had no one to gripe with now, no friend like Molly around.

The book of Bonnard color reproductions sat on her table. It was opened to a color plate that displayed a woman in a long pink dress about to serve her cat a bowl of milk. Behind the woman a window and the sparkling sea—a paned window that would later emerge in the paintings of Matisse. Dahlia had seen such windows all over France. She had stood by one, overlooking the Mediterranean when she had been unthinkably young and studying art.

Saul didn't write until the next morning. It was a Thursday, and the beginning of Shavuot.

Good Yontif, beautiful. Our first B & B over the Mackinac Bridge. He sent her a link. And another text: *Sea kayaking on Lake Superior. Daya, it looks so lovely and relaxing, maybe we should skip Toronto and stay out in nature? Yr birthday, yr call.*

Wanna c u, she wrote back. *Wantchu bad, bad. Anywhere.*

He said nothing for two long days, which were Friday and Saturday, his family days. She wished he could have sneaked off to text her from the bathroom. One word from him would have changed her whole day.

But he didn't manage anything until Saturday afternoon. *Girls graduate from middle school and have their fifteenth birthday. Mother coming up from Florida.*

The words burrowed into her on Saturday at the gallery.

Weekend art shoppers were sifting through, as they usually did, and Michelle, one of the owning partners, was ingratiating herself to a cluster of them. "The lithographs are by Haley Thames, our emerging printmaker who's on the verge of selling four prints to a designer in New York..." by whom she of course meant Molly.

It occurred to Dahlia that Michelle should be grateful that Dahlia had produced a sale, but as Molly had aptly observed, Michelle lived in "the perpetual business present"—elated as a deal transpired but more or less numb an hour later, like a person who's wolfed down a good meal and finds herself hungry again.

While Michelle was distracted by the Saturday art shoppers and their prospective deals, Dahlia reread Saul's message. He'd mentioned a while back that his mother would be staying with them, and that they needed to schedule her dialysis treatments weeks in advance. Saul and Cheryl would host her for ten days, and then his sister Julie and the notoriously boring husband, Bob Herman, in Michigan would take over. "While she's here, she'll want attention—especially from me and the girls," Saul had emphasized.

His mother's name was Shirley, which had always struck Dahlia as suspiciously close to Cheryl, and according to Saul she'd been a diva mom. She wasn't loud, like Dahlia's parents, "but I suspect she's not as loony or loveable as they are," Saul had suggested. "She's just the kind of person who gives marching orders, and you march." His father, he often recounted, had been more kindly and indulgent. He died just before Alex was born; Saul had passed on the initial *A* from his deceased father, Arthur.

Shirley loved the family fiercely. "She'll often tell us, 'You're all I've got,'" Dahlia had heard him say. She wanted to celebrate the girls' graduation and their birthday, under the appropriate twin sign of Gemini, and Saul's birthday—over the Cancer cusp—before they'd all disperse to points around the country and, unbeknown to her, Saul would be Dahlia's for a week.

Duz this mean I won't c u til August? she texted, as Michelle showed some clients into her back room, where she kept a portfolio of unframed works on paper.

No way, he wrote back. *Miss u bad. Need u to bear with me til u can be bare with me.*

Early summer was always prickly for them, between the end of school and the Fourth of July weekend, which encompassed his birthday. Such occasions collapsed him into the family, leaving Dahlia to a season of roses, ripe peaches, and nervous waiting.

At this time she grieved his touch, how his hands sculpted her into a beauty she didn't feel when she was alone. He shaped her the way children shaped a beach into castles and hills. Without him she felt like the beach at dusk, when everyone leaves and the sea softens those castles into formlessness.

The following day, a Sunday too splendid for even the most devoted art collector to forego the outdoors, Dahlia's phone rang at her desk. This barely happened, and Michelle looked surprised across the long, empty room. It was clear that she didn't expect Dahlia to have a social life and was disgruntled by the reminder.

Dahlia checked the incoming number and felt alarmed—because her busy and beleaguered sister hardly ever called, especially not on a weekend with Matthew around. She opened her phone and whispered, "Tam?"

"Can I speak to you-ou-ou-ouuuuu…" her sister's words ended in a flurry of boo-hoo tears. Dahlia remembered her crying like that as a little girl, the same choppy rhythm and prolonged wail.

"What's going on? Are you okay?"

"Nooooo!" screamed Tamara. "I am not okay."

"Is Daddy okay?"

"Daddy's in his glory. He's just…" she was so loud that Dahlia had to hold the phone away from her ear. She worried that Michelle could hear the racket across the room.

"Daddy's *kvelling*! With a son-in-law joining the tribe now and a grandson. I hate our fucking sexist creed…" She fumed, she ranted, and Dahlia felt relieved. She was afraid their father had died. She'd rather have him *kvelling* over Matthew's conversion to Judaism and a grandson.

"Is it that bad?" she asked her sister.

Tamara cried out so boisterously that Dahlia nearly dropped her phone.

"I can't be with Matthew anymore! I've asked for a divorce."

"Are you crazy?"

"No, I'm saaaayyyyyyyne! But I'll go crazy if I spend one more day with that lunatic hypocrite."

"Tam, calm down," said Dahlia firmly. "Now look. Do you need me to come to New York?"

Tamara was suddenly so silent that Dahlia worried that they'd lost the connection.

"Hello? You there?"

"You'd really come here?" Tamara asked, sniffling.

"If you need me to, yes."

After reading about her negligence in Tamara's diaries, she felt determined to be more of a sister, to not let this one fall on Molly's shoulders.

"Have you spoken to Molly?"

"Oh, poor Molly. He's such a jerk to her. He's such a jerk, and now he's using my religion to stick it to me…asshole."

"Tam, try to calm down…What happened with Molly?"

She glanced up and fortunately, Michelle had gone to answer her own phone call in the back room, so Dahlia was free to focus on Tamara's story.

"The day Molly returned from visiting you last week we needed her to watch the kids—one of our sitters was out of town and the other had a cold. Last-minute favor, and she was completely nice about it. But when we came to pick them up from her place the jerkface had a conniption because she was—catch this—playing Irish music for the girls. You know, a jig and a hornpipe."

"What was the problem?"

"Well, it's not Jewish music, you see! He accused Molly of not respecting his wishes to raise his children with a 'Jewish identity.'"

"Because she was playing Irish music?"

"If Molly's friend Eugenia hadn't been there, he would have gotten obscene. Eugenia's this super-gorgeous blonde—the type that has a calming effect on men. I said to myself, 'I should be jealous,' but I so wasn't. I so didn't give a pig's bum."

"Oh, I've met Eugenia. At the *bris*. Remember when Kayla got chocolate on her white jacket?"

"God, that feels like ages ago. So you could imagine Eugenia cracking the ice age with a smile and saying, 'Matthew, it's happy music. That's what the children hear.' I steered him out the door and told him we'd talk later, when the kids were asleep. But he pretended to conk out early himself."

"How do you know he was pretending?"

"When you're married, you know from pretending. Then yesterday, he shlepped us all to a—trust me when I say, God-forsaken—Shavuot ceremony in Borough Park." Tamara started to cry again. "Daya, it was so awful. Not even a—pardon my French—fucking synagogue. But a mess hall with folding chairs, shabby curtains, and a screen that separated the men from the women."

"Borough Park? Where's that?"

"Not far from Aunt Renie. Who do you think gave him the grand idea?"

"Sound like serious turf."

"No kidding! And true to form, behind that screen the fellas were whooping it up, you know, dancing, singing and davening to their heart's delight in their dumb-looking Jewish cowboy hats. But we girls just sat twiddling our thumbs. Mira looked sad, and Kay looked pissed. Even they knew we didn't belong. I finally opened my shirt and started nursing Oren. All the women in their *sheitels* tried not to look."

"But why the Hassids?"

"That's where he's studying to convert, you know."

"What's gotten into him? Doesn't he know they're crazy?"

"Crazy?" yelled Tamara. "Why Dahlia, they have the word of the Almighty."

Now Michelle was heading purposefully out of the back room toward her.

"Tam, we must talk more about this, but I'm at the gallery…"

"I'd better get off, too. The baby's waking up from his nap. The two-month-old baby, I mean."

Dahlia worked conscientiously for the rest of the afternoon, filing Michelle's receipts and drafting a press release for the upcoming show. She didn't look at her phone until evening, when she got home and found two messages. One lifted her heart, from Saul, saying that he would try his best to come see her tomorrow (*my sweet honey apple cake,* he called her). The other she assumed was from Molly, since the email handle was m_douglas.

But it was from Matthew. His subject line was *family crisis/need your help.* Dahlia poured herself a shot glass of brandy to sit and read it.

Hi Daya,

Please forgive me for appealing to you in this way, over email. But I didn't want to put you on the spot by calling. If you wish, we can speak once you read this. Or maybe you'd prefer to stay out of this sad mess. I leave the choice to you.

I'm sure you know that Tamara and I have scaled our hurdles, but you may not know that yesterday she asked for a divorce.

I'm shell-shocked, didn't see it coming, and absolutely oppose it.

We've just had a third child, and I strongly believe we should be more of a family, not less of one.

Daya, you're the only person I can think of who might help us through this.

Tam and I can't even agree on where to turn for counseling. Of course, I don't want to go near that so-called Buddhist (except-when-it-comes-to-accepting-dona-tions) temple of hers, and she has developed an equally strong aversion to her own faith, which is now becoming mine.

This, I think, is part of the problem. Strange as it may sound, she doesn't want me to convert. But stranger yet, I feel I'm already a Jew.

I never used to understand people who said they were "'born the wrong gender'" and wanted operations—used to think they were nuts. Now I completely get it.

Because Daya, it's no accident that my wife is Jewish, my children are Jewish, and even my close friend and business partner, Lenny, is Jewish. I feel much more warmth from your mishpachah *than I do from my own. While I admire my mother's dignity and social command, I haven't had a real conversation with her since she reconciled with Molly. My father has always been too much the dry, sardonic Scots-man, and he's always preferred Molly, never known what to make of me. Our time together has become formal and awkward. Meanwhile, I speak candidly with your dad ("Daddy"), and he asks me good questions and speaks naturally, not like I'm an afterthought to him.*

Maybe "the grass is always greener," as Tamara says. Certainly, she appreciates the Jewish value of discourse and education, but she feels it was traditionally encour-aged in men at women's expense. I can't counter that claim or rewrite history. But still I treasure the special vitality of Jewish life.

As a gentile, I must commit to a strongly religious Jewish life, should I elect to convert. Tamara doubts my ability to adhere to the laws over time; but laws and structures keep my feet on the ground. She's seen me go to seed in periods of paralysis and depression that I'm prone to. She finds the Halachic laws excessive, but I want her to understand that they will help me be the best husband and father I can be.

Tamara trusts you more than anyone on Earth.

You'll probably hear from her.

If you feel moved, perhaps you can urge her to reconsider such an extreme deci-sion as divorce? Any words of guidance to either of us would be so welcome.

I don't want to lose my precious family.
Your brother,
Matt

Dahlia texted him instantly: *I'll help you! T. called me yesterday. Will talk 2 her.* Within the half hour he replied: *Bless you.*

Monday morning Dahlia's weekend began. As the city outside geared up to shuttle commuters on its trains and buses, to serve the coffee and pastries that would launch a new week, Dahlia found herself under blankets. As she opened drowsy eyes, Matthew's words about needing structure came to her.

She didn't know whether to expect Saul later. If he were definitely coming she'd feel motivated to get up and clean the apartment, and she wouldn't go to the exhibit at the Art Institute. She felt compelled to see him in those arbitrary slots of time he had for her—especially now, before his mother's long, disruptive visit.

She reached from her supine position to check her phone. Anything? Nothing. She tossed it down again. Sleepy but not tired, though not ready to be awake, she gazed across the room to the bright blue rectangle of sky wavering through her lace curtains.

An hour later she sat at her table drinking the chicory coffee Molly had left her and reading the paper. She dropped off halfway through articles about places in which she had no desire to set foot and was dismayed that any woman had to—Juarez, Mexico; Afghanistan; the Sudan. She dropped the paper to her knees and pondered an antonym for *lonely* or *lonesome*. *Close* was the opposite of *distant*, *happy* the opposite of *sad*. You couldn't necessarily say: "I'm not lonely, I'm happy" because someone could feel both lonely and happy in a strange land—as her forebears had felt coming here. And it was certainly possible to feel close to someone, yet lonesome for him.

Suddenly she received a text and bolted over to her phone, worried that Saul would show up soon and she hadn't showered or done her hair. He always said those things didn't matter, that she was beautiful to him "groomed or informal."

But the message was from Matthew: *Daya, don't tell Molly about my family crisis. Tks*

She wrote back: *won't.*

Two minutes later, another text. She knew it would be from Matthew, but shut her eyes for one hopeful moment before reading: *Glad you enjoyed Molly's company, but she and I have different values.*

Upon the heels of that, more from Matthew: *No surprise if Molly suggested that Tamara divorce me.*

Dahlia texted, *Highly doubt it.*

And Matthew replied, *Whatever the case, pls don't tell her anything.*

Now, to remember all the mandates:

> *Molly not to know about Tamara's bid for divorce*
>
> *Tamara and Matt not to know that Molly loves Eugenia*
>
> *Saul not to know that I saw his daughters at the Congress Plaza Hotel*
> *from beneath blonde wig disguise*
>
> *The world at large not to know that Saul is my lover,*
> *and I am not to know whether or not I'll see him today.*

As it turned out, he was not going to make it.

Please don't be mad, he wrote by noon. *Next week, I promise. IOU.*

Wednesday afternoon at the gallery an email came in from Molly with the subject line good news/bad news.

The good news was that her client had raved about Haley's print and wanted to purchase two others. They admired how she didn't print editions of replicates but added surface variations of grit and ash with chalk and pencil shavings. They'd already chosen their other favorites online. Michelle would be overjoyed, which might bode well for her extending Dahlia's vacation in August. Dahlia was thinking about visiting New York for a week after traveling with Saul.

The bad news, Molly had written, is I'm worried about your sister. Do you have a moment to speak?

Can speak later but not now, Dahlia wrote back. She had to update the mailing list and research ad prices in some new press kits and didn't want to risk speaking on the phone after that long phone call with Tamara on Sunday.

Eventually she heard again from Molly, who emailed, I can speak now but not later. I'll write, if that's ok? Read when you can.

Dahlia did so, between her dull responsibilities.

Yesterday evening I came home to your sister on my doorstep with Oren in her arms, like a gypsy mom on the steps of an Italian church. She stared up at me and begged to come in.

Between us, Dahlia, I didn't feel like seeing anyone. I'd been in conferences all day and expected Genie later, so I wanted to rest. But I welcomed Tamara and gave her some tea – over which, in a barely coherent diatribe, she conveyed that she's dog miserable with my brother and thinking of divorce.

I advised her not to act rashly, and she burst into tears. She says she spoke with you over the weekend, and that you'd also urged temperance.

I understand that my brother's driving her to the brink, but I asked her how divorce would help – it hardly means you're out of someone's life if you have three young kids together in the same city.

Years ago, Dahlia had thought the same thing about Saul and Cheryl. Even if they divorced, Dahlia realized that Cheryl would hardly be out of the picture.

What did Tamara say? Dahlia eventually wrote back.

Says she loves him but can't bear how he simplifies and idealizes Orthodox Judaism. He's become what's known as a Philosemite.

Dahlia couldn't help writing, *Well, so many people hate us...I say, bring on the love.* ☺

There's love and there's fervor. Take nudity, for example. I adore being nude with my lover, and I wouldn't get into a bathtub any other way. But do I need to mill around a nudist camp with adults who'd look better in clothing...?

You can push good things too far, and my brother's got that knack. The other day Genie and I were looking after the kids, and we put on a CD from an Irish band that plays at our bar. Matt completely went berserk -- accused me of being provocative, because our mom likes Irish music, and of undermining his new Jewish values. Tamara was standing there with her eyes shut, incanting the Heart Sutra. When they left, Genie said: "I like them, but they're both up the wall." And she's seen plenty of that, with her fundamentalist Christian brothers and sister-in-laws.

I care for your brother.

Well, you're at the right viewing distance for Matthew. Some people are best at arm's length.

I'll call Tamara, Dahlia promised, but found herself leaving messages on her sister's voice mail.

A Painfully Elusive Antonym

When Saul appeared at her door that next week they fell into each other like a decomposed tree falling at last to Earth. Barely pushing the door closed again, they hobbled to bed, grabbing at each other's buttons and zippers and laughing breathlessly.

Once they landed on the duvet she traced a nascent goatee that flowered around his lips. He kissed her fingers, sucking them into his warm mouth—two, three at a time.

"Why...in summer?" she asked, rubbing her cheek against his new stubble.

He mumbled something with his mouth full of her fingers, which she slipped out again, and he repeated, "Tell you later."

The fan was on, and her lace curtains flailed in the warm July breeze. She kicked her bare feet at his loafers, trying to push them off. He eventually shook them to the floor and scared both cats under the bed.

"Missed you," he whispered. "So damn much. Weeks of thorns and you're my rose petal."

"How long can you stay?"

"Forever."

She unbuttoned his shirt, finding the Star of David on his chest. But his ribs protruded more than usual against his skin. Above the goatee his cheekbones too seemed prominent, and she realized he'd lost weight since she'd seen him. She unwrapped the rest of his clothing like tissue paper, peeling away the shirt and pants. Poking from his wiry nest of pubic hair, his penis lay against his thigh as though it had been carelessly flung there.

And he moaned something between "Dally" and "Darling"—but not "Daya."

She lifted her shirt over her head and then worked her skirt down her hips and legs, where it fell to the floor in a poof hoop.

Nude except for her black lace bra, she climbed upon his loins, one leg to each side. He stared at her for a moment then shut his eyes, his penis still not moving.

She clasped his hands and instinctively opened herself and drew him into her, soft as he was, as she rocked gently from side to side.

"Snap, crackle, pop," he whispered to offset their embarrassment over the slick sound of their contact. Gradually she felt him stiffen, and she increased her gyrations like a belly dance on him. They had never done it like that before. Usually, it was her delight to lie back and let him work his magic upon her, to vicariously share his excitement. But in that moment, she admitted something to herself: lately she had been imagining Molly and Eugenia together before she fell asleep—just trying to figure out what the heck happened when they did it—and the concept of Eugenia's pelvic movements made her shiver with arousal. Now she owned that female force in her own belly, feeling herself transfer voltage to Saul as she surrendered to the large warm hands that clutched her buttocks. Then he sat up, his face flushed and blue eyes bright.

"You are fucking amazing," he growled into her ear, biting it sharply.

Now he was hard inside her, their hips snug and legs overlapping as they drew closer, and he thrust into her in this unfamiliar position while they grasped each other's backs with fingernails, and he cried out as though he were hurting, "Jesus! Oh, Jesus, Dahlia!"

After that, the thump, thump, thumping of his heart.

"Sorry," he whispered. "I let that cat out of the bag a little fast."

"Did I hurt you?" She stroked his face with its sharper cheekbones and new goatee.

"I never feel this good without you. Guess that hurts." He swallowed, seemed disoriented. "Hope I didn't let you down, after all this waiting."

"It doesn't have to be the same each time." Then she whispered into his ear, "I love you."

The new goatee tickled her cheek as he responded. "I'm crazy about you."

And it struck her that the antonym of *lonely* was *together*.

They lay side by side beneath her sheets, unable to move.

Ashes and Phoenix tugged her skirt over the floor, but she didn't care.

She heard someone text her, but she didn't care about that either.

It was probably Matthew or Tamara, and she'd given plenty of her time to their problems lately. All week it had been one thing after another.

"Your phone," he said distractedly.

"Did I tell you my sister might get divorced?"

Saul sighed and said, "Must be in the air. So might I."

Unprepared for that one, Dahlia sat up beneath the sheets.

"Are you kidding me? What—did Cheryl find out about us?"

He shook his head sadly, and now it all made sense: his weight loss, the new goatee, his impotence and quick ejaculation.

"She doesn't know yet," he said. "But she won't be surprised."

"What happened?"

He knotted his brows and pouted at her.

"Don't be mad at me…"

Now her heart started thumping too.

He shrugged himself up into a half-seated position against the pillow and backboard. "Look—how to explain this? She read an article about marriage and intimacy in some women's magazine at the hair salon." He shook his head with shame or annoyance, Dahlia couldn't tell. It was an emotion he reserved for Cheryl. "So at her initiation we started making love again, for the first time in years. Or trying to."

Whodathunkit?

Dahlia's heart bit itself.

"That's part of the reason I just—I couldn't see you for a while. Between that, and my mother visiting. Old crab apple that she's become…"

The bite bled discrete droplets, one after the other.

"But it just—" He shook his head again as if denying something, pursing the lips that were accented sensually by his new goatee. "No chemistry, nothing changed, we shouldn't have gone there."

"How can any woman not have chemistry with you?"

Her heart stung.

He smiled meekly and said, "With the finest ingredients, a busboy is a master chef. Our time together is beautiful because of you."

She shook her head in protest, but he reached out to stroke her arm.

"Cheryl yawned like she was waiting for it to be over so she could make phone calls." He blanched, then gazed fondly at Dahlia. "It wasn't like being with you, where we're both so—present. Alive."

His voice went low as though he couldn't speak anymore. Ashes jumped up on the bed, and Dahlia stroked his fur downward, over the soft pocket between his little shoulder blades. The cat rumbled and purred contentedly as Saul found his voice again.

"The next day, when I tried to talk with her about it, she laughed me off in this cutting way. Didn't want to get into it. She went to help Alex order pants and a rain parka from LL Bean for his bike trip, and I found myself watching her with resentment. Usually when she helps the kids shop online or something, I appreciate what a great mom she is.

"We had it right, staying away from sex all these years. We still liked each other."

Dahlia continued to stroke Ashes vigorously, aware that Phoenix was eating dry food across the room and that she was almost out of dry treats.

"But when I got ready to shave the next morning, I stared at myself in the mirror—like a classic moment of truth—and had a word with this old boy…'Buster,' I said, 'you turned forty-nine last week. There's time left, but not much of it.'"

He reached over again and took hold of Dahlia's hands that were grazing Ashes' soft, lumpy back, holding them still. "You know, Dally, we're not young. But we're not old. What's most important is we should be with each other. I was always afraid of how my kids would deal with you, but I see how they still talk about your friend from New York—they liked Molly so much. It occurred to me that they might like you too."

"I'm not clever and outgoing like she is."

"Oh," he said, "but you're lovely and dear and intelligent. Sure, at first it might be touchy for them. In time they'll be as crazy about you, in their own ways, as I am. It's worth a shot. Isn't it?"

Through her absolute shock, Dahlia wondered if this might rate as a variant of the philandering 'I've Met Someone!'

"Well," he continued, his hand still warm and sweaty on hers, "that morning I decided not to shave my whole face…I thought, 'Let me grow this little beard as kind of a boundary, an omen of living separately from Cheryl.' So you and I can have a free situation, like you've always wanted. Who knows? One day we could even have a pad of our own. Waddaya think?"

Dahlia was so unaccustomed to talking like this that she thought again of dry cat food. She couldn't recall whether it was cheaper to get it at the pet store or the grocery store.

"Here's another part of it," he said, raising his other hand to stroke her hair. "When Papa died, he left Mother a shitload of insurance and investments. The old bird has more money than God these days. Ten years ago, she opened an account with Bernie Madoff—you ever heard of him?"

Dahlia shook her head. If he'd asked her whether she'd heard of The Beatles or The Grateful Dead she couldn't have answered at that moment, so this name was already gone.

"And he turns over quite a profit. So part of her reason for visiting was to offer some of this nut to Julie and me—you know, for our kids' college funds, and for our households. Trust me, there's enough to go around. Mother hasn't exactly been generous. Now she's old and in pain much of the time. She didn't say as much, but I sense she doesn't want to die in an embarrassment of riches in her Florida condo. And this is what Papa would have wanted for us, kind of a living will.

"Julie and Bob are keeping their share with Madoff, but I've got a better option than some hotshot on the East coast. Developers from the mall just asked me into a deal that could top any charts…and then the liens I bought three years ago. Honey, we could get ourselves a big apartment by the park. My kids could go to the schools of their choice, and Cheryl wouldn't have a day's worry if she lives another two hundred years."

"Are you serious?"

Saul's hand continued to stroke her hair and cheek as he stared into her eyes.

"You," he whispered, his breath warm on her face. "Oh apple cakes, you're the love of my life. It's crazy that we're not together. It's crap. Mind you, this all may not happen at the speed of light. But I can't see it taking longer than a year or two."

"Won't Cheryl be devastated?" Dahlia asked, and he shook his head, his hand now falling lightly down her neck.

"She's…checked out. Not with me anymore."

"But she'd flip if you tell her, 'I've met someone.'"

"Best not to say that. Though the ironic truth is, I might have left her years ago if you weren't around to keep me happy. But things don't stay in one place, do they?"

"I don't want us to hurt her unnecessarily."

He shook his head again and cleared his throat.

Conference Call

The next day Dahlia learned that Matthew and Tamara had gone to a marriage counselor and talked circles around the poor woman.

Her mother called, saying dolefully, "Have you heard? The kids are having troubles. I told them, 'Enjoy your good health. Nothing else is so important.'"

Their father's take, which Dahlia learned later that day, was decidedly less charitable.

"You don't have problems," he'd scolded Tamara. "My mother had problems in Budapest, shacking us up in the embassy while we waited for the Schutz-passes and visas. Your mother's aunts had problems with the Cossacks. You want problems, the world will give you problems. What you have with Mattie is trifles. Don't let it break your spine."

It was little surprise to hear Tamara's voice-mail the next day, claiming: "Not that I don't get Daddy's point, like a slap in the face. But it looks like we're rounding that corner of separation. There's no way back now."

Still, she sounded remorseful, and Dahlia perceived an opening.

Of course she, who never interfered, would tread carefully. This was not her situation to change or judge. And she hardly wanted to immerse herself in Tamara's strife. Much to the contrary, Dahlia had worked herself into a superstition that too much contact with Tamara might jinx her own joy. Every day Saul spoke or wrote her about living together in an apartment overlooking the park. He said he could support her, that she could go back to school for the PhD in art history that she'd always wanted—or she could hang out all day reading books.

She was beginning to acclimate to this lovely prospect the way she acclimated to warmer days in spring: not quite trusting them, flinching from every gust off the lake, but realizing the winds no longer pricked her nose. Mulling over this potential new life, she felt tempted to avoid Tamara's onslaught of tears and complaints, and the new irony that lurked behind all of it: that soon Dahlia might live with someone, while Tamara might become a single mom.

She could have withdrawn from Tamara and enfolded herself in the silken chrysalis of dreams, watching them twirl, strand by strand. But she had promised to help her brother-in-law keep his marriage and to help her sister keep her soul. Knowing too that Saul would respect her dedication, she picked up the phone and called New York.

"Couples therapy was a bust," Tamara sourly reported. "We both knew more than the frigging professional. She hadn't had a relationship in years."

"At least it gave you a way to bond with Matthew."

"Yeah, our last connection before the blade falls."

"Tam, you sound really sad."

"Should I be popping champagne? I have a baby and two preschoolers, and I'm going to fucking get divorced. We're going to find a mediator. I kind of can't believe it's happening."

"Well, it doesn't have to. Matthew's not abusive, and he's not a drunk slob. He's workable if you want him to be."

Dahlia's heart thudded. She hardly ever took so strong a stand for anyone else's life, even her sister's. She hardly held such ground with anything in her own life.

"And how would you work with him, if you were me?" Tamara huffed, sounding, nevertheless, grateful for the attention.

"I don't know exactly, but look...if you both want to try talking to me before you go to the mediator, trial-run it with a third person who cares about you..." She felt instant apprehension as Tamara began weighing this option.

"You seem to think highly of Matt."

"I do."

"Why?"

"He's got a good heart, he's intelligent, he's reliable. And he's pretty cute—may I ask you a frank question?"

"I can guess what it is, and the answer is that when we don't revile the sight of each other, we're pretty happy between the sheets. That hasn't changed. Actually, it's gotten better lately. Which is weird."

"Well, Tamara, come on," Dahlia cried, shifting her position on the bed where she laid back, bunching a pillow beneath her head.

"Sex is an animal act. It's easier to have sex with someone you can't stand than it is to have dinner with him, because dinner is a civilized act."

"People complain bitterly about their sexless marriages."

"*People*? You mean Saul."

"Um, I have news for you. He's hardly the only one in that situation."

"You're suddenly an expert on marriage? *You*? Ms. Single America?"

Dahlia groaned. "It's not rocket science. Look at any study on the subject."

"'My wife doesn't understand me,'" Tamara mimicked in a low, masculine voice. "What a crock. What a cliché."

"Cliché? Listen to you...'Oh, my husband doesn't understand me—'"

"Anything that man says you believe, don't you?" her sister interrupted.

Dahlia felt a hot bubble at her throat.

"I agree with Daddy," she spewed, sitting up at the edge of the bed now. "You're acting like a spoiled little princess and the pea; everything isn't perfect, so you're ready to toss it in...can't even give your baby son the memory of having a mother and father in one home."

Her heartbeat was deafening, and she realized the other line had gone silent.

"Tam? You there?"

Sobs began to squeak out of her sister.

"I'm sorry, Tam. Tam? Are you still there?"

"No, you're right," Tamara finally said, sobbing and gulping. "We'll talk about this. But Molly should be there too. I think she has a better understanding of just how insane Matthew can drive a woman."

Of course Matthew vetoed the idea of Molly having any part of this "trial-run mediation," though he expressed gratitude for Dahlia's prospective input. She offered to travel to New York so they could speak together in person, but Matt and Tamara insisted that a conference phone call would suffice. He volunteered to initiate the call from his office, after hours. Tamara would stay home with the baby while a neighbor took their little girls to the park.

Dahlia waited that evening for Matt's call, which came five minutes late. "Hold on, Daya," he said. "I've got Tamara on the other line." There was a short click, and Dahlia's phone went dead. She shook it, slapped it, threw it on the bed, shut it down, and rebooted. When she called Tamara she got a rapid busy signal.

Twenty minutes later Tamara called her, complaining that Matt had completely bungled the call and that it was too late to speak anyway; she had to start dinner.

Dahlia felt faintly relieved, as she told Saul when he called later.

"So why exactly are they counting on you to mediate?" he began.

"I guess I'm premediating before the real mediator, who precedes attorneys..."

"Oh, they're not going through with it," he said flatly. "This is all hopscotch. I've gone straight to an attorney."

"Have you?"

Dahlia was flitting around her kitchen area, slicing tomatoes for the grilled cheese on pumpernickel she was preparing in her toaster oven as the cats shadowed her feet. She was shocked and thrilled that he'd sought an attorney.

"Well, I called this guy that a colleague used. Haven't hired him yet—hell, I haven't even told Cheryl I want to separate—just checking him out. I'm already beyond Matt and Tamara. We have friends like them, always griping and grousing and interrupting each other and threatening divorce—it's foreplay. Mark my words: those sharp edges bind. Cheryl and I are smooth enough to slip away without half the fanfare. You just watch."

A few days later, Matt and Tamara tried the conference call again. Dahlia was starting to believe that Saul was onto their delay tactic: the more they scheduled a conference call with her, the more they could postpone the misery of their further steps, and the more calm and relieved they seemed.

Now she'd been given a number to dial with a code that would enable her to access their particular call. "Welcome to live conferencing," a robust recording greeted her. "Please enter your five-digit pin, followed by the pound sign."

Dahlia did so, and the same voice advised that she was now entering the conference.

"Hey Daya," said Matt. "How are you?"

"Okay. Is Tamara on?"

"Not yet. So…I guess this will work…"

He sounded nervous.

"Are you at home or at the office?"

"At the office. We were thinking that would give us more breathing room."

Ten minutes later, they had chatted about Mira and Kayla's day camp in Central Park, and Matt had asked about her birthday plans—Dahlia was evasive—but Tamara was still not on the line.

"You want to call her?" he asked.

"Sure."

"Oh, wait…looks like I've got a text here. Says she's tried this conference number three times and dialed the correct pin—38612—yeah, that's it—but she keeps getting bumped into the board meeting of a business school in Iowa. She refuses to try it once more."

Matt started giggling boyishly and Dahlia doubled over in hysterics. If one of them stopped laughing to sigh or groan, the other found it even sillier, and before they knew it two minutes had slipped by.

"One of us should call her," Dahlia managed to gasp.

Matt said that his eyes were tearing so much that he was losing a contact lens. Another phone rang in his background. He said genially, "That's probably her. I'll get it and call you back."

Ten minutes later Tamara called to say they were attempting one more approach.

"I'll get him on my cell and you on the landline, and we'll see if you can hear each other if I hold the receivers together. What a bunch of techno-dopes we are! If Molly were on the case, you know this call would've happened by now. I wanted to include her, but of course he won't think of it."

"Well, we may need her, simply to set up the call."

At this suggestion Dahlia and her sister burst into their own peels of laughter. It had been a while since they'd laughed with each other in their special way, and the bond felt welcome. Outside her window sunset burned clouds into shadow, gently shading the walls. Dahlia knew only that whether or not this call ever occurred, she had already brought mirth to the unhappy situation, and she could travel with peace of mind in two weeks when she and Saul left for the Upper Peninsula.

What I Wasn't Looking For

The next morning as Dahlia was leaving for work, her mother called.

"My heart sang when Tamara told us you offered to talk to her and Mattie. They need perspective, support…I believe in what you're doing."

As Dahlia locked her door she heard Phoenix meow inquisitively as he often did once she was on the other side of it.

"Daddy's proud of you too. He's tired today; he's resting. But he wanted me to let you know."

"Wish me luck."

Dahlia trotted down the small steps, one hand on the banister and the other around her phone.

"You were always such a calm and happy child," Mama went on. "It didn't take much to make you smile. You know, Daddy and I want the best for you, darling."

"Good things are happening."

"Oh?"

Her mother heard the difference in her voice that morning.

Dahlia pushed the front door open to a vibrant summer day on her street with lush elms and canopied storefronts. Though soon she wouldn't live here; she and Saul would have a grander and more open home with big sunny windows and a view of the park. Every evening they'd cook together or sit on the sofa and read, their legs entwined, or they'd slowly undress each other for hours of languorous love. But of course, she could not say anything to her family just yet.

In fact, she had to remind herself that there would be less than stellar days in store, when he might be short or condescending with her—as he was from time to time. She would have to be careful about depending on him for money. Then there were his children, who would undoubtedly resent her. She recalled how Wendy had given Molly the once-over at the Congress Plaza Hotel. Still, despite such occasional abrasions, she believed that the life her mother wanted for her was beginning.

Two days later she met Saul at a building on North Clark Street with Marianne, a real estate agent in a rayon pants suit with frosted hair the color of lemon ices and lipstick the color of sangria cherries. They'd presented her with phony names: Saul called himself Arthur, his father's name, and Dahlia decided upon Molly—too superstitious to call herself Tamara. She would rather have Molly's luck than Tamara's. They had told Marianne that they were fiancées, and Saul had removed his wedding band and slipped it in his shirt pocket for this occasion. Still, he wore one of his visor hats and sunglasses to "keep a low profile."

They were viewing an apartment that he'd come upon online and insisted they view in person. Marianne led them to a 1920s brick building with a lobby of orange marble.

"An elevator," Dahlia commented. "Never lived anywhere with one."

"Me neither," said Saul. "Except in my student dorm a million years ago."

"You'll enjoy many conveniences here," said Marianne, and as they rode to the tenth floor, she chirped them off in a Canadian-sounding accent: a gym, a sun deck, laundry room, permit street parking, basic cable service.

Dahlia's heart leapt when Marianne, struggling for a moment with the stubborn key, opened the apartment door. The smell of fresh paint and summer air greeted them. Lights and a ceiling fan had already been turned on. Their footfalls echoed on hardwood floors.

"Wow," said Saul, pacing around the airy living room. "Nice."

The city views struck Dahlia as quintessential, between the glass high-rises and low, flat buildings, the park's greenery fading into lake and sky. They might as well have been overlooking Rome.

"What do you think…Molly?" he asked.

Dahlia nodded nervously.

The real Molly wouldn't be fazed. She already owned a beautiful apartment in New York and was accustomed to decisions of consequence.

Saul took off his sunglasses, went over to the window, and looked down briefly as though he were peering down a long chute.

"Let's see the bedrooms."

Marianne obediently led them through a small corridor, past a bathroom with shiny black-and-white tiles. There was a disconcertingly large master bedroom and a smaller one beside it. Dahlia took his hand, careful to suppress any response, remembering her parents famous tussle about showing too much enthusiasm to a real estate agent before they'd bought their first home in the suburbs.

Marianne walked them back to the kitchen, pointing out the microwave and large refrigerator, the double sink and dishwasher. Even the tiny kitchen window afforded an impressive vista.

"Is it possible that Molly and I could speak alone here for a moment?" asked Saul.

"Sure. I'll go to the sun deck and come back in a little while," said Marianne.

"Thank you."

When she shut the door they walked around again, oohing and ahhing more freely through the bright, bare rooms.

"This is a damn nice place," he said several times. "Damn nice. Thought it would be."

He pointed out where her lithographs could hang between the windows and described how they'd have bookshelves and a large-screen TV on the other wall.

Then they sat side by side on the newly polyurethaned floor of the living room, their legs overlapping. She slid her arm around his, dropping her cheek to his shoulder and savoring the rich scent of his skin and cologne.

"You like it here, Daya?"

"Love it."

She took his hand, which was nicer to hold without his wedding band.

"Shame we can't just—move in."

"I know."

"We're gonna talk later, Cheryl and I. I'll break it to her."

Dahlia lifted her face from his shoulder.

"You haven't done that yet?" she asked, trying not to sound upset. "You've contacted an attorney. We're here looking at an apartment, talking about hanging my lithographs…"

He pressed his lips together, taking in her words.

"There's been—well, over the last week, there's been some trouble with Wendy," he said, in tones so low that she had trouble hearing him even though he was beside her. Still, he faced outward, across the room. "Hasn't made for the best atmosphere to talk about separation."

"What trouble?"

"It's been brewing for a while. But everything came to a head when my mother was here."

"Why haven't you told me?"

"I was hoping it would go away."

He clutched her hand.

"Hoping *what* would go away?"

"Wish I knew. To begin, Wendy and Cheryl were at each other's throats; Wendy called Cheryl a bitch in front of my mother. Ooh, that did not go over well."

"What about Lisa?"

"Lisa's become the good twin, the quiet and pleasant one. She's also been… well, Wendy isn't her best friend anymore, though she is Wendy's—if you see what I mean. Wendy's still attached to their exclusive twin society. But Lisa's becoming close to other friends at school, and since April, she's started spending time with a boy."

"You actually *let* her, Sasha?"

Dahlia sidled closer to him and he gripped her hand tighter.

"Honey, don't kick me…Jared is just what an overprotective dad would want. Handsome, polite, a year older than Lisa, from a good Jewish family—both of his parents are tenured professors at Northwestern. He accompanies Lisa's flute on piano. They play Bach duets three evenings a week. Wendy's unhappy about it. She's made some disparaging remarks about Jared that are not well-founded. I even said, 'Sounds like sour grapes, Wendo—find yourself a guy buddy too,' and she declared that she hates boys and finds them disgusting."

"Typical for girls that age," said Dahlia uncertainly, because she knew that she already had developed heartrending crushes by then.

"It's typical for a nine- or ten-year-old," Saul rejoined. "Lisa is typical for a fifteen-year-old. Her eyes light up when she talks about Jared. She always wants to go over there for dinner, and I gotta say, his folks have been kind about having her. They're nicer than Cheryl and I. We haven't had him once. Well, I've always trusted academic Jews more than schmucks like me that do business," he said with a laugh.

"Which is why Wendy was so off-base. He's a nice boy. Just realize, Daya, that my typical conversation with Lisa is agreeing to pick her up from Jared's. My typical conversation with Alex is making sure he wears his helmet when he bikes. My typical conversation with Wendy is trying to find an answer when she asks: 'Why do religions teach us to love each other and not kill, when God kills so many people in fires and floods?'"

"She asked you that?"

"Among other ponderous questions."

"She just sounds intelligent."

"No doubt. She makes top grades, and her teachers love her. But it's not the whole story, Daya."

He then dropped Dahlia's hand to prop it on his knee. And he sat for a while, not saying a word as Dahlia gazed across the room to the kitchen nook and the large, bright windows on the eastern wall.

"Sasha, I hope my cats will be safe; we might have to cat-proof the windows," she began, and at the same time he divulged, "I think she's anorexic."

"Well, we *know* she's anorexic," she said.

He regarded Dahlia with incomprehension.

"What do you mean, we 'know' she's anorexic?" he asked in a plaintive voice she'd never heard from him. And when he charged, "You've never even met her," Dahlia felt humiliated, remembering her disguise in the hotel lobby where she had seen Wendy. She also remembered the many times he had second-guessed Tamara, her parents, and even Molly.

"Well, you always talk about her not eating enough."

"Always?" He balked. "Am I always talking about that? Seems you and I have a lot of other topics to talk about."

Dahlia unmoored herself from him, stood up, and walked toward the window. She lingered there, watching traffic lights change on North Clark Street as people dashed across the striped lines. She glanced at her wristwatch. Eventually he came up behind her, grazing her elbow with his index finger.

"I wonder when our friend Marjorie will be back," he said, sounding more like the Saul she knew.

"Marianne."

"Oh that's right. Remember that old Zeppelin song, '*All of my love, all of my love to you, Marianne*?'"

"No," said Dahlia.

"You think she's onto us?"

"Who?"

"The real estate chick. Marianne."

"Onto us?"

"Do you think she knows we gave her fake IDs?"

"I think she sees ten million people and doesn't give a damn."

Dahlia fixed her gaze outside, to the crossing stripes, the traffic lights, the promenade by the park.

"I like this place," Saul said firmly. "Maybe I could put down a deposit and hold it for six months."

Dahlia continued watching the street.

"You haven't even broken up with your wife. You just made your real estate investment last week. You told me it takes a couple of years…"

"That one will take some time. But I invested in the liens years ago."

"And you cashed out?"

"That's coming," he said. "Daya—this is business. You act fast. That's what I'm about. I should hold this place for us, right?"

"Getting ahead of yourself, seems to me."

"I live ahead of myself and behind myself. What do you think? Should we do it?"

She didn't hear from him until two days later. He called in the morning, on her way to work—perturbing her so completely with an update about Cheryl that a cyclist nearly hit her, and at the gallery she had to triple her efforts to concentrate.

She couldn't process what he'd told her until much later, at home, when she sat with her phone drooping her skirted lap like a body in a hammock. Long ago she'd lazed in a hammock, which—like everything else in her parents' home—had become too fragile to use but literally hung around for years, its pillows musty and the ropes frayed. For a while she thought it could hold her, and for a while it did. Then one visit she sat in that hammock and fell right through it.

She tinkered with the idea of calling Molly on Tamara's behalf—but also relaying her own breaking news. According to her sister, "Matt's agreed—miraculously agreed—that Molly can be in on our premediation powwow. It's a golden opportunity, but I can't push it with her."

"Why?" Dahlia had asked.

"Molly's wearing thin on all this," her sister explained.

"Who isn't?"

"Molly thinks it's inappropriate to talk with us about our marital problems. So now I'm in the unusual position of having Matt's approval but not hers."

Restless, Dahlia had understood Molly's misgivings.

"Can't you just go to a marriage counselor?"

"Not like we haven't tried—but you and Molly are smarter, and you know us better. None of these people *get* us. They think I should be glad he's converting."

Yesterday Dahlia had protested, but now she was glad for an excuse to call

Molly. She had to talk about Saul's phone call that morning.

So she sat with the phone in her lap, almost dizzy in the fan's warm breeze. Finely splayed stalks that were embroidered upon the mesh of those curtains from the Old Country danced before her. News of escalating violence between Israel and Lebanon didn't help her paralysis—"last fucking thing we need," Saul had said—with her parents panicking about Nurit. And everyone at the gallery regarded her delicately, as if by merely being Jewish and having a sister in Israel she offended their Yankee conviction that global problems could be solved by bottled water and nice words. As it happened, she suspected Israel was not on the right track, but didn't want to get into it with them.

That day, nothing had felt right.

Saul was lying to her.

On the phone that morning he claimed that he'd called Marianne to offer a deposit, and she hadn't called back. But why wouldn't she? It didn't make sense. Something in his voice had seemed unconvincing, though Dahlia couldn't say what.

"Maybe someone else has already taken it," he suggested.

"She'll want our business…you'll probably hear from her."

"Yeah maybe," he'd said dismissively.

Since they'd seen the apartment he'd taken on an almost offhand tone, a new liberty that she didn't appreciate. As she acknowledged this disappointment to herself, her phone's familiar ring tones startled her.

"Have you reached Molly yet?" Tamara asked eagerly when she answered.

"I was just going to try."

"Daya, please do it before Matt changes his mind."

"I'll do it right now."

"Tell me how it goes, okay?"

"Sure."

"Hey, did you get the email from Nurit?"

"What email from Nurit?"

"She wrote to me and Mama that she's fine and not to worry. She was playing volleyball on the beach—said the media's exaggerating everything."

"Yeah, well, I doubt that."

"Me too, but you know Nurit."

Why hadn't she been included in this email from Tel Aviv, Dahlia wondered? It occurred to her in a dull, remote way that her older sister so disapproved of Saul that she was withholding calls and emails. Dahlia almost wanted to tell Tamara everything that was going on with him. But she figured that it wasn't worth losing both of her sisters.

Molly was hard to pin down by phone, a better bet by email or text. But Dahlia actually reached her on the phone to loud cheering in the background and the hum of a sportscaster.

"Do you have a second?" Dahlia asked.

"Sure," said Molly. "Hold on."

The din quieted, a door squeaked closed, and she explained, "Genie's here with 'the girls,' watching a Yankees game. A couple of them," she lowered her voice, "go all out. They light candles, kneel, and pray for the Yankees to win."

"Haven't you been with guys like that?"

"My boyfriends were artists and introverts with no appetite for televised sports. But this fever runs high with in buzz-cut set. Speaking of buzz, I know why you're calling. We're enlisted to be Matt and Tamara's new therapeutic saviors…"

"That was my brilliant idea. You weren't supposed to be part of it, but we couldn't get our phone conferencing act together." Dahlia swiftly added, "It's important for Tamara to have first-hand support, you know, about dealing with Matt's attitudes."

"He'll feel ganged up against. It's not going to help them."

"What *will*? What can?"

Molly sighed. "If I knew, I'd be more willing to play counselor. It's not like I want to see those children lose a stable home."

"I agree; they're so young," and Dahlia inserted: "unlike, for example, Saul's son, Alex, who'll be out of the house in two years."

"But Saul isn't planning to leave them."

"Now he is."

"Are you kidding me?"

"A lot has changed since you've been here," Dahlia told her, getting up to pace around the room, to toss magazines and unopened junk mail into the trash.

"Do tell."

"He's trying to put down a deposit on a two-bedroom apartment for us on North Clark Street. He called the real estate agent, but he hasn't heard back. Or so he says. I don't even know if he's telling the truth."

"It's moving suspiciously fast."

"Wait 'til you hear the rest of it."

Dahlia ripped a paper towel from the dispenser and dampened it in the sink. Then she began scrubbing the morning's coffee stains from the counter.

"When we went to see the place he'd stuck his wedding band in his shirt pocket."

"Why?" In that moment she remembered, uneasily, that her sister had also removed her ring when she'd courted Phil.

"To hide it from the real estate agent," Dahlia said. "And he forgot to put it back on, but apparently Wendy asked him at dinner about it. She noticed it was gone—Wendy, not his wife."

"That sounds like observant little Wendy. How'd he get out of that pickle?"

"He told them he had to check oil in the car and didn't want to stain it."

"Which went over like a wet sandbag."

Dahlia laughed sadly, crumpled her paper towel, and discarded it. Apparently, once Saul slid the band back on his finger, the subject had been dropped until bedtime. From the way he recounted it, Dahlia could imagine Cheryl in a bulky bathrobe pointing a long-nailed finger at him and insinuating, "Who is she?"

He'd said something like, "Who is who?"

"Don't play dumb, and don't play like I'm dumb," she'd warned—at least, according to his account. She asked for "the real story about the ring."

"Understandable," said Molly. "Wouldn't either of our moms ask that? Wouldn't we?"

"I guess so."

The next part of the story was what Dahlia most doubted. He'd told Cheryl that he'd seen an apartment he liked in town and hadn't wanted the real estate agent to know he was married.

"What apartment?" Cheryl had demanded. "What are you talking about?"

He then said he felt their marriage was ending and that he was looking for another place to live. Just like that.

"She acted like I was coming from out of the blue," he'd reported to Dahlia. "She was shocked. I said to her, 'You know perfectly well what's on my mind.' She said, 'Look, we're not a couple of twenty-year-olds.' I said, 'Speak for yourself.'

"She went on to say that she was considerably past her baby-making years, and that she resented 'the fuss this world makes over sex,' that she didn't want to 'fake anything' or feel uncomfortable in her own home. Her whole deal was, 'I know what the magazines say, but it's only part of marriage. You don't toss out a pie that's missing one slice.'"

"He told her, 'You also don't buy one that isn't whole and take it home to your family.'"

After a moment Molly remarked, "She doesn't miss making love, for herself?"

"According to him she doesn't—which I don't get. He's really good. The way he puts it, he's a wasted resource. I'm inclined to agree."

"Of course, we're hearing only his side," Molly reminded Dahlia.

"Seems she told him he could find a girlfriend—who is 'disease-free and not going to make trouble for the family.' But he asked her, 'Suppose I fell in love with said girlfriend?' She said: 'You won't.'"

"Or else?"

"She'll make it excruciating for him to leave. Said she'd take him to the cleaners and hang him out to dry. If we're to believe him, those were her words."

"How very fond of him she sounds. You know that my mother's a shrew. You've seen her in action, right?"

Dahlia felt sorry when people described their parents that way. Hers could drive her up trees and down rivers, but she didn't speak unforgivingly of them, especially now that they were older.

"My mother," Molly continued, "would never say something like that to Dad, shrew that she is. Not after being married for years and having children together. She sometimes addresses him as if she's chairman and he's but a board member—but she'd never talk about 'taking him to the cleaners.' Wow. You're contending with someone tougher…Cheryl must be a battle-axe."

"In some way…and Wendy's not eating much. Said she wants to be really thin and fit for gymnastics camp. Saul thinks she's anorexic, and now he's asked me—if he does separate from Cheryl—could Wendy live with us?"

"Dahlia, if I may say so, you need the phone shrink session more than Tamara."

Dahlia swallowed again. She'd been furious with Saul earlier. If her parents had ever parted, she'd told him, she would not have wanted her sisters yanked away too.

"You know," she said to Molly, "I just can't tell what's real anymore…"

"And what's spit in the wind?"

"Exactly."

"I'm tempted to say 'run while you can.'"

"But I can't," moaned Dahlia.

"I know."

Televised cheers suddenly blasted into Molly's background and a breathless voice uttered something about "first and third, top of the ninth…"

"Honey," said Molly. "My hetero roots are showing. I'm talking to a friend about her love life."

"Molly!" groaned Eugenia—clearly it was Eugenia. Dahlia remembered that tall, sculpted and intimidating presence.

"I'm being co-opted, Dahlia," Molly said into the phone with a euphoric-sounding giggle.

"Enjoy the game," said Dahlia.

"Listen," Molly continued, "let's just do this crazy call with Matt and Tamara on Thursday night, okay?"

Dahlia knew he'd told the truth about the shakedown with Cheryl because he was different when she saw him next—on edge, almost comical, like a hunted bird continually scanning his periphery for danger. "We're being watched," he insisted. Everywhere he went, he explained—alone, with his colleagues, or with Dahlia— he felt wary. "Too much surveillance in this country now. The government knows everything we do, every red light we run at midnight. No privacy anymore. No privacy." As he ranted on, his suspicion morphed away from the government into Cheryl's planting a detective in their midst.

They sat outside beneath a canvas umbrella at a neighborhood spot near Dahlia's gallery, drinking iced tea during her lunch break. It was the last they might see of each other before next week, when they'd meet in the rented sedan and head out of town for their long-awaited vacation in the Upper Peninsula. She was surprised that he agreed to sit outdoors with her, but he felt so convinced he was being trailed that he said it didn't matter where he sat or what he did. In fact, sitting outdoors might seem less dodgy.

He showed her photos on his phone that were taken when his mother had visited. The first thing Dahlia noticed, aside from Saul's anxiety, was how cute his son was becoming. For a while, at least in photographs, the boy's frame had not quite adapted to his longer limbs and his nose and mouth looked big for his face. But in the last year Alex's chin had stretched becomingly, his neck had thickened, and his eyes held a new twinkle—all augmented by reddish-brown hair that was pushed behind his ears.

"Strapping," Dahlia said.

"He's a sweet kid."

Saul glanced over his shoulder in a twitchy way, then back to Dahlia. "He was good to his grandmother. Helped her get around. I was proud of the common sense he showed. Well, guess I got two out of three of them right."

More photos swept by as he thumbed through them. Comfortable and respectable Midwestern Jews, not nutty immigrants like her family. Cheryl, in designer sunglasses, radiated the kind of proprietary smile that was intended for wives in such photographs…never suspecting the humiliation that would follow soon.

His mother, Shirley, was hunched over, though perky in her bold Florida colors with a shock of white hair. She was still pretty, and tan as a walnut. She looked more alive to Dahlia than Cheryl, more like someone to actually talk to—though maybe Dahlia was imagining that. In a series of posed photos Saul stood behind her, the loyal son with a hand on her shoulder and his smile obliging, bracketed by a goatee that was thinner than it had grown to be now.

There were close-ups of the daughters—Lisa, in love for that indelible first time, head tilted and eyes misty. Saul, however, stared at Wendy.

"Look at that—she's possessed."

Wendy's little face was so gaunt that her chin stuck out, and her eyes seemed large and spooky. "Twin girls," he muttered. "Same DNA. Same womb. And you know, Daya, this was no Petri dish stint. Cheryl and I both had twinning in our families, and these girls came into the world the old-fashioned way. Raised in the same household, went to the same school. But one of them is a little stick figure and the other a dreamy teenager. What the hell happened?"

"Staking out their own identities?" she suggested to Saul.

Dahlia knew that in her family, as in most, each sibling had assumed an identity based on birth order and a salient character trait. Nurit, the eldest, was the eternal contrarian, so their father had dubbed her "Eyore"; Dahlia, or "Pooh," was the agreeable, slightly gullible middle sister; and Tamara the baby, "Piglet," or "The Caboose" was smart, intuitive, and fussy. Mythic tales often presented three sisters, like the Graces or the Fates. It seemed to Dahlia that the first and second sisters were always flawed and the third was magical, like Cordelia or Cinderella. She found some consolation in the parallel tales of brothers who also didn't get it right until number three came along.

Saul suggested that Wendy might be grappling, for the first time, "with the human condition. What I mean is that loneliness most of us feel as little kids when we let go of our mother's' hand. All her life Wendy's had a mirror image right beside her, a twin sister, even wearing the same clothes. Imagine that security."

"I wouldn't like it," Dahlia decided, sipping iced tea through her plastic straw. "Too close for comfort."

"That's because you're forty years old and accustomed to being one of a kind."

He reached out and pinched her arm.

"Ouch," she grumbled, though it didn't hurt.

"See, this kid never had to wing all the chitchat that we feel is 'normal life,' even though we can't stand it. When she was with Lisa they were one composite being. She didn't have to stand alone at parties and answer to 'how are you? What are you up to?' like other kids. She had the luxury of a union that exempted her. But now that her sister's migrating to a new union with a boy, Wendy's left in the lurch. That hurts, doesn't it? That sucks. Oh, poor little Wendy. It's why we seek our soul mates. Life is so much sweeter with our better halves."

Dahlia suspected he was priming her to agree to Wendy's living with them when they began this hypothetical life that felt more unnerving each day. It was clear that he'd be dragging baggage into this life, even eighty-five pounds of a waif daughter who was freshly contending with the human condition.

But then he surprised her by saying: "You know, darling, you're my soul mate."

He lay his phone with its family album face down on the slatted table and looked at her from beneath his visor hat. She couldn't see his eyes, as a midday shadow struck a sharp angle across his face.

"Really?"

"Who else would be?"

His words came out shyly, and she couldn't match them. She suddenly wasn't sure if he was her soul mate, but she couldn't say that he wasn't.

The humid sun was clamping her, slowly baking her hair. She curled paper from her plastic straw around in her fingers, feeling almost trapped by his proclamation. These were words she'd longed to hear for years. Even a month ago she would have savored them—yet now she felt strangely inclined to step back and to withhold confirmation that he was her soul mate too.

He took off his hat and scratched his head. When she looked up she noticed that his hair was thinning slightly at the crown. She remembered how black and thick it had been six years ago when they met.

"I don't talk to anyone like I talk to you," he continued, gazing warmly at her and replacing his hat. Now she could see his blue eyes.

"But do you tell me the truth?"

"Of course."

"Like, what happened with Marianne?"

"With who?"

"The real estate chick." She used his expression, though she found the word *chick* annoying.

"Oh. Well. Seems another agency had already rented the place the day before we saw it. There was some contention about whether the listing had been exclusive." Saul waved his hands in a shrug. "Look, it's why I say jump when you want something. Anything worth wanting won't stick around forever."

Except me, she thought.

As if he could read her mind, he reached across the table to grab her hands with both of his. "And I'm not waiting around anymore with you, kiddo. Word is out in the town square and gallows are set to fall."

Dahlia scrunched her face into a question—what did he mean?

"Cheryl's been so hostile, like I was never anything more to her than a reserve of cash and baby seed. Now that I'm pulling away I see it more clearly. We're not the close friends I thought we were. We haven't gone on vacations alone in, God knows, years. We don't have much in common except the kids and the house. That's all we talk about."

He turned his head abruptly, as though to make sure nobody was overhearing his invective, and dropped Dahlia's hands…just in case.

"Do you think she'd ever hurt me, Sasha?"

"Hurt you—how, baby?"

"Break my legs or something?"

"She doesn't care that much," he emphasized, lowering his voice. "She's not passionate about me. And besides, Cheryl's the most law-abiding citizen on the block, coming from her line of tax attorneys and accountants. She cares about our savings and insurance, her standing in the community—that sort of thing. But she doesn't care about another woman having sex with me because she's made it clear that she doesn't want to."

"What about her weird brother?"

"Oh, Richie. Yeah, he might have stronger feelings about all this than she does. He might try to knock me off, but I don't think he'd touch you. I'd see to it that he doesn't."

"If he knocks you off, how will you do that?"

"You report him to the homicide squad if he knocks me off."

"What's his last name?"

"Stein—Cheryl's maiden name. Don't look now, but Daya, we're being watched. Don't look around."

He leaned in, speaking barely above a whisper, as though he were chewing a thick piece of wood. "Not surprisingly, she too has chatted with a divorce lawyer, they may have a detective on me. There's a guy several tables away—don't look now—holding up a cell phone like he's trying to track the wind."

"Are you sure?"

Dahlia felt suddenly ill, her guts pinched as though she'd have the runs.

"Actually…looks like he's taping that silly little dog. You can turn around."

Dahlia turned to see a chubby guy in plaid pants taping a girl eating ice cream with the tiny shih tzu whose leash was tied to their table.

"Of course it could be a set up. You never know."

"This isn't a setup," Dahlia stated. If it was, they wouldn't need both the girl and the dog.

"We'll have to be vigilant. More than we've been."

"But we're still going on the trip next week, right?"

"Damn right. Look, I even have explicit permission now to have a girlfriend. She's made these kinds of noises before—as you can imagine, it flatters me to no end. But now she's presented it as a tactic: *have girlfriend, will stay married*. She can still present a respectable front to her buddies at Hadassah. What she doesn't realize is that we're past that phase."

"If you take her up on it she could still turn around and say, 'He cheated on me,'" Dahlia pointed out. "If she wants to make trouble for you."

"Right: 'His word against mine that I gave him permission.' She may be setting a trap. But I'm not quite the chump she thinks; I emailed Julie and my own attorney about it, made it seem like she was denigrating me. So at least two other people can vouch for my fidelity, as I couldn't very well ask you to be my witness."

Dahlia finished slurping her iced tea through the plastic straw, still queasy.

"I'm also starting a fund with my sister so my own investments aren't entirely construed as marital property. Julie agreed to say that we worked this out when Mother was visiting. If we can position the Madoff stash as a gift from her to Julie and me, Cheryl might not find it so easy to shake out at the cleaners. Well, I can hope. You know, a man's got to live too, after divorce."

As promised, Dahlia's parents sent her "a little birthday *gelt*."

Their check was for a greatly needed thousand dollars, "two hundered fifty for each decade you've lived, with our love and wishes for many more." The Hallmark card in which they'd enclosed it was a relic from the seventies, adorned with daisies and butterflies. Dahlia knew exactly which shoebox it had come from, because she'd still been living with them when they decided they should store greeting cards in shoeboxes for various occasions.

What she hadn't expected was the cardboard box from Amazon that waited on her doorstep when she got home from work on Thursday. She never ordered books from Amazon—she patronized bookstores, preferably small and struggling ones. But when she picked up the package she read her name and address on the UPS label. Maybe, she thought, someone had sent her a birthday gift. The postmark was from Evanston, where Saul worked.

Dahlia sliced the box open with a kitchen knife. For a moment she flashed on opening the UPS box of Tamara's diaries, "like a crazed Pandora, with my cardboard courier boxes."

The cats watched her unfold thick pink paper that was wrapped around a manila envelope. When she tore open the envelope, wads of rubber-banded cash tumbled onto the table—Ben Franklin lifting his brow, Ulysses S. Grant scowling sagely. A sheet of paper slid to the floor.

Daya, she read, as she stooped to retrieve it. *I liquidated some holdings. Keep this supply handy. We don't know what will happen next. Cheryl is angry, and she's talking to people. Call me when you get this. S.*

She immediately texted him, *Got Amazon.*

A second later her phone rang.

"Have you counted it up?" he asked nervously.

"Not yet."

"Should be twenty-eight thou."

"Twenty-eight!"

Now she was lowering her voice, afraid that nonexistent spying neighbors would overhear her revelation.

"I know you're clever," he said in his own husky whisper, "at hiding cash in unsuspecting places. You're clever at hiding love in unsuspecting places…and listen, I've been thinking about something. I want you to know that when we're together, honey, you're not going to sneak around on me. You're a little too good at it."

"Me? Who am I sneaking around on? My pets?"

"Oh, you know what I mean."

"I really don't, Sasha. I should be saying that to you, who's cheated for years."

"And now paying the price. My knuckles are getting rapped raw. You should see what a mess it is here, Dally. Cheryl's getting these weird, secret phone calls and looking at me like I was a lizard in bright green slime. She and Lisa are packing for their trip, but Lisa doesn't want to be away from Jared for even two weeks. She's grief-stricken."

An unfriendly thought seized Dahlia: Two weeks? Try waiting a lonely lifetime. *You wanted me to, and I have.*

"Wendy's taunts just made her feel worse," Saul continued. "I'm going to give her a talking-to when I drive her to camp tomorrow."

"Stay out of it," said Dahlia. "Sisters handle themselves best. And look, I don't think I should leave all this cash hanging around here." She glanced at the pine-green stacks on her table. "I'll put it in the bank with my parent's check. Maybe I'll stick my birthday card from them into it so the teller will just figure it's all from my crazy family for this big birthday…retro Hallmark card and tons of cash."

"A tip from the master," said Saul. "Don't deal with tellers. Do it through ATMs."

"All that money? No way."

"Little by little. Keep good records, and keep some bills at hand. Hide them like the *afikomen*. You've always been good at that."

And now she was supposed to preside over a conference call about Tamara's marriage? Dahlia stomped around her room so fraught and frazzled that she sent the cats into hiding under an armchair. She had less to tell Tamara about mature love than Wendy had to tell Lisa. Maybe she'd let Molly take over. Molly seemed to be in a thriving, hot relationship. And it would remain so because she had a built-in obstacle with Eugenia: society would never give its blessing to two beautiful women gratifying each other. They'd be permanent outcasts. They had nothing to worry about; they could always enjoy their big, nourishing problem.

But by divorcing Cheryl and moving in with Dahlia—money first—Saul was pushing their relationship into the box. Of course, it was the very box she had longed for and at times even insisted upon with tears and foot-stomping. It was the box she'd wanted even last week.

But now that it was closing in on them, she realized that it brought with it every cliché faced by a couple in their position: how to handle the fallout from his separation, the presence of his children in their life—especially Wendy, their prospective roommate—and how to start over with integrity on their own. They'd no longer enjoy carefree assignations. They'd no longer text clever and saucy missives as they yearned for each other. She could no longer count on being his special underground treat, or on being favorably compared to Cheryl. It occurred to her—and not without some shock—that, in the interest of sustaining their romance, Cheryl might be the best thing since sliced bread.

She called Molly half an hour earlier than they were scheduled to speak, and Molly apologized. "Did I get this wrong? I thought we were on for seven, Eastern time."

"You're right," said Dahlia. "But I wanted to talk to you first."

"Okay." Molly sounded unenthused. She was busy, perhaps finishing something in that half hour. But Dahlia was too upset to stop herself.

"We told Matt that I'd conduct this session. But I'm just..." She bit her lip. Molly waited. "I'm in no shape to do this."

"What happened?"

Dahlia explained the box of cash. Molly asked: had she expected it? Dahlia told her of course not.

"Calling the shots again, is he?"

Dahlia had forgotten her own complaint about Saul. And now, as Molly reminded her, she nabbed her source of her disappointment—their relationship would not change. Whatever they became, or didn't become, would still be his call. If he wanted Wendy to live with them, she would live with them. If he wanted to send cash from God knew where, Dahlia would do what he asked her to do with it. He called her "soul mate," but he walked her like a dog.

"It's not going to change," she admitted.

"Are you okay with that? Because if you're not, now is the time to walk away."

"I don't know what to do!" Dahlia found herself shouting, as though Molly were to blame. "How can I tell my sister what to do?"

"You're not going to tell them what to do," said Molly, with maddening steadiness. "You're going to moderate the session. Because my brother won't go through with it if I do. He's got his hackles up."

"Yeah but..." Dahlia was hyperventilating. "He's asking me this favor. I can't."

"Did he ask you? I thought you volunteered your services to Tamara. Then she solicited mine too. Isn't that how it happened?"

Molly was correct, and Dahlia realized how aggravated she found herself with the drizzle of actual facts.

"You have this great relationship," she pleaded. "I'm in a mess..."

"Yeah, I have this great relationship that neither of them know about." Now Molly's voice cracked. "They both know about you and Saul."

"Not about the latest development."

"So tell them, if you want," said Molly. "They're not going to disown you. And they won't say anything ridiculous like 'ooh, you're playing for the other team' or 'what do you actually do when you're in bed together?'"

Dahlia sighed and threw herself backward on her bed holding the phone to her ear. "Can't we both play umpire?"

"That's not Matthew's wish. He and Tamara are meeting each other halfway. Let's not get between them."

With Molly managing the conference call, all four of them joined easily at the appointed time. Matt and Tamara were on phones in separate rooms of their apartment. The children were with a sitter. Everyone chuckled over how smoothly it happened with Molly at the helm.

"But Dahlia is running this show," Matthew declared. "Molly does not get to Pass Go and Collect a Hundred Dollars because she managed to set up this call."

"Agreed," said Molly.

"Actually," Dahlia countered, "Matthew, I know you want me to oversee everything. But—just saying—I'm in a really crappy mood right now."

Her disclaimer was somewhere between an honest plea and a call for attention. She lay back on her sofa bed gazing across the room at fifty- and hundred-dollar bills, her parent's birthday card, and ripped envelopes stacked on her table.

"I've been in a crappy mood for three months straight," said Tamara. "If not longer."

"Oh Tamara," Matthew moaned. "Three months ago was Oren's birth. How could you say that?"

"It has nothing to do with him."

Matthew didn't address his wife, but instead asked Dahlia: "What's getting you down, Daya?"

"Let me guess," inserted Tamara. "Does it begin with *s*, as in snake?"

"He's leaving Cheryl," declared Dahlia. "Really, this time."

There. Now everyone knew.

"Nawwww…" crowed her sister with the usual inelegant sarcasm.

"Really?" asked Matt, sounding surprised.

"Hello, he's been leaving her for years!" cried Tamara. "And sticking around at the same time."

"So you think," asked Dahlia slyly, "that when someone betrays a spouse they're actually leaving them?"

That put a lid on Tamara—and it was intended to. But like all of the Szabós, she wasn't silenced for long.

"If it's a long affair," she replied, "then it undermines the marriage. If someone just does it once or twice, I don't think that's the same thing."

"Because it's just a…momentary lie," suggested Dahlia. "Like an acute disease versus a chronic condition?"

"Maybe," said Tamara.

"What do you think, Matt?" Dahlia asked him.

"It's sleazy to deceive your spouse," he said. "But I agree with Tamara that the long-term charade is more problematic than a one-time slipup."

Dahlia wondered if Matt knew about Phil, and if he had pardoned his wife's "one-time slipup."

To everyone's surprise, Matt then asked Molly's opinion.

"There's a difference," she said, "between an extramarital affair and ending a marriage. Some marriages survive because of affairs. Maybe that's the case with Saul."

"We can always count on my sister for cynicism."

"She's just being honest," snapped Tamara.

"You asked about marriage," Molly pointed out. "Not about good marriage."

"Which you, having had neither, would know nothing about."

"I know more than you think about both."

"What?" he asked. "Are you secretly married?"

"Not far from it."

"Did you elope?"

"Didn't need to."

"Told ya so," Tamara blurted out. "Didn't I tell you she's with someone, Matt?"

"And why have we never met him?" Matt asked in the kind of scathing, melodic cadence he and Molly employed, which was less soggy and petulant than Dahlia and Tamara's family style.

"Why should I subject anyone I love to this family's enmity?" Molly replied, in that same tart and sing-songy tone.

"Okay, who are we talking about now?" Dahlia commanded. "Molly or you guys?"

"We're talking about you and Saul," Tamara cried. "My favorite TV soap."

Dahlia felt the phone shake in her hands. "That's really not funny, Tam! I am ready to hang up..."

"Okay," inserted Matthew. "Let's just hold it here. Ladies and gentlemen of the jury, please note that Tamara's managed to provoke her own sister into hanging up on her. You all heard it. It's not just me. *Her own sister.*"

No one said a word.

"You'd agree that she's really provocative, Daya?" Matt continued.

"She sure has her moments."

"Well so does he," Tamara said quickly. "Wouldn't you say, Molly?"

Dahlia realized that they were playing doubles, and that she and Matt were in the court across from Molly and Tamara.

"I'll avail myself of the Fifth Amendment," Molly deferred.

"See?" sneered Tamara.

"So we can conclude," said Dahlia as Phoenix jumped onto the bed and cuddled beside her, "that you're both really difficult. You're both pains in the ass."

"Yay us!"

"Loveable pains in the ass," Dahlia qualified. "At least I find you loveable. And the question that's brought us to this venerable phone call is: do you two loveable pains in the ass want to stay married, or to part? And how can we help you get clear on this?"

"I'm not the one who wants to split," responded Matthew. "When I said 'I do' I meant forever. This isn't a 'Matthew question.'"

They waited in silence. Someone coughed slightly, probably Tamara. Dahlia brushed Phoenix's fur, watching flaxen hairs drift to the floor and remembering how Cheryl had noticed them on Saul's shirt.

"I mean, in theory I want it to work," Tamara began.

Matt interrupted her with "this equivocation is the kind of—"

"The kind of *what*?" she barked.

Shit, thought Dahlia, wishing someone else were on the line, like Saul or Eugenia, someone farther from the epicenter of siblings.

"This is the kind of, pardon me—bull dung that Molly brings out in you," Matthew explained.

"Huh? Molly? Did anyone else hear Molly influence me? Mediator?"

"The words came from my sister, Matt. Not yours," Dahlia said as she continued to stroke Phoenix's back.

"And if you'll let me finish, Matt, I was going to say that in theory I do want to be married to you, but when it comes to moments like this, which happen too damn frequently, I'm ready to blow a gasket. I fear for my mental health, even for my competence as a mother."

No one dared to rebuke that statement.

"I'm getting worn fucking down," Tamara reiterated. "And it's wearing enough to deal with a baby and two smart little girls. Oh, and a job. And a household, and a body, with all its fun new kinks, brought on by age. Marriage should support a couple in the face of this pressure, not destroy them."

"In theory," said Matt.

The conversation transformed from a tennis game into billiards, with colored balls squireling around the green felt table, sometimes swallowed up by holes, but more often remaining in place no matter how many eight balls were aimed at them.

Dahlia could feel her palm sweating as she petted Phoenix, who eventually flew off the bed and joined Ashes in batting a stuffed toy around the floor.

Molly said barely anything as they swept from Israel to Asia, from Orthodox Judaism to Pseudo Buddhism. When Matthew called her a "Jew for Bu" Tamara began to cry, as she had with Dahlia on the phone back in June.

"If I'd wanted to marry an observant Hassid I would have gone to Jerusalem and plucked one from the Wailing Wall."

"Must you speak so disrespectfully?" Matt implored.

"Disrespectful? You know that they forbid women to study Talmud?"

"I'm aware."

"And you know the Orthodox don't serve in the IDF."

"And you know that I didn't invent any of that."

"But you want to bring it home, Matt. You're ready to live by it, and I'm not. Six hundred thirteen laws, most of them archaic and inapplicable to our lives. Who are you kidding?"

"Well look," he said meekly, "my conversion is on the local track anyway. The rabbi's biding time, having me read tomes of Jewish law…"

"You never even asked me how I felt about your converting."

"I assumed you'd welcome it. Silly me."

With this last round of potshots, Dahlia's head felt ready to fall off. Still, a "marital cease-fire" was declared—for the moment, Tamara emphasized. "Which is better than we're faring in the Middle East."

Matthew said he needed time to think about everything. He wouldn't make false promises to change his ways. "But," he added, "I'll try not to look for open wounds with my saltshaker." Reluctantly, he agreed to reconsider becoming an

Orthodox Jew in a secular family. It was clear that he had no intention of caving too fast.

Then he and Tamara laughed about how he'd bounded about with the other men at Shavuot in Borough Park. Her earlier tears transformed into giggles. Some problems, Dahlai found herself thinking, evaporated. Some melted slowly, while others persisted like floodwater.

By the time they all said good night, over two hours had elapsed. After performing the briefest ablutions, Dahlia shut the lights. Her cats had already settled into their baskets and now they soaked in moonlight through the window as the lace curtains heaved like a slow-moving ghost. She plopped her head on the pillow until her phone jarred her dizzily back to awareness. Before she could think about whether answering was a good idea, she found herself clearing her throat and muttering "hello?"—interrupting someone's garbled rant.

"Hello?" she repeated.

The voice became Saul's, saying, "I just had to get the hell out and walk!"

"What?"

"Lame duck marriage," he grumbled. Now he was coming in more clearly. "She's sleeping in his room. I mean, I'm miserable too. No reason to dump it on the kids. She's sleeping in Alex's room. Can you believe that?"

"But Alex is in France on his bike trip, isn't he?"

"I wouldn't send him to that land of ingrates and dishrags. He's not even on the continent. He's in the U.K."

"Oh, sorry." She yawned, covering her mouth instinctively. "I just meant he's not in his room."

"Well, would you have wanted your father to sleep on your bed when you weren't there?"

"I wouldn't have cared."

"Course you would've. It's invasive and incestuous."

In her eardrum his voice sounded familiar but winded, like he was exerting himself on this walk. Dahlia began giggling sleepily.

"What's so funny?" he asked.

"Incestuous?"

"Well, what is a *mother* doing on her *son's* bed?"

"Sleeping," Dahlia managed to reply, between giggles.

"We're not some extended family in a clay hut in India, you know, with every-one sharing a pillow with their grandmother and four sisters."

Dahlia began to rock with laughter.

"In the West, family members observe interpersonal boundaries—"

"Okay!" Dahlia interrupted him, feeling more awake. "So she's making a boundary between you. You tell her you want to end the marriage, so guess what? She doesn't want to sleep beside you. You say you don't even have sex."

"Are you on her side now?"

"I'm not taking anyone's side. I'm over 'sides'…just got off the phone with Matt, Tamara, and Molly, you know, our 'let's save their marriage' phone call?"

"And did you?"

More panting.

"Saul, are you jerking off or something?"

"No," he said crossly. "Just walking. So, did you save their marriage?"

"I didn't do anything. They needed a sounding board. They needed to know that other people care about them. This isn't going to be resolved in one phone call."

"Is she at least cutting him some slack?"

"They're cutting each other slack."

"Cutting each other's slacks. That could be sexy," he mused. "I read a scene like that in a book once, some guy cutting up his girlfriend's pants before going at her. We should try it sometime."

"If you're careful with the scissors."

"I'm careful with everything. Speaking of, did you hide the cash yet?"

It remained out on the table, but she didn't want to tell him.

"I'm…going to do that."

"What does that mean? When are you going to do it?"

"Tomorrow. I'm going to the bank…"

"Daya," he said sharply. "This is important. I've got to trust you with stuff like this."

"I promise."

"It's our kitty, our sea chest…" He stopped speaking and she realized that these auxiliary sound effects—the sighs and panting—suggested that he was sobbing but didn't want her to know. What he said next confirmed her hunch. "What have you done to me? My life was good enough. Now, it's like I'm on the road to Damascus—blinded, as they say, by the power—of what? What is worth all this upheaval? I never wanted to put Cheryl or my kids through it. For what? A good lay? Even a good friend? It's got to be more…"

He was rambling, but she smarted.

And she decided to fail his test outright and not respond. At all.

"But can you turn back," he lamented, "when you're Saul, on the road to Damascus?"

DAVID

Memory Motel

The next morning as she sat in the gallery filing receipts, Dahlia imagined his household splitting in half: Cheryl ferrying despondent Lisa to the airport; Lisa madly texting Jared about how she'd miss him; and Saul driving cryptic Wendy to gymnastics camp—Wendy with visions of vaulting and leaping around with other emaciated teenagers. Even the twins were separating for the first time.

She wondered if either of them noticed that their mother had slept in their brother's empty room. Somehow, she doubted it.

Paintings for a new exhibit were being delivered that day, and Michelle was working with Trey, the art handler, who often transported pieces to and from the gallery. A perfect specimen of Tamara's WASPy type, Trey was tall, with butter-nut-brown hair and steady blue eyes. As he shuttled large canvases into the room, holding them in his arms or wheeling them on dollies, Dahlia observed his striped shirt and white shorts that revealed long, summer-brown legs as he and Michelle stacked artwork against one wall.

Trey was probably eight years younger than she, so Dahlia had never taken his brief flirtations seriously. But they caught eyes as he helped mount a large piece, placing a leveler along its top edge.

"It's reading okay…what do you think, Dahlia?"

"Looks even to me."

"Nudge it down to the right," Michelle insisted.

Too far down. Dahlia had been correct, and he knew it. His smile crept through Dahlia's nerves like a shot of tequila. But in the same instant, she buckled with self-consciousness. She was now in a committed relationship, and her boy-friend had preempted such gratuitous flirting: "No sneaking around on me. You're just a little too good at it." She would have to adjust.

At her lunch break she ferreted off to Federal Express with a sturdy, bub-ble-wrapped envelope. She had called Molly in the morning, asking how to handle the bills that had flown to her doorstep from the road to Damascus.

"Is it wise to keep all of it in my apartment?"

"Home-sweet-home is the most underestimated repository," said Molly. "Better than the bank or trading floor, in the event of some electrical grid fluke. But I wouldn't keep everything there."

She confided that she and Eugenia had "scads of backup cash" folded into the pockets of shirts they rarely wore, tucked into a chafing dish on a high shelf in the pantry, "and other places that no burglar would think to look."

Dahlia decided she'd put a thousand of Saul's dollars into the pocket of some baggy and unflattering pants, "and keep them at the bottom of your drawer," Molly advised. She would put two thousand more into the bank with her parents' check and overnight the rest of the cash to Molly, who said she could deposit it into her payroll account and send her a check for twenty-five thousand dollars.

"Anything flammable, liquid, or perishable?" the clerk at Fed Ex had asked nonchalantly, and Dahlia shook her head.

"Just paper," she said.

She texted Saul about what she'd done, aware that he was driving Wendy to camp and probably couldn't write back.

But by the time she returned to the gallery he'd sent two words: *Good Girl.*

I'll write u a 25K check when Molly's clears, she replied.

He didn't answer, probably too far in the woods.

Trey had apparently left for the day, and Dahlia knew that her own help would now be enlisted. This ordeal could be grueling, the frontline of Michelle's perfectionism. For some reason, Dahlia was the only employee who could withstand the fuss of hanging a show; it was no secret that Michelle had come to depend on Dahlia over the years to absorb her excesses with poise.

"They want lilies at the opening," Michelle mentioned, as they finally hung the last painting in the space that awaited it. "Tiger lilies and calla lilies."

"I won't be here," Dahlia reminded her.

Michelle looked slightly horrified.

"I'll be on vacation, remember?"

The expression on Michelle's haggard face didn't change, and she continued to stare at Dahlia. She was a scrawny, limber woman who wore turtlenecks all winter and polo shirts all summer.

"My birthday," Dahlia said.

"Oh, yes. That's right. What are you doing?"

"Traveling."

"Where?"

Dahlia shrugged and quickly lied: "Lake Tahoe."

"Who are you going with?"

"My boyfriend."

Michelle put her hand on her waist in a scolding position.

"I never knew you had a boyfriend."

"I didn't either," said Dahlia.

Molly received the Fed Ex package of cash the next afternoon, which was Saturday. She called Dahlia to let her know, but Dahlia was too busy at the gallery to pick up the phone. Typically, Michelle had declared that the show must be entirely rearranged, just as she decided after every hanging. She wasn't convinced that anything was right unless it was picked apart, raked over, and redone several times—even if all that trouble found them precisely where they'd started.

Few visitors were shuffling about just then. The new show would open on Thursday, when Dahlia would be in the Upper Peninsula with Saul. But Michelle still encouraged people to come in for a preview, to look at catalogs and unframed pieces in the back. Their eager publicist, Cindy, spoke to reviewers from the press and online zines. One reviewer with long, choppy hair and granny glasses tried to interview Dahlia as she and Michelle dragged canvases around the room.

"I'm not the right person," Dahlia told him. "I'm just the assistant here."

"You are the right person," he insisted. "You are more the right person than you'd ever dream."

"Watch it, Frankie," Michelle warned. "She's a hooked fish."

She tried calling Saul in the evening but got only voice mail. Still out of range in rural Wisconsin, he was staying until Sunday morning at a motel near Wendy's gymnastics camp, apparently making sure that she felt comfortable—granting his daughter concessions that infuriated Dahlia. Or maybe it was anger left over from his "got to be more than a good lay or a good friend" dig. Whatever the case, they'd snapped at each other about it the day before, when he'd told her of his plans.

"You say Cheryl's incestuous for using Alex's spare bed, but you won't just drive Wendy to camp and trust that she'll be okay if you leave her?"

"Dahlia, when did you become Dr. Spock? This is Wendy's first solo flight, without her sister, and she's very nervous. I'm helping her make the transition."

Dahlia had to back off. It was a minefield, as he was helping the family "make the transition" to his absence…for the thrill of a good lay.

I'm just not sure, she wrote to Molly the next morning, *what I really am offering him. Maybe he's right to question whether it's more than good sex.*

I thought you were his "best friend and his soul mate," and he "doesn't talk to anyone like he talks to you.

Sometimes the air pockets of recent words with Saul suctioned Dahlia away from the bigger picture. But now she had a confidante who listened and remembered. Molly was on her way to DC on business, even though it was Sunday. She was apparently on some kind of shuttle coach with Wi-Fi, so she could email but not speak on the phone. Dahlia had returned her message about receiving the cash and then took the occasion to launch into her latest woes:

It's really stupid. Or I should say, I'm really stupid. When he's sweet and romantic I don't believe him. When he says lousy things, it hurts—but I trust it.

Molly asked for explanation.

Seems more real for him to have second thoughts about tearing his home apart because he's having great sex than to risk all for a "best friend" and "soul mate."

Sounds like both are real.

When Molly's words appeared on her laptop screen, Dahlia stared at them over chicory coffee. She would have to leave for the gallery soon, but not just yet.

Can he be my soul mate if I'm not his?

And now, the gift of a tear trickled down her cheek, because this doubt was hers, not Saul's. Five minutes passed, and Dahlia didn't notice the time go by until Molly's words came again: Don't worry about whether you're soul mates or not. Don't worry about if it's 'only a good lay.' Those are his concerns, and he'll handle them. What's there for you?

The new show looked promising—they had certainly spent enough time arranging and rearranging it so they were back where they started. Dahlia wondered what Trey did when he wasn't shuttling pieces between artists' studios and galleries and back again. Maybe he was an artist himself...but wouldn't he be showing somewhere? Did he have a girlfriend? He seemed easy to be with. She imagined herself sitting behind him on a motorcycle—he would have one, maybe a chopper—her arms encircling his waist. They'd stop for a beer. What would they talk about? He'd probably look at a map. Could he make her laugh the way Saul did? She almost chuckled aloud when she remembered him fuming about Cheryl's "incestuous" invasion of their son's empty bed and that rat's nest of cash he'd mailed her in an Amazon box.

What would she laugh about if she were with Trey? His friendly blankness had appealed to her, and she finally understood Tamara's interest in these decorative WASPy men who were so different from their family. But after a certain point, what did anyone do with them? Even Tamara had found someone thorny for the long haul.

The gallery was abuzz with phone calls and full of photographers circling the exhibitor and his family, who'd shown up on a lark. About an hour into her shift, Dahlia dared to check her own phone to see if Saul had texted. He had not.

But she found an email from Molly when she got online and was surprised to see that it was rather long:

We're stuck in traffic because of an accident on I-95. Good thing I've got my laptop. This is the problem with driving, but I didn't feel like airports today. No simple answers. Like the old predicament from my straight days: my taste in men was so lousy that the minute I considered seeing a guy, I had to wonder what was wrong with him.

You'll appreciate this, Dahlia. Back in my "boy days," when I met one – before we'd barely uttered five words – my first thought was "is he single?" Without knowing the answer, my second thought would be: "are we flirting or talking?" My third thought: "if we got married, what would my mother think?" My fourth thought: "is he hot? Are we even attracted to each other?" By the time we got to the fifth or sixth thought, I was wondering if I could bear his face over dinner for the next fifty years.

Now that matrimony is moot, it's like looking at the same terrain from an airplane window. I can see that the mountains are foothills, and the river I thought had frozen just has ice patches.

All by way of saying – and pardon my diverging – that I have a more panoramic perspective of men since I'm not dating them. I even have a more panoramic perspective of women. I watch them bitch about men they chose to share their lives with. Complain, complain, complain, like they're some great shakes. I was probably like that. Actually, I know I was.

Back in my heterosexual days I would have been like Tamara, railing for you to "dump that jerk Saul." But now that I don't have the chip on my shoulder, I can empathize a bit with Saul's terror. I know what it's like to turn your life upside-down for someone you adore. I know that well. I'm more impressed with him than I thought I'd be. Most people are pitiful cowards when it comes to their private lives. Mind you, his rap about "more than a good lay" was hurtful and DUMB. But he's facing more uncertainty than he might ever have before. I'm sort of reading between the li...

Wi-Fi meltdown left Dahlia to choose between *lies* or *lines*.

Before she had to take another call for Michelle, she dashed off an email to Molly, asking: *What do you think now when you meet guys?* That topic held more interest for her than Molly's newfound compassion for Saul. But of course, Dahlia also checked her phone again eagerly for a text from him and scolded herself for sulking when nothing was there. Eventually she heard again from Molly.

Being with men is delightfully normal now. Of course I still notice if they're charming or sexy. Flirting isn't off the table. Gene and I grant each other a long table, because we both enjoy flirting and are kind of naturals. But we save the last dance for each other, because that's where we really want to dance. Which means I'm never put on the spot with men — truly relaxing, when it doesn't make trouble.

That's what happened with David.

Who IS David?

Sticky rice, now a friend.

Dahlia was up for a story about anything other than her life. And now that the artist and his family were leaving the gallery with Michelle, she had time to read. She welcomed the distraction from brooding over Saul's return from Wendy's camp and their trip next week. In fact, she was battling a premonition that it would all crumble, either before or during the vacation. She realized that she didn't share Molly's estimate of Saul's courage. There was such a thing as being too fair to men, and Dahlia had made that error pathetically often.

So, Dahlia, traffic has just started budging again. If I write the story, time will go faster. This kind of memory would have been impossible to describe when it was happening — I had no distance, I was too craven — but I understand it now as a fertile tempest whose fruits I'm still harvesting.

Imagine spring of the year before Matt lost his job. He still worked for Schmuckface and your sister was pregnant with Kayla. No one in the family spoke to me. My mother had written a brutal letter about how "abnormal" I was to give birth to my friend's child but not my own, and to be "single" when I was pushing forty. Of course she didn't know about Gene and me, and still doesn't. But even spared my most radical departure from her designs, she declared herself "too hurt and confused" to face me, so please pardon her if she didn't.

My father didn't feel quite so strongly, but he lives to appease her. They all shut me out until Tamara ended the silence two years later, and eventually my father brokered a more general truce.

But none of that had happened yet. Eugenia and our friends were my family. And I was not easy to be around. Basically, I was emerging from a postpartum/midlife stew. Even through that murk I walked into Eugenia's Cajun one day with a vision of how it should look, and she loved it. So we made it happen.

One spring evening, restaurateurs from Easthampton were having a drink at the bar and they asked who decorated the place, and might I be interested in doing something for them? I'd have to make detailed sketches and go to Easthampton intermittently. Larry wasn't crazy about my taking time off over the summer from our agency, but I couldn't refuse. This was the stint that hooked me on decorating.

When I went out to brainstorm with the owners about what they wanted, Fred and Claudie showed me their collection of early American quilts. You probably looked at quilts when you were studying textile design and know that they are consummate works of art. I suggested that we take them out of storage and display several in the restaurant, under museum glass. That was when I got the idea to decorate a room around artwork.

Inspired! What kind of food do they serve?

Seafood and local produce, like many places out there. Lobster bisque and summer squash soup, skirt steak and Cornish hen — tasty fare for rich vacationers.

Tell me about the tables and plates you chose.

Mission-style oak tables and stoneware. Simple, to offset the complexity of the quilts but carry on the early American theme. They have vases of wildflowers as a centerpiece. Roses in June.

Is it still open?

On Old Montauk Highway. Does well during the season, of course. The Hamptons essentially hibernate for winter. And Fred has had some health problems now, I hear. But The Cherry Basket forges on.

Do people remark on the décor?

That's how I got my subsequent referrals. And a write up in *Town and Country*.

You really could start a new career.

In as much as I can manage that with my other responsibilities. I spoke about it at great length with the architect who was gutting and rebuilding the interior. David had a lot more on his plate, so to speak, than I did. He was out there full-time for a while, revising blueprints, meeting plumbers and electricians, supervising the contractors. He'd recommended another decorator, someone he always worked with, so he wasn't very forthcoming at first. But eventually we took walks down the beach, sometimes with Fred or Claudie or their other guests. And sometimes by ourselves.

I know Matt and Tamara have friends out there — have you ever been to the Hamptons, Dahlia?

No.

Lovely as any beach in the world. Genie and I have seen a bunch by now. Of course you don't have palm or almond trees in Easthampton — it's flat and scrubby, even moorish as you get out toward Amagansett. But you walk along and get hypnotized into a misty, exhilarated mood.

Looking back, I realize it may have been a mistake to walk with David by the surf and chat about architecture and geography, or to lie one day side by side on a big beach towel after we'd finished work. Everyone knew I was involved with someone called Gene, whom I didn't speak about much since I was even more "undercover" than I am now — didn't want Fred and Claudine and all those other people to know about my personal life.

You don't have to explain that to me.

So I figured it was fine to hang with David in this informal, friendly way, and that he wouldn't get the wrong idea. I'd often mention, for example, "Oh, Gene and I saw that movie," or "Gene and I are going to Block Island at the end of August." And everyone saw me getting calls from Gene all the time.

Then one scorching afternoon I asked David to spread sunscreen on my shoulders because my pale Irish skin burns to a crisp if it's given half a chance. When Genie and I were in the Virgin Islands, I got sun poisoning — I was really careless and didn't put lotion on my legs before we went sea kayaking. Well, the next day I couldn't walk. In fact, for the next week I couldn't walk.

Lesson learned: I need a shitload of sunscreen, and as David slathered it on my shoulders, he said something about how petite and delicate I was. I just laughed and said thanks.

Putting the lotion in the bottle.

Or the shoulders. That's how comfortable I felt, Dahlia. He was my friend. It was nice to have a straight guy friend. Seemed a long time since that had happened. Both Eugenia and I preferred hanging out with boys when we were kids. She was a tomboy, and I was a nerd — although an active, running-around kind of nerd. We both found boys more interesting companions than girls. Of course we lost that natural connection to boys once everyone started playing spin the bottle, and the new world order of adolescence set in.

But out in Easthampton that summer, I appreciated how fun it was to be with David in a prepubescent way, not flirting or desiring him or wondering anything — just hanging out.

Is he cute?

David's Armenian and has golden skin, big brown eyes, and a mound of black hair. He's exotic-looking and appealing, though not a drop-dead movie star like Eugenia. A little hefty in the middle. I've seen him in a bathing suit. He has "love handles." Can you tell what's going to happen?

He fell in love with you.

I noticed him staring when we spoke. It was a disappointment, like: oh please don't ruin this! I like having a guy friend again. One day we were looking over his blueprints, and he suddenly dropped his pen and said: "Does Gene ever tell you how amazingly beautiful your eyes are?"

I said, "Yes. Often."

"Why don't you live with him?" David asked.

I told him we're not ready. But we might be one day. I hated being cross-examined. David was not doing the right thing, so I stayed clear of him for a while.

Well, July became August, and the sea air began smelling more like apples than wild roses and honeysuckle. David and I regained our friendly, collegial manner. I was generally in such good humor, seeing my plans for this restaurant come to fruition. I had my life with Gene in the city. I'd finally gotten over the birth of my surrogate son and was slowly coming to terms with my family's stonewalling me.

When you're loved — and Gene loved me, heart to heart and body to body — people find you easy to love. But you're the last to know it.

Try me, Dahlia thought. I'll have this chance next week in Michigan for my birthday. Try me.

Late August, I went to Easthampton for a weekend to approve the décor for their grand opening. On that Monday I would meet up with Genie in Montauk, where we'd booked a beachside condo for a couple of days. Then we'd head to an inn on Block Island for a real getaway.

On Saturday night Fred and Claudie had this party on their wraparound porch. Dignitaries from the Easthampton and Bridgehampton town boards were there — mostly WASPs over seventy, making David and me the kiddies in that crowd.

So everyone concluded that we were "an item" and kept remarking on how lovely and dear we were. I let the compliments fall on me like sea spray. Figured it was only an evening. It had been so long since I'd been publicly recognized with any guy that it felt like punching into some cosmic time-clock.

What you tell the world when you can't say the truth.

Dahlia thought of her own lie to Michelle about going to Lake Tahoe. Why exactly had she suggested that? So as not to take risks—on Saul's behalf, of course.

Lolling in that illusion, it seemed beside the point to explain to people I'd never see again, "no, I'm actually not with David but with someone else." Though I certainly didn't confirm their impression that we were together. I just smiled. I guess I did it for Fred and Claudie, who were starting to feel comfortingly parental in the wake of my own family.

The next afternoon I strolled on the beach with David, I in a bathing suit and gray sweatpants with a flannel shirt tied around my waist, hardly feeling seductive. I remember the day so well, how I told him that the imprint of tide on the wet sand resembled mountain peaks. And he said, "Or rose petals unfolding." Then we spoke about whether or not I should apply to architecture school if I wanted to design interiors.

I stopped walking for a moment and watched the waves stretch to the sky and slap the shore with spray. It was a bright morning and the sea was so clear you could look right through it.

Suddenly an arm slipped over my shoulders.

"See where the sunlight pierces those waves?" he asked. "It's the green of your eyes."

Then he started kissing me.

Dahlia, I was so taken aback that I let it happen for a second – before I pushed at his chest, told him to stop it, crying out to him, "You know I'm involved..."

He stepped away, breathing heavily. I almost thought he would cry. Then he said, "You don't have to pretend."

What did he think you were pretending?

It took a while for Molly to write back.

You know, it still pisses me off. Not David per se. This is old stuff with us. But the default condescension. Guys think you're bereft if you're not with them. Ya know?

All. Too. Well.

Well, David stared in a patronizing, obsessive way and told me: "Last time you were out here you said you were going to meet Gene in Sag Harbor."

"Yes – and so?"

"You didn't meet Gene."

"Sure I did."

He tried to take my hands, and I grabbed them away, suddenly feeling like I was with Jordan or Tom, my last two boyfriends before Eugenia. Came over me like a straightjacket: David slipped out of being my friend and into this controlling male.

"There is no Gene," he said. "Just as I thought. I followed you in my car when you went to the Jitney, and I saw you meet another woman, a blonde."

I actually started to cry.

"That is Gene. Eugenia."

After I said her name I ran down the beach, back to Fred and Claudie's. David didn't follow. In a frenzy, I packed my bags and toted them out to my car.

Fred asked me what was going on. He'd been out on the lawn with their golden retriever and a neighbor. I told him that my plans had unexpectedly changed, and that I had to rush back to the city. In a fatherly way, he asked if everything was okay. At that moment I can't begin to tell you how much I missed my dad.

You weren't speaking to him yet?

To none of them. No matter how difficult it must be to miss our parents once they're gone, it is agony to miss them when they're alive.

Did you see David again before you left Easthampton?

Before he could tear his feet out of the sand I was on the highway, speeding to Montauk — as much as I could in Sunday traffic, though most of it was heading back to New York. But the "East End," as they call it, was mobbed and the beachside condo that Gene and I booked wouldn't be ready until the next day, when she'd join me.

So there I was, alone in Montauk on a hot, discombobulating Sunday afternoon in August, looking for a spare room. I finally found one in the Memory Motel, if you could believe that. A depressing shack on 27, the main drag out there.

The Stones' Memory Motel?!

Maybe I stayed in the same dark little room as Mick Jagger and Hannah. Or was it Keith? Well, I got a mind of my own ... I could hear the roar of traffic outside, not surf. I was almost relieved not to be on the ocean. Strange to feel that way in a seaside town, but the tumbling waves brought back David's compliment.

Under other circumstances, Dahlia wrote hesitantly, not sure if she was emotionally trespassing, *those might have been nice words to hear.*

That's why they bugged me. It's also the kind of thing I've said a lot to Gene. A woman's beauty inspires such tributes. But it's a tough line to walk, between true appreciation and fawning flattery.

What did you remember in the Memory Motel?

In the eighteen-hour stretch I spent alone there, I kept hearing the Stones' song in my head. I mourned my family and failed relationships with men. I'd had good sex with guys and good, discreet little experiences — but never good relationships. I was incapable. Too bossy. Maybe even cold. Eugenia's brief history was the opposite, but her paradigm seemed nobler. She really cared for her high school boyfriend. She loved him. But she didn't desire him.

You'd think we could sail into the sunset and leave such vexation behind. Sometimes we do. We don't even notice how great things are, and they become greater. But sometimes both Gene and I succumb to feelings of staggering ineptitude.

Like you've disappointed everyone.

Including ourselves. We get into this "what is my problem?" routine, as in: "why do I have to dredge up the same issues, why must I meet them over and over in dreams and counseling, and why can't I get used to myself?"

But the examined life takes a lot of examining, swimming beyond waves to where the sea is calm. We can't tell anyone that's easy. Not everyone makes it back.

The fact is that under other circumstances, as you said, I might have been interested in David. He's more mature and educated than the men I dated. Would he have been as ecstatic a lover to me as Genie? I doubt it. After the birth of Andy, would David have cared for me with Gene's power and empathy? Hardly. But I did reflect, when I was alone in Memory Motel, that — as a sheer template — he was a good Plan B? Yep. Though of course, for me, it's Plan A or nothing.

Did you tell Eugenia about him?

Before I met her at the Jitney stop the next day, I decided I wouldn't mention the whole incident. There was no reason. The job was over and so, I thought, was my friendship with David. He'd ruined it, or maybe we had both ruined it. I don't know. Something had ruined it. Nothing that pertained to her.

I knew only that my heart leapt when she stepped off the bus in her leather boots and jean cutoffs, her long embroidered shirt and straw fedora with blonde hair flowing from it, a backpack dangling off her shoulder.

I had checked out of Memory Motel that morning, and as we loaded her suitcase into the trunk of my rented car and headed to the beachside condo, I felt my life was ready to start again and I knew things would be okay. Deeply okay.

Out there it was just Genie and me with the sea and sky and sand dunes. It's amazing how peaceful you can feel after even two days like that. Less talking and more touch and movement, more walking along the shore or hiking to a lighthouse, renting bicycles, swimming in the bay, sleeping late and making love.

The party at Fred and Claudie's, the walk with David in Easthampton, seemed remote as a TV movie. I did notice, the one day I checked my email, that I had a message from David. But I would wait to read it until I got home. I didn't care what he had to say. It was surely more about him than about me. And even if it was about me it wouldn't matter.

I read it a month later, at the end of September. He hadn't written much, only: "I'm sorry for being presumptuous. Please can we talk sometime?"

My silence spoke to that. Or so I thought.

Then Molly fell off and Dahlia checked her watch. Over an hour had passed, and she'd felt so engrossed by this gnarled tale that she'd momentarily forgotten her own. The gallery was quiet without Michelle, and only a couple of Sunday afternoon drifters. They seemed pleased that Dahlia was occupied, allowing them to peruse paintings and the price list in a leisurely way, to dream more than deliberate. Dahlia understood. She disliked saleswomen approaching her in boutiques as she leafed through silk dresses on a rack, inhaling their faint perfume as hangers squeaked softly, imagining herself in something…and Saul taking it off.

Did she need any help? No, she did not.

Michelle didn't understand such privacy and often threw herself at brows-ers. That was how she closed an impulse sale and why she owned the gallery and Dahlia worked for her.

Hey, you there? Dahlia wrote. *I must hear the rest of this.*

A few minutes later Molly replied: Pit stop. We needed one. Looks like I'll be on time for the meeting after all. My fingers are tired of typing and my heart's tired of remembering. But it's good for me to look back on how things happened, and yes, I owe you the denouement.

It took a little while to come, though.

In early October David wrote me an ornate letter, on parchment paper with a foun-tain pen no less, about how he'd fallen unscrupulously in love with me and was sorry he'd been out of line. Said he hoped we could meet sometime so he could apologize in person. But I didn't feel he owed me an apology, or that I owed him an explanation.

Besides, I was raw enough from surrogate motherhood and being dumped by my family. The last thing I wanted was to jeopardize my life with Gene. While she was the rainbow in my stormy skies, she also felt wracked with ambivalence back then about getting close to "a straight woman." I sure didn't want to stoke those coals. Suffice it to say that I left well enough alone, figuring it was best for David to have me out of his life anyway.

But Dahlia, you know how guys are – the more you're off-limits, the more they convince themselves they want you. Think Stanley Kowalski howling for Stella.

Maybe that's why I've found the unattainable man.

Dahlia noted that Saul hadn't called or texted yet. He should be out of the Wisconsin woods by now, even if he wasn't home.

Well, caveat emptor. You may find he's attainable yet.

She didn't write to Molly that when Saul seemed within reach, he frightened her. But when he seemed unattainable, she terrified herself, and life terrified her.

I was not prepared when Genie came to me one day with a melting look in her blue eyes. She held up an envelope and asked, "Why'm I getting letters like this?"

"Like what?" I said. Because let me tell you, my gorgeous and adorable girlfriend has gotten fan letters that have turned me more jealous shades of green than a rainforest. Well, she handed me the envelope and tossed her head, inviting me to open it. I instantly recognized David's handwriting, and my jaw dropped. I must have gasped "what the?" because I remember her saying, "No. You tell me *what the.*"

Dahlia wriggled in her seat. Even if Saul had texted just then, she would have been too riveted by Molly's story to reply.

David actually wrote to Eugenia?

It gets better. He not only wrote to her, he'd started hanging out at her bar. He told her something like, "By now you know me as Dave, the architect from Astoria who has sat at your bar. What you don't know about me is that we're both in love with the same woman."

Oy, wrote Dahlia. Or, as her father would often cry: "Oy, America!"

He elaborated that he'd been single for four years and hadn't met a woman with my ineffable attributes. He told Gene something like, "You are so blessed and lucky that I had to perform my own research to see if you were worthy of her. Because after Molly rebuffed my ham-fisted advance last summer, I admit that I felt hurt and jealous. So I got to know you myself. And not only do you pass muster, Eugenia, you surpass muster. You are as beautiful, tuned-in, and creative as Molly. This fool stands corrected, and in awe of you both."

Then he said he was dating a woman his friends had set him up with, and he had tickets to a Broadway show—would we care to join them? He wanted to "extend this olive branch" and be friends with us both. And because I'd never answered his email or letter, he was now appealing to Eugenia.

You must have been…a little moved by his valor?

Frankly, I was aghast. When Gene asked me, "Who is this guy?" I explained how we'd met at Fred and Claudie's and worked together on the restaurant. She wanted to know why I hadn't mentioned him or what had happened. Well, I told her, what was there to say? I'd rebuffed him and not answered his letters — just as he described.

Before she could ask anything further, like how we'd left things, and had I ever described her as anything besides "Gene" with no pronoun, I ambushed the dialogue. Not my finest hour. I pivoted, by bewailing her legion, drooling fans. She said: "So every hick with a hard-on and every bi-curious bizarro wants me, but they're bugs on a windshield. You made friends with this guy in a professional setting. That's a little different, missy." She calls me "missy" when she's furious.

Well, I broke down and reminded her that neither my father nor my brother spoke to me anymore. I had no straight men in my life. We heard plenty from the female camp, through the outspoken cabal of women and gay boys around us — but there were few straight guys in the mix. Alessi's husband, Pete. That's about it. I said, "It's like never getting the E in Scrabble. I enjoyed Dave's perspective. Not because I wanted to sleep with him. I actually liked talking with him."

I expected Gene to storm out on me. As we've worked through various issues, we had our share of wrenching scenes. But to my relief, she listened. The upshot? "Look, he's your friend," she said. "Decide how you'd like to handle this invitation, and I'll go along." My first instinct was not to reward his nosing into my life. But she pointed out that he'd tried honorably to contact me by mail and email. And rather than being pushy with me, he'd forged another option.

Good of her to see it that way.

Gene's not petty. She made me realize that by getting to know her, David was acknowledging us as a couple. Which is beyond many fools we've suffered. In fact, once you get together with Saul, beware — parasites will eek out of the woodwork for their piece of your apple pie. Women have stood beside me, at a party or on the dance floor, propositioning Gene, like I wasn't in her arms or holding her hand. One South American hussy took a business card from her cleavage and asked Gene to "give her a call sometime." Gene handed it right back and said, "I won't be needing this."

Then there's this Jamaican guy. Not bad-looking, mind you, but too aware of it. He lurks at the bar when I'm around, soliciting Gene and me into a "reverse Oreo cookie garden of delights." We've had blunter renditions of that one from motorcycle trash on their benders.

So relatively, David's appeal for our friendship came off as sweet and harmless. Still, I was on the fence: So much for E in Scrabble. MANY WORDS CAN DO WITHOUT IT.

Later that week I changed my mind. Eugenia's ex called from Columbia, where she'd been deported years back, threatening to put a gypsy curse on us if Gene didn't dump me and return to her, *iinmediatamente!* The day after that, my own ex, Jordan, called to ask for a loan. By that point Gene and I were just laughing.

People do what they'll do, but nobody outside a relationship is the deal-breaker. Not our exes, or any Latina hussies or Oreo cookie monsters. Once we got clear about all that, Gene and I could hang out easily with David.

We took him up on the Broadway tickets and sure, it was a little awkward. Luckily, the woman he was with was so bland that she neutralized the tension. Alas, David specializes in dating bland women.

And we've met them, because over the years he's become the good friend he said he wanted to be. He's been there to cheer Gene on in the triathlons, with or without his lackluster girlfriend of the moment. He and Gene designed a stage at our Cajun place for musicians – it's really cool, built into the wall and it unfolds. They loved doing that. And when my dad made his first bumbling attempt to break the family silence, David came with me to meet him. I introduced him as a friend and colleague, and it really helped to have him there.

That's why this story has a happy ending. At least for us. I hope it's happy for David. I'm aware that he's never found a woman worth his salt.

How so?

It's surprising how many straight women are shallow or neurotic. When I was a straight woman I thought we were all the king's caviar.

WENDY

Peaches and Cream

At home later, Dahlia sliced some peaches and dropped them into a bowl of crème fraîche with a smattering of blueberries and some clover honey. As she began eating she called Saul and said brusquely, once he answered: "Hey."

He'd texted at the gallery that he was back from Wisconsin, but she decided not to call him immediately. Michelle had been breathing down her neck.

"Hey," he echoed. "You home?"

"Mmmm, yeah."

"Ready for the big trip on Tuesday? Ready to turn forty?"

"Actually…" She chewed her peaches and crème fraîche for a moment. "Yes to all."

"How do you live alone?" he asked her. "I'm finding it creepy here. I've never been in this house without Cheryl and the kids. It's making me squeamish. Feel like I hear every damn sound in the cellar. Then I turn on the TV and I can't stand to watch coverage of this misbegotten war. So I turn it off, and it's too quiet. How do you do it?"

Dahlia had spent years carving space away from overbearing personalities. She'd been raised in a home where her mother cracked open a window for fresh air and her father wailed about contracting pneumonia. If Nurit tried to cook she'd burn something, and their mother would run around fanning her hands in the smoke, screaming about asphyxiation. Life in a college dorm had been no better, with brooding, suicidal undergrads.

"Peace and quiet becomes the faint of heart," she explained.

"You'll have to train me."

Dahlia slid another scoop of peaches and cream into her mouth and asked, "How's Wendy?"

"Huh?"

"Sorry, I'm eating. I said, 'How's Wendy?'"

"Let's hope *she's* eating. I mean, she will be. I chatted with the nutritionist there. They've been dealing for years with campers who are skinny as rails. I was glad to hear that a lot of them come home with more muscle tone and appetite.

"And you know, Daya, my poor kid needs a break. As we were driving up there Wendy told me that she's been bullied at school. A group of kids have been stealing her notebooks, pushing her around at her locker. Some of the boys call her 'Lisa turned ugly.'"

"But she's a lovely girl, not ugly."

"Of course. Though she is getting too thin, and Lisa's more popular. It's a problem. That's why I wanted to give her some TLC and support."

Now Dahlia felt terrible about carping on him the other day. She swallowed her fruit, reflecting that she'd always been too hedonistic about tasty food to go anorexic. Maybe she'd be a good influence on Wendy.

"I asked her why she hadn't told me or her mother about the bullying, and she said she didn't think we could stop it. And then—like, out of the blue, she said, 'I know you're breaking up with Mom.' I said: 'What? Who told you that?' No one told her. Apparently, Cheryl even denied it. But somehow, she and Lisa have caught on.

"She asked me not to go, Dahlia. She said, 'Don't leave us alone with Mom.'"

Dahlia stopped eating.

"Well, what did you say?"

"I assured her no decisions had been made, and that her feelings and Lisa's are very important to me."

Dahlia balled a paper napkin and flung it against the wall. Ashes thought it was a game and pounced on it.

"So I don't know," she said, suddenly feeling ill from the rich cream. "Maybe you shouldn't leave them."

"It's too late. I have to. What, now you don't want me?"

"I don't want to ruin your daughter's lives."

He sighed. "It appears that Wendy's life has already taken a beating. And Lisa's life won't be ruined so long as Jared's nearby. It's not the way to think, Daya. Protecting them at my own expense isn't going to help anyone. Sure, some days I ask myself what the hell I'm doing, and I want to crawl under a rock and cut my nerve endings. But I know…Look, honey, I was thinking on my long drive back…it was a long time, and I couldn't do anything but brood…I've been a nuisance lately. I mean, to you. I've been…Jeez, I've been fucking crazy. I don't blame you for snapping. I don't know how you've put up with me."

She sat down, tapping the spoon on her thigh.

"You've been different lately," she agreed.

"Yeah, different." Another sigh. "You look at the person who's been your dependable teammate for twenty years and see a stranger who's got it in for you. You look at the place you've called home for twelve years and realize you won't be welcome here soon. It's the damnedest thing. Makes you want to take up slam wrestling and write poetry. I'm jumpy, I'm edgy, I start muttering to myself. My sister doesn't know about you and me, but she knows there's trouble with Cheryl. She thinks I should go into therapy, and I'm starting to agree. How would you feel about that?"

Dahlia was shocked. He never asked how she would feel about anything he did. And now he was silent, waiting for her answer.

"I think it would be helpful," she said, stirring the last slice of peach and blueberries in cream.

"You wouldn't think less of me?"

"Of course not."

"I might even want you to join me, sometimes. We're taking a big step here. I'll be starting life with you while I'm buried the rubble of Cheryl. And I don't want to get you dusty."

Dahlia put down her spoon. Phoenix and Ashes played with the napkin she had wadded up and thrown just a minute ago—Phoenix sparring aggressively with his paw, Ashes feinting retreat as they scurried circles around it.

"I want to protect you, and us. I think you've already taken too much. I just don't know how I'll ever make this up to you."

"Sasha," she interrupted him tenderly, "I can't believe you're saying this."

"Why?"

"It seems too good. I've always wanted you to—I don't know. To be yourself, but more aware of how I see things. And a little more caring."

"So you're saying I've shut you out?" he sounded discomfited.

"I mean, not always. But—yeah."

"Too much of the time."

She nodded, even though he couldn't see her, and watched her cats abruptly lose interest in fighting over the crunched napkin.

"Even my sister and colleagues say I get tunnel vision when it comes to other people. Lousy habit," he said. "It will be hard to break. But not impossible. And for you, every bit worth it."

She swallowed.

"I wish I was with you now," she said.

"You are with me," he answered. "We haven't been together this way for a while."

"I know."

"You were starting to have second thoughts, weren't you?"

"How could you tell?"

"I'm not as idiotic as I seem."

They both laughed.

"Just one more day," he reminded her, "and we'll be off to Michigan. God, sweetheart—I can't wait to see you in a bathing suit. Hope the water will be cold enough to keep me well-behaved in public."

"Sasha, I'll probably look awful. I haven't been exercising."

"You don't need to exercise. You've got everything in the right place naturally."

"Flattery will get you nowhere."

"I'm actually being honest. Even I manage that now and then. Though it sure hasn't been the ticket around here lately. On that note, I was thinking that maybe you should pick up the car from the rental office Tuesday morning and meet me a couple of blocks away?"

"In case the spies are out?"

"The politics of a dissolving marriage can get bloody."

"But isn't she at her mother's?"

"She may have left dirty work to her emissaries. I don't know which of our friends and neighbors to trust anymore. Can't wait to get out of here for a while."

"What about her crazy brother?"

"Last I heard, he was telling Cheryl's aunt, whom he lives with in Springfield, that the CIA was spraying their backyard with 'potent military chemicals.'"

"What?"

They laughed together again.

"He's also convinced the CIA's impersonating him. Like those overextended fools have nothing better to do. Oh, jeez, don't ever let me start sounding like that."

"You bet I won't—and look, okay, I'll pick up the car," she said. "Just bear in mind that I'm a hopeless city driver."

"Well, I'll meet you at the Dunkin Donuts around the corner, on Wabash. You won't have to drive far."

"When will you be there?"

"We get the car at ten, so I'll just be there from nine forty-five on. You can call me."

"Sounds good. What are you bringing?"

"Lots of love for you, chocolate-covered cherries, a bathing suit, and swimming goggles. How 'bout you?"

"A copy of the *Kama Sutra*, the negligee you got me for Valentine's Day, and hiking shoes."

"This will be the best vacation I've ever taken," he said. "It already is."

"Sasha," she agreed, "this is the best talk we've ever had."

After she hung up, she remembered Molly saying: *I knew things would be okay. Deeply okay.*

And before climbing into bed, she texted Saul: *Dreaming of the one I love.* It sounded cliché, paraphrased from yet another seventies song. But clichés were consoling, like freshly laundered sheets and fluffy blankets.

The one you love says catch yr dreams b4 they slip away. He too paraphrased shamelessly.

She read it with a smile, her head tipped and hair falling over her cheek.

Help me catch those dreams.

That's what I'm here for. Put me in the outfield.

She slept with her phone beside her on the pillow, like a teddy bear.

A Case of Mistaken Identity

On Monday Dahlia vacuumed cat hair, scrubbed her counters, mopped down her floor, and packed and repacked her bags. Saul called in the morning, reporting that he'd slept poorly, awakening with every creak and drip emitted by the empty house.

"And I could swear someone was breaking into the cellar. Look, I know that no one did, because our alarm system would sound off to Timbuktu. But I need you to sleep beside me. I'll catch your dreams if you chase away my nightmares."

"Deal."

"Dally," he whispered in a husky voice, "I love you even more than I thought. This is crazy."

She tried calling him in the early afternoon, upon receiving the check from Molly for twenty-five thousand dollars, express-mailed from New York. Molly had deposited the cash into her payroll account, as she'd promised. Dahlia wanted him know that she was getting it to her bank, so she left him a voice mail. She was always careful on his phone, even now. She said, "Hi, Mr. Finerman. I'm depositing the check from Molly Douglas."

She called again in the early evening just to ask how he was and what he was doing. Again he didn't answer, and she figured he was at his office. He'd mentioned a "formidable litany of last-minute matters" to address before taking off tomorrow, said something about "sticking around 'til seven or eight if they need me. I'd actually rather be there than in that empty house."

Dahlia had calls to make herself. She decided to let Tamara know that she was spending her milestone birthday with Saul, so they chatted for a while. Tamara sounded distracted, but didn't scorn her plans.

"He is leaving his wife," Dahlia reminded her sister.

And Tamara replied, "Yeah, yeah," with little conviction.

"I guess some things take a while," Dahlia went on. "Maybe we needed these six years to test the waters and make sure we have a connection. We've both had our doubts. But after we spoke last night..." Dahlia shut her eyes, smiled to herself.

"After you spoke last night, what?" asked Tamara flatly.

"We know this is for keeps."

Around nine Dahlia knocked on Mrs. Johnston's door to discuss her mail and where she kept the new dry cat food. She received a text as she was showing her neighbor around the cabinets—but it was from Michelle, asking if she had left town already. She didn't reply. She tried calling Saul again, once Mrs. Johnston left. This time, she got a recording that his voice mailbox was, surprisingly, full. She knew she'd left only three short messages all day.

Whattup? she texted. *Mailbox full?*

When he didn't reply for forty-five minutes, Dahlia knocked on Mrs. Johnston's door. Her neighbor answered in a housecoat, television purring behind her.

"I'm so sorry to trouble you," Dahlia apologized. "But I'm charging my phone before I leave and don't have a landline anymore. Can I use yours to make a quick local call?"

"Come on in," said her neighbor, and Dahlia walked into an apartment the reverse of her own, with the kitchen facing south and windows overlooking the same yard and oak tree as Dahlia's. But the curtains were thick and coarse, and every wall was painted toffee brown and held too many crooked photos. Dahlia had taken Saul's home phone number and figured she would try him from this random, area-code-312 number that could not be traced to her.

Her fingers shook so madly as she punched in his home number in Highland Park that she had to start over again. The phone rang three times, and she heard Cheryl say officiously on microchip: "You've reached the Finermans. We'll call you back if you leave your name, number, and a brief message at the tone." The voice was squeaky, as though Cheryl hadn't quite cleared her throat. Dahlia felt a flicker of repugnance as she hung up without saying anything.

After another hour of silence, she texted Saul: *Is something wrong?*

And by midnight she was frantic. They hadn't spoken since morning, and he hadn't replied to her calls or texts all day. She kept telling herself that he probably ran himself ragged at the mall and his office, then came home and collapsed. He wasn't a late-night person, and they had hours of driving tomorrow.

But why hadn't he replied even once, and why was his voice mailbox full? He always listened to messages and kept his line clear. He had to. He was paid too much.

She started remembering phrases like, "I could swear someone was breaking into the cellar" and "he was telling Cheryl's aunt that the CIA was spraying their yard with potent military chemicals." Dahlia reflected as she brushed her teeth, spitting vigorously into the sink. Suppose all those other messages on Saul's phone were threats from Richie?

"*But her brother Richie, now he's got a gun, and that crackpot would shoot. He's never liked me.*"

Cheryl and Lisa were at Cheryl's mother's—that would be Richie's mother too. Suppose Cheryl had trilled about her marital strife, how she "never realized what a schmuck he is." Maybe that was all the incentive her brother needed.

"*Oh, Richie...He might try to knock me off, but I don't think he'd touch you. I'd see to it that he won't.*"

"*If he knocks you off, how will you do that?*"

"*You report him to the homicide squad if he knocks me off.*"

Dahlia rinsed her face, blotted it with a washcloth, and applied a dab of hydrating lotion that smelled of plant extracts. She tried not to imagine Saul in a white undershirt walking downstairs to check sounds from the cellar, calling, "Hello? Hello? Someone there?" and then Richie bursting out with his Uzi, rattling bullets through Saul's chest as he flew to the floor, blood soaking his undershirt, his heart exploding—just after he'd found the courage to open it to her.

"You watch too many movies," she berated herself. "You read too many terrible stories. Now stop. Get some sleep. Everything will be fine in the morning."

But the minute her head hit the pillow, the image mill whirred faster. Maybe

Richie hadn't shot Saul—Maybe he'd just held the gun at Saul's temple and locked him in a closet. Maybe Saul had heard the phone ring when she called his home from Mrs. Johnston's. His family would come back and smell him rotting…Dahlia shot up like an arrow, sweat pouring down her face.

She needed to call someone. Michelle snaked across her mind but no, no one in Chicago at this hour, and New York was an hour later. She'd call Nurit in Tel Aviv, where it would be tomorrow morning. She liked the thought of a sun rising, and—when she wasn't determined to be a wiseass—Nurit could be uncanny. Dahlia turned the light back on and hunted for her sister's phone number. But she found too many and had no idea which was current; in fact, she wasn't certain which of her own phone books was current, since she called people other than Saul so seldom. No one else's number was even entered in her phone. She tried a number for Nurit in Tel Aviv and didn't get through. It was good to do something, though, to keep herself occupied. So she tried another and heard a voice mail announcement in Hebrew, with her sister reciting "Nurit Szabó" before the tone.

"Hey," Dahlia began. "If this is still your number, could you call me? Doesn't matter what time. I'm, uh, in a very strange situation…leaving town with my boyfriend tomorrow for my birthday and he seems to have, well, vanished. I know, it sounds like magical realism or…true crime. God knows." Dahlia's brief laugh turned into a surge of tears, and her teeth chattered for a moment. "I'm just so worried for him…"

She hung up fast. Blubbering to herself, she deliberated calling Tamara, who might be awake nursing Oren. She'd be cynical after Dahlia's declarations earlier that same day about the tenacity of this love and would say that Saul was getting cold feet. But Dahlia sensed he wasn't, because she knew precisely how he would bail and what he would say, in that case: "Don't be mad at me, Daya." He would let her know if anything was awry. He always did. Sometimes he'd been known to delay communicating, for impact. But he'd never stood her up, in all their years.

After getting the full mailbox message yet again, she dialed Molly's home number and was relieved to hear a sleepy woman's voice mumble, "Hello?"

"Oh Molly…forgive me…I'm so sorry to call at this hour…I'm just a wreck.

Can I please talk to you?"

After a brief silence, the voice one the other line said, "It's Gene. Molly's sleeping." And a little sharply: "Who's this?"

"Oh, Dahlia here. Tamara's sister from Chicago. We met at the *bris*."

"I remember."

"Look, I don't want to disturb you, but my boyfriend has been…I don't know, attacked or hurt in an accident. We're supposed to leave for a trip tomorrow, and he's not answering his phone or texting…"

"Has he done that before?" Eugenia asked reasonably.

"Only when he's really mad at me. And I know he's not mad at me. I *know* that." Dahlia realized she was sounding more ludicrous by the second but was too upset to feel embarrassed. "Has Molly explained my situation?"

"Molly never gossips."

"Well, he's leaving his wife. Everything's a mess…" She found herself ranting about Saul sending her cash in an Amazon carton, about Cheryl's paranoid schizophrenic brother with a gun, and how Saul had felt frightened alone in his house last night. "I just don't know," she concluded, "if I should call the police. If I do, I'd be busting our love affair."

"Keep the cops out of it," said Eugenia, sounding tired. "You know, it's probably nothing you think—just some crazy-ass reason, like his phone's broken or the sucky day on Wall Street. Some guys in business don't answer their phones on days like this."

It appeared that even the most counter-cultural person in New York, like Eugenia, was tuned in to the stock market's pyrotechnics. Dahlia herself couldn't give a damn about it.

"His voice mailbox was full. Still is."

"For what it's worth," said Eugenia, "last time I didn't take calls was when I heard my dad was in the hospital having bypass surgery."

Then Dahlia thought of Saul's mother, on dialysis. That would account for his voice mailbox being jammed, probably with calls from his sister, Cheryl, and other relatives. She was relieved to think of him alive, even if upset, on a plane to

Florida. On the other hand, she was livid that his family was once again interfering with them. In fact, how dare something so ponderous happen on the eve of their trip?

"I've been with this guy for six years," she squalled to Eugenia, "and now the iron curtain of his marriage has lifted and we're going away—so his mother has the nerve to keel? Now?"

"Lotsa lousy scriptwriters in the heavens."

"But why wouldn't he *tell* me?"

"He'll call you tomorrow. Maybe he needed a day to just be with it. I sure did."

"What would you do if you were me?"

Dahlia heard Eugenia breathe softly through her nose. She was probably exhausted.

"Try to reach him in the morning."

"And if I can't, and he doesn't call?"

"Then call Molly. She gives the best advice for weird situations."

Dahlia awoke uncertain if she'd slept. For one moment she enjoyed a buttery patch of sunlight on her moldings, the shimmering lace shadow of her curtain. But then she remembered the trick life was playing on her: an apartment ready for her to leave it, down to the last shiny glass in the dish rack. She felt remote even from the cats, who seemed to have noticed her suitcase and pulled away preemptively. But as she had dreaded, there were no messages from Saul on her phone, no texts, no emails. She tried him again and got the full mailbox recording.

If only she could call his home, but she didn't dare. He'd never forgive her. Perhaps she could get some haphazard male to do it—maybe she could go to the grocer across the street and offer to pay the delivery boy ten bucks. She certainly had plenty of cash at hand. She stuffed bills from the pants she kept at the bottom of her drawer into a her purse and zipped it shut, then pulled her suitcase out the door, bouncing it down the staircase. The limpid August morning wasn't hot and felt somehow promising. She put on sunglasses and instead of approaching a delivery boy, hailed a cab to the car rental. Maybe Saul would be at the Dunkin Donuts around the corner from it, as he'd said.

Sure enough, once she'd picked up the car and made her way to Wabash, she caught sight of him inside paying for coffee at the register. "Silly, silly man!" she cried, pulling the brake as she careened into the parking lot, throwing herself slightly forward. "Bastard! What was he doing to me?"

Relief flooded her, tempering her heart rate. She hadn't realized how distraught she'd been, how barbed, even in sleep. Now she could breathe. She slammed the car door and raced inside Dunkin Donuts, grasping the keys in her sweaty fist, not minding how the ridges of it bit into her fingers. He sat at one of the messy little tables with crumbs and coffee stains, and she clawed his shoulder, nearly ripping his rugby shirt and crying: "What's the idea? You think you're funny or something? I thought your mother was dead!"

It took a moment for her to realize that the face she was looking into was completely unfamiliar. Yes, the hair was dark and curly like Saul's, but the features were older and saggy, the eyes bloodshot, the nose big, and he was mouthing syllables at her in some language like Kurdish.

Horrified, Dahlia ran out to the car again and locked herself in. She whipped out her phone and called Saul's number. This time she got his normal voice mail and could actually leave a message: "The number you have reached," recited the merry female voice, "has been forwarded to an automatic voice message system…" then his resigned, factual cadences, as she'd heard many times. "Saul Finerman" the recording continued cheerfully, "is not available. Please leave a message at the tone or stay on the line for more options."

"Where the fuck are you?" she cried. "What happened? Your mailbox was full, and you've clearly listened to it, or at least wiped everything off. Damn, I hope you're hearing this. I'm in the car at Dunkin Donuts. It's ten forty-five. I'll wait here for a while. Call me or just—just show your face."

As she hung up she realized dolefully that perhaps it had not been he who had cleared off all the messages.

Perhaps it was a detective who'd found his phone.

By noon, she had watched many people enter and leave Dunkin Donuts, and none had been Saul. Obese teenagers had stuffed their faces with colorfully sprinkled cupcakes; cops had slugged coffee from Styrofoam cups. She'd kept her window rolled up in case the man she'd mistaken for Saul came around, and now felt more suffocated than a goldfish in a plastic bag. She kept reviewing their exchanged texts: '*Catch yr dreams b4 they slip away.*' There it was, in her phone. She had proof that she hadn't imagined everything. But how could she catch his dreams if she couldn't catch him?

She finally called Molly, who seemed well versed in her predicament. "I'm terrified that his brother-in-law shot him," Dahlia mumbled. "Either that, or he has some secret fetish with chintzy prostitutes, and he's in Vegas with a pack of them."

"Gene said you were thinking that his mother may be on her last leg."

"That was the sane version, which my imagination's had time to edit. Gene was precious, to talk me through it all last night," Dahlia added.

"Gene is precious, and I am her ardent fan forever. Assuming there's merit to the explanation you concocted with her, do you know his mother's name? I can call, pretending to be a telemarketer. Let's see if she's alive and answering phones."

When Dahlia gave her the information, Molly rapidly found a listing for Shirley Finerman in Fort Myers, Florida—the putative paradise for Midwestern retirees. "God's waiting room," Saul had proclaimed it, and now perhaps his mother had been summoned by the receptionist. Molly would sleuth, and they also agreed that she'd call his office in Evanston on a pretense and get back to Dahlia with a status report.

As Dahlia waited, rocking back and forth in the stuffy car and finally rolling down the window, Saul's voice came to her vividly: "*I don't know how I'll ever make this up to you…This is crazy, Dally. I love you more than I thought.*"

"What happened to you?" Dahlia whispered. "Sasha. What happened?"

When her phone tinkled its ringtones, she jerked up from her seat, heart in her throat. But it was Molly.

"His mother's nasty, isn't she?"

"I've never met her. Just seen photos."

"She's not kicking the bucket anytime soon," Molly declared. "I asked if I was speaking to Shirley Finerman, and she kind of sneered, 'And who am I speaking to?' So then I launched into the 'do you know that you qualify for a one percent rate on an option ARM mortgage?' racket, and she hollered, 'I requested exemption from these calls! I'm on a government list!' Many expletives later, she hung up. Now, admittedly, we live in a world of spin, spam, and scam; I can't blame her. Here I am in a lesbian relationship getting hit up with Viagra ads over email—you know what I'm saying?"

Though Molly's energy was refreshing, it was hitting Dahlia that Saul wasn't with his mother. So much for the "sane explanation." He was a notch closer to having been shot in cold blood, or to suddenly not giving a damn about her.

"Did you reach his office?"

"They told me he's on vacation and that he'd be back late next week," Molly reported.

"That's all they said? I wish we could try his home. But I don't dare, from any of my phones. Not the way Cheryl's been watching him. I need a guy's voice."

"Maybe I could get Larry," mused Molly—and then she stopped herself. "No, he'd sound too swishy. Not what we need now." And she mimicked Larry's coy, feminine lilt: "Hey Saul. What happened to you? I'm waiting."

Despite her anguish, Dahlia giggled for a moment over that.

"Oh, you know who'd be great for this?" Molly exclaimed. "Good old David. Let's have David check Saul's home number. I'll give him a call and get back to you."

"David of the fountain-penned love letters on parchment paper?"

"That would be the one."

Going back to her apartment was not an option. Dahlia was prepared to camp out in this parking lot and spend her fortieth birthday at a coffee-stained table in

Dunkin Donuts eating trans fats and sugar. At least she'd be "away from home." She remembered the vistas she and Saul had savored on those travel sites of Nova Scotia or the Greek islands—steep hills rising behind stone churches, overgrown hedges of bougainvillea, sylvan waterfalls, coastlines with breaking waves and sea spray.

Who'd said "sea spray" to her recently? Even at thirty-nine her memory was lapsing. She knew it was a woman for whom she felt warmth. Not Michelle. Oh, it was Molly, writing about her escapade with David at the seashore. He'd said her eyes were like sunlight piercing the green waves before he kissed her. Dahlia started to weep, leaning her head on the steering wheel.

It was just as well when, ten minutes later, Molly conferenced her into the call with David and instructed her to "mute yourself." As Dahlia did so, she heard David pick up the phone and say, "I called those numbers you gave me and just got voice-mails. 'You reached the So-and-So's and the Who-nots, and nobody's anywhere.'"

"Did you speak?"

"When don't I do what you ask, Molly?" There was something familiar about David's low, resonant voice, but Dahlia couldn't say what. "I said, 'Hey Saul. David here. Hope everything's okay. Not like you to miss a meeting. We'll wait a little longer.' Now what is this about? Who's this guy?"

"I told you—a friend's waiting to meet him in Chicago, and he's AWOL."

"Why doesn't she call him herself?"

"She's tried."

Dahlia knew that Molly and David had weathered storms together, but now their voices sounded carefree. They were trying to help, but they couldn't know her anguish. The odds were narrowing into a scenario of spousal revenge. Saul's mother was fine, his colleagues were clueless, and his kids were in camp or on bike trips. Out for blood, Cheryl must have somehow seen to it that his breakaway wouldn't happen.

"Between you, Genie, and your cohorts," David said, "you've got more intrigues than the late-night movies. And my life is so drab—cat food, vet appointments, drafting table, new client on the phone."

"That's why we share our joy with you."

He laughed in an easygoing way.

"Happy to oblige."

After he said goodbye, Molly got back to Dahlia: "Okay, so we've rooted around, and the drawers are empty. Shirley's alive and telling mortgage banks to go fuck themselves. Saul's not answering his Blackberry or landline."

"We're back at square one," muttered Dahlia. "Either he's tied up with duct tape in his cellar or in Vegas with cheap women. You got me. I'm not the world's best driver, but I guess I should get out to his house and make sure he's not hanging from rafters. Or maybe I'll find a ransom note."

She found his street with difficulty, between her choppy steering—a near brush with death as she hurriedly changed lanes for the exit, another car's horn wailing into her silence—and the misleading GPS tracker, whose sugar-sweet, canned directions reminded her of the recorded voice that announced Saul's mailbox was full. When she got to Maribel Lane, in its splendor of oaks, red maples, and mansions stretched upon green lawns, she parked at the corner and decided to walk to number 27. On this road to Damascus the addresses weren't clearly indicated. But she was relieved to see that the estate likely to be Saul's didn't look like the scene of a murder. No yellow police tape embraced it, and no ambulances were stationed in the driveway.

She was also glad that it wasn't an engorged "McMansion" or some trifle with aluminum siding but a staid and classical stucco. Not Mediterranean-style, with a tile roof and iron balcony, like the one where she'd lived with her family in Southern California—but rather, a Tudor with a slate roof that sloped into various peaks. It was painted a bright, no-nonsense white with black trim. She thought again of the house her family had owned and the patches on crumbling stucco where Daddy had begun to paint it then stopped because of rain or some spat with Mama about how they should hire professionals.

By contrast, 27 Maribel Lane was painted so crisply that it looked more like a photograph than a house. Hesitating before she set foot on the driveway, Dahlia noticed one open window on the second floor where a fuchsia-colored drape crept out, like a furtive tongue. She thought somehow of Wendy, then proceeded to the front door. When she saw the mezuzah she felt reassured that she'd found the right place but decided to open the tin mailbox beside the door and inspect the envelopes in it. Sure enough, they were addressed to Mr. Saul D. Finerman, and she recalled his middle name was Daniel; S. Finerman; Ms. Lisa Finerman; Resident, 27 Maribel Lane; and Saul and Cheryl Finerman.

Tapping the envelopes in her palm, she noticed a sign in the window beside the door that said *Notary Public.* How strange, she thought, to post that in a residence. A neatly coiled green garden hose was affixed to a spigot below that window. As she admired the coiffed lawn, as verdant as the house was white, she heard a girlish voice cry, "Hello? What are you doing here?"

Dahlia whipped around to see an ungainly woman with a little boy approaching her from around the garage. She heard hoarse barking inside the house and wondered if she'd found the right place after all, though the letters in her hand attested to it. The dogs continued to bark—little doggie yips and yelps—and the woman called out to her again, "Who are you?"

"A friend of Cheryl's!" Dahlia called back, regretting that she wasn't wearing her sunglasses.

"Oh. I'm Marsha Traubner from across the street."

At closer range the woman's skin was blotchy, and she appeared to have recently contracted poison ivy—her arms were slathered with pink lotion whose scent brought to mind the word *Calamine,* and hikes Dahlia remembered through forests and campsites. She looked like a "Marsha," Dahlia decided, with small, squinty eyes, stringy dark hair, and protruding teeth the color of sour corn. Still, a kind of friendliness emerged from these mousy features. Dahlia couldn't say that for the surly, restless boy beside her.

"So what's with—?" Marsha pointed to the envelopes in Dahlia's hand.

"Oh," said Dahlia quickly. "I work with Cheryl at Hadassah. I, uh, came by because she's not returning anyone's calls, and we were worried about her."

"She's out of town. I'm looking after the dogs."

"Dogs? She never said she had dogs."

"Can we go?" whined the little boy, pulling Marsha's colorless shirt while Dahlia slipped the envelopes back into the mailbox. The child observed this dourly. He hadn't believed her lies for a second. "She wouldn't let us get ice cream cones," he griped.

"Who, Joel?"

He pointed to Dahlia and mumbled something that Marsha understood.

"When you play at Brett's you have to do what his mommy wants," said Marsha, to both of them. She asked Dahlia, "Do you keep kosher?" and Dahlia nodded. Now that she appeared to be "Brett's mommy" and had referenced Hadassah and Cheryl, Marsha felt free to gab about how the dogs were "basically housebroken," but "needed to be let out into the yard a couple of times a day. Good thing I was around, or that parlor would've been one poop fest, and Cheryl would've had a fit. Saul, her husband, tore out of here a day early. You know him?"

"Is he the notary?"

"They both are. But he's so different from her. God, he's—he's funny. I laugh so hard when I talk to him. Have you met the twins?"

"Once," said Dahlia.

"Gorgeous girls," Marsha swooned. "You know, to look like that…"

She spoke as though Dahlia too was some dumpy middle-aged woman who should be coveting Wendy and Lisa's appeal.

"*I'm still technically 'in my thirties,*'" Dahlia ached to remind her. "*For two more days. And I've never had teeth as disgusting as yours.*"

"Well, the girls take after him," Marsha continued. "He's rather—handsome."

You don't say.

"Can we *go*?" grumbled Joel again.

Dahlia heard her phone ring and rifled through her purse to find it.

"I just heard from Saul," Molly said, without the usual fun in her voice. For a moment Dahlia's vision doubled.

"You *what*?"

"I got a message from Saul. I was at lunch. Look, I've—"

"Is he all right?" Dahlia whispered, her heart thrashing.

"Well, *he* is. But something terrible has happened."

Cheryl must have found out about the money he'd skimmed and sent to her. Or maybe she'd gotten a private detective on Dahlia. Maybe she was spying on Dahlia now. Joel whined on to his mother like a buzz saw, and Marsha stooped beside him, trying to appease with funny faces and promises.

"I'm going," Dahlia said to them, beginning to back away. "Nice to meet you." She stumbled on a small flagstone step and regained her balance.

Marsha called, "Watch yourself!"

"Where is he?" Dahlia demanded to Molly as she marched across the lawn to the road. The day had grown humid, and it was now hitting her that she'd barely slept last night, and had not eaten. "I'm at his house. So why did he call you?"

"Who were you just talking to?"

"Oh, some neighbors of his—" Dahlia tuned Molly out for a second, glancing back at Marsha. Why hadn't Saul ever said that he had dogs? He knew she had pets. She suddenly remembered the night Cheryl had slept on Alex's bed, when he'd been pacing around, out of breath. He must have been walking the dogs. She felt faint and heard her belly screech with hunger. Why hadn't she packed a donut? Why hadn't he told her that he had dogs?

"Dahlia?" Molly was calling from her phone. "Are you there?"

"Yeah," Dahlia grunted.

"Did you hear me?" Molly asked.

Feeling faint and dehydrated, Dahlia said nothing.

"His daughter's in critical condition."

"Which daughter?"

"Maybe it's best that you hear his message. But I want you to sit down somewhere, and we'll talk about it afterward, okay?"

"Okay," she said, coming upon her car.

"You're not alone, Dahlia. I'm here, and we can speak as long as you need to after you hear this. Hold on."

As Molly set up the phone to replay his message, Dahlia climbed into the driver's seat of the stifling car and sat sideways, with the door open. If only she'd bought a sandwich. Her stomach creaked like a dying bird. She put the phone to her ear again.

"Molly. Saul Finerman. I understand you called my office." His voice was dull, strained. "As you probably know, I was supposed to meet Dahlia today. Well—as it happened—Wendy fell on her head, at camp. It's very serious." He sighed deeply. "There's been bleeding, in her brain and she's in the trauma unit here in Racine. My wife and Lisa are flying in later. Look, Dahlia's called me, but I can't talk to her now. I just can't. We don't know—" his voice faded for a moment. "It's not a simple concussion. We won't know how critical it is for a few more days."

Then, such a long silence occurred that Dahlia thought the call had ended. But he continued. "Maybe you can break all this to her, Molly. Dahlia doesn't seem to have many friends. Maybe—you know what? Tell her to use the cash I sent her to visit you and her sister, in New York." Then he muttered, "Look, sorry to dump this on you. We barely know each other, and it's not the best day of my life. I appreciate whatever you can do," and he hung up.

"Now you have it," said Molly.

Dahlia asked if she could hear the message again, and a third time.

"But why," she finally moaned, "did he call you? Why didn't he talk to me?"

"He said he 'just couldn't.' He's probably too upset."

"Is Wendy going to die?"

"I hope not. But it doesn't sound good. At worst, if she remains in a coma, they might have to—*decide* if she'll die."

Dahlia's stomach screeched again, and her brain seemed to spin, to convert the greenery and sunlight around her into Cubist blades.

"This is just—can't be. How could it be?"

"Let's pray it won't. I'll ask Gene. She knows about sports injuries."

"How could this happen?" Dahlia repeated, leaning out of the car and staring into the asphalt of the road to Damascus.

"It's still your birthday," Molly said kindly. "Why don't we book you onto a plane to New York this evening? Would you like that?"

Tears burned Dahlia's eyes. Her long-awaited trip with Saul, and her life with him, had vaporized. Her head fell into her hands, and she snapped her phone off.

She spent the night in a motel near Toledo, sick to her stomach. She didn't remember what she'd eaten until she saw it again in the toilet bowl. Six hours later she awoke to rapping on her door. They needed the room; she was two hours past checkout. God—or any lesser deity—only knew who would so urgently need this wedge of bed on the state line between Michigan and Ohio, within a stone's throw of four gas stations. She now understood the term *splitting headache*; her skull felt sliced down the middle in a throbbing rush. But she found aspirin and a new hotel room nearby.

Sometime that evening she turned her phone back on to see volumes of calls from Tamara and Molly. There were also calls from an area code she didn't recognize, probably the mountainside inn where she and Saul had booked a room on her credit card. She read these names and numbers over with disturbing numbness and slept until one the next afternoon. When she awoke, she found new calls: from Saul, from her parents, and from Nurit.

It was her birthday.

She skipped immediately to Saul's message. "Daya," he'd groaned with a familiar rasp that made her shiver. "Oh, Daya. Jeez, could it possibly be worse? I trust Molly filled you in. Wendy's on a respirator, still unconscious. They can't tell us anything about paralysis until the swelling in her brain subsides. Thank God Jared and his mom are driving up tomorrow. Cheryl's furious with me. Some kids at camp said Wendy cried when I left her on Sunday, you know, 'I miss my dad, he's my best friend,' and like that. So now everything's my fault; I had 'upset her.' Truth is, some prick from Canada wanted to seduce her by showing off on the fucking trampoline and—look, Cheryl's coming. I gotta go."

A swift click. No birthday wishes.

But that was compensated by an exuberant call from her parents, with both of them trilling "Happy Birthday, Dear Daya" off-pitch. "We're thinking of our sweet, beautiful daughter and wishing you the best today," Mama announced. They were hoping to travel east for Thanksgiving to be with the kids. "Can you come too? Maybe you can stay with Molly Picon."

Dahlia felt cast in lead to imagine New York without meeting Saul in some hotel. Before turning off her phone, she listened to a couple of Molly's and Tamara's entreaties for her to call them back and let them know she was okay. Well, she wasn't okay. And she would leave Nurit's message for another time too.

It was helpful to have cash in her pockets so long as she was alone in a rented car pulling into downtown Cleveland on the evening of her fortieth birthday. She treated herself to a Grade B summer adventure movie with greasy popcorn, and after that, even worse food at a Chinese restaurant with plaid carpeting and a looping soundtrack of 1970s Musack. She spooned down a bowl of wonton soup to wordless versions of "Mr. Tambourine Man" and "Imagine." But the real challenge came with diluted Kung Pao Chicken and Lou Rawls' "You'll Never Find Another Love Like Mine." She almost wished the lyrics had been obliterated by synched violin, and she left in the middle because she couldn't finish any of it.

Her most worthwhile purchase that day was a spiral notebook with a parakeet and palm fronds on the cover in which she resolved to start a diary. She penned her first entry back in the hotel room. *August 6, 2006: I am now forty years old and, in case anyone's wondering, it bites.* Unlike Tamara, she did not go into detail. She couldn't convey on paper how lanced she felt by every reminder of where she'd planned to be this evening—and how different it felt, where she found herself. Nor did she describe the parking lot view from her window, or the steady pounding on the wall, like that Simon and Garfunkel song about the prize-winning couple in the next room. She was not a writer; she was a summarizer, a receptionist, an assistant.

Saul had called twice while she'd been in the movie, once at 3:58, and again at 5:16. She cracked open a bottle of Jack Daniels from the bar in her room and poured some into a glass on her bedside table.

"The good news," he began, his voice echoey, "is that her brain isn't herniated.

And so the Lord, in a spate of generosity, spared us the worst. But she's still in a coma. Lisa's been at her bedside for hours, staring at her, willing her back to us. But even that hasn't broken the spell.

"Hey, you remember all those release forms I went through last spring? You'd think we were applying to leave the gulag. And at camp Wendy signed even more papers, like an agreement to practice skills only under supervision of her staff coach. So the damn next day she breaks her word. Lisa says she was worried something like that would happen. She tells us that Wendy, for all her bookish smarts, completely lacks common sense and relies on Lisa to make decisions. Not that I'd ever been clued in on that. Some shithead tells her he can teach her the double somersault—we're going to meet this Philippe Arnot tomorrow and get the full story. Of course he'll be expelled. The camp never had anything like this happen, in decades of operation. He should've left her alone. Goddamn males.

"Reminds me, I'm pacing around the men's room since I have no privacy anywhere else. Cheryl's on me like a vulture. Only place I can take refuge is by a urinal, and," he added, lowering his voice, "some schmoe's coming in to make it smell worse. Pardon me if I forego the fanfare."

Dahlia thought fleetingly of Matthew's bad luck in the men's room at his office. The association should have brought to mind her worried sister, but she just sipped her whiskey and listened to Saul's next message. "So, uh, guess you're too busy with your pals in New York to call or text me any consolation, Dahlia. And for Chrissake, who's David? Cheryl said I got this call, at home—had to make up something fast. New friend? Well, at least one of us is having fun on your birthday. Better that it's you, popping corks and eating oysters with Molly. While I'm hearing words like *intracranial pressure, cortical tissue, MRI, head trauma*—well, as Dr. Zhivago says: *Think of me now and then, my sweet!*"

Dahlia lifted her glass to him and drank up.

She slept as though trying to settle upon roiling waves—lunging upward, she groaned, pulled the covers around her, flopped back down, then tossed to the other side. Behind Dahlia's eyelids Wendy wavered on an August afternoon, her long, bare legs in shorts, bony arms by her side. At the rec period after lunch, she's approached by a tall, muscular boy with a French accent. *"Bon après midi, Mademoiselle. Je m'appelle Philippe Arnot. I am from Quebec. And you?"*

Highland Park, Illinois.

"Do you like it there?"

Wendy shrugs. "It's okay." She follows Philippe to the trampette, where he shows off for a while, then tries to teach her how to do it too.

He's a little pushy and keeps saying, "Don't worry. Trust me. You can do it." He has all sorts of plans for this sad, mysterious girl. It's the beginning of a long summer, and she needs someone to tell her what to do; he can sense that....

At 3 a.m. Dahlia kicked off her covers and stomped to the bathroom to pee, sitting on the toilet with her head in her hands. She remembered so many hotel rooms with Saul, climbing back beneath covers and rubbing her cheek against his warm back. Now, as she slid between the sheets alone, she thought of the woman who legitimately shared a bed with him. What was Cheryl going through, with a daughter poised between middle school and paralysis? And Lisa, what was happening to her? Sighing and muttering, Dahlia acknowledged that she couldn't even grieve with these people. As she finally fell asleep she imagined herself and Wendy, tugging the same rope from different ends in a dark room, never looking upon each other.

The next morning she watched TV in bed until 2 p.m. with her phone off. Nobody wanted this mildewed, musty room. Nobody disturbed her. Management was glad to have business. She turned the sign on her doorknob to Privacy rather than Service, as she didn't need new sheets or towels. And her next diary entry read: *Privacy, not Service.*

He didn't call that day. Out of curiosity in the late afternoon, she played Nurit's message from a couple days back. Dahlia was surprised by a high-pitched voice saying, "Hi...Ben! Hi, Da, Daya." Then Nurit took over: "Got your call, kid. Hope you found your boyfriend and are off on a good birthday romp. Let him do something right by you already! So, guess who that was? Look...you gotta keep this secret, okay? You out of anyone, Daya, can do that. Ben' is Kayla's age. I named him for Walter Benjamin. He looks like those childhood pictures of Daddy and Uncle Gabor, you know, where they wore knickers and stared into the camera like the cocky young Kafka.

"I've been meaning to tell Mom and Dad, but they're going to flip out because I'm not married—hell, I'm not even in touch with Ben's dad. It was four years ago, you know? And he's Moroccan. I almost called Tamara because—trick or treat—her kids have a cousin! A secret cousin. So what do you think? Maybe I should bring him to New York this year? Give me a call. You got the right number. Hope you're painting the town red—or at least painting your boyfriend red. Live it up—*Zei Gesunt!*"

While she'd been listening to Nurit, it seemed that Tamara had been calling her. At first Dahlia didn't want to listen. Trick or treat! Her kids have a cousin. It sounded like a new reality TV show: *Secret Cousin.*

"Look Daya," Tamara was saying on voice mail, "this isn't cute. Matt, Molly, and I are out of our minds. If we don't hear from you in the next hour, we'll call the cops in Chicago and report you missing. We haven't wanted to upset Mama and Daddy, but we can't keep them in the dark indefinitely. And no, we didn't call what's-his-name. Sounds like he's got enough to worry about. We know you're listening to our messages because your mailbox didn't max out, so maybe it's time to cut the shit already and come out of hiding?"

Dahlia put her head in her hands and laughed from her belly. They were worrying about her the way she'd worried about Saul, making all these rational guesses, figuring out little clues. How hilarious! She fell over on the bed. And Nurit secretly having a kid with some Moroccan? Even better.

Leaving Cleveland's Lakefront Station at midnight in a backward-facing seat, she sent two text messages. The first was to Tamara: *Coming to NY by train. Don't worry, I'm great.* And the next to Saul: *Wendy's in my prayers.*

As the train crept through Erie, Pennsylvania, she ruminated. Neither Nurit nor Molly had sustained a relationship with a man as long as she had with Saul— and yet they had more to show. They'd both given birth. It didn't matter that the father of Nurit's child was some crazy fling and that Molly had been shot up in a fertility center with eggs, sperm, and the whole nine yards. Dahlia had created neither children nor works of art. She hadn't started businesses, written books, or taught classes. She'd made sure to keep a job that gave her time on the weekdays for assignations with her married man. She'd lost friends. She didn't travel overseas. She led a more restricted life than a housewife.

Of course she knew that she could do what Nurit had done and find a guy to father her child. That was hardly difficult. She could even look into the pool of eligible men and marry someone impressive—a doctor or professor. But the fact was, she hadn't. And she didn't want to think about losing Saul and getting to know someone new. She lacked the bootstrapping spunk that both her sisters possessed. There was a vacuum around her, like the unrelenting darkness outside as she rattled through upstate New York, nodding out between Buffalo and Syracuse. By morning they dawdled for an annoying hour in Albany-Rensselaer. A call came on her phone from someone named Lauren Albert with a Chicago phone number. Chicago felt far away, and Dahlia ignored it.

When she got to Penn Station and washed up in the ladies room, she noticed that she looked ridiculously well. In fact, she looked great. She had avoided mirrors since the day she left Chicago but now realized that all the inedible Midwestern food had chiseled pounds from her, and for some reason, her skin was radiant and her hair shiny, stylishly unkempt. She tipped her head and smiled ironically to herself as she prepared to brush her teeth, which she'd been doing avidly since she'd met Marsha. She never wanted graying, yellow teeth. A woman coming out of a toilet stall looked at her as though she found her strange, in that blunt way New Yorkers had.

She would now head to Eugenia's bistro to pick up keys—Molly had been nice enough to say, "Use Eugenia's apartment in the Village...it's yours, it's empty, Eugenia will be with me. Don't feel like you need to stay at Tamara's with the kids and chaos."

Dahlia decided to walk the twelve blocks uptown. As she began, she noticed another call coming in from Lauren Albert. She knew no one by that name and felt pestered by this person, whomever she was. Doggedly, Dahlia pulled her suitcase behind her, block after block, with the unsettling sense that all the New Yorkers she passed—the young and chic, the down and out—could see that she'd missed the boat.

When she heard a text coming in, she stopped walking for a moment to check it. *Who are you?* Saul had written. Dahlia stared for a moment, then shoved her phone into her jacket pocket. Was it not enough for her to text that Wendy was in her prayers? What did he want? Maybe he was puzzled because they'd never spoken about prayer, and in fact, Dahlia didn't pray unless she was completely panicked. "Oh God, I pray that I find my keys and my wallet...I pray that Saul is not hanging from the rafters." Real prayer would be performed every day, no matter what. Real prayer might include gratitude. "Give us this day our daily bread, and lead us not into temptation..." But Dahlia had become too secular to put any stake into praying. So maybe that's why he was asking, "Who are you?"

At 43rd Street and Ninth Avenue, Dahlia felt an impulse to listen to the calls from Lauren Albert. She stopped at a small plaza with benches and sat down for a moment. To her surprise, Saul's voice greeted her: "Hey Daya, I'm using Jared's mom's phone. Cheryl has seized mine. Look, uh, she came upon some of our texts. She has only your screen name, 'Dodaya,' and I don't think she knows how to text. But you may hear from her. Don't pick up your phone if you see my number. She says she has 'proof of infidelity,' and she'll throw me in the can if I 'try to walk out on this family now.' Well, we all know that's moot, but she's very upset. She's calling me 'The Playboy of the Midwestern World.' Cute, eh? Wendy is stabilizing. Unconscious, but breathing off the respirator now, and they say the swelling is beginning to go down. Keep her in your prayers, baby."

In the next call, which he'd placed five minutes ago, he sounded frantic: "Okay...she's texting you now. I'm getting food from the cafeteria—before I left, I overheard her ask Jared and Lisa to give her texting lessons. Don't do a thing! In fact, Daya, just take that twenty-five grand and start a new life. Study Italian in Siena, like you always wanted to. Go to the Sorbonne for a semester. Open a gallery in Key West. Rent an apartment in Brooklyn. As luck would have it, my daughter's in shambles, but all my ships are coming in—the tax lien investment, the mall

204 · SUB ROSA

deal. We're rolling in so much dough that Cheryl won't notice what's missing. So this is your chance to cut the hell out of Chicago. Go honey, and don't look back. If you need more help, I'll get you more. And once I'm back home I'll get a new phone number. Just pray that Wendy pulls through…"

As his call ended, another text rang in: *Answer me, Dodaya.*

It was a crossfire: one finger pushing her out of Chicago, the other trying to pin down her identity. Dahlia shut her eyes for a second and then proceeded to follow the command Cheryl had issued.

Cheryl, she wrote, *can u 4give me? Marsha.*

She sent it off, then quickly wrote another: *don't tell him i told u.*

The Big Easy meets the Big Apple at Eugenia's Cajun, read the review in the window. *"We go light on fat, heavy on flavor,"* says founder Eugenia Drury. *"If you care to be adventurous, our Hot Tamale Pie and Crawfish Etouffée will not disappoint."*

Dahlia had exchanged her own piquant words onscreen with Cheryl as she'd dashed up Ninth Avenue. Her lover's wife hadn't let up. *You never fooled me, Marsha*, she'd charged. *I knew you were trouble.* Then: *whose phone are you using?* And: *For shame.*

no shame in love, Dahlia had answered.

Then what am I forgiving?

4give me if i hurt u.

We;ll talk when I;m back home, Cheryl proposed.

no, Dahlia wrote. *no talk. over + out.*

Hand quaking, she'd shut her phone and distracted herself with reviews in the window. *Zagat* had given Eugenia's top billing for food, service, décor, and price. Dahlia shut her eyes, then opened them again: *Pecan Catfish, Lime Grilled Shrimp, Jambalaya Lafitte*, she read. The logo, which Molly had undoubtedly designed, substituted the *j* in *Cajun* with a shrimp, dotted with a whole note. Clever. Dahlia pushed open the door, still not believing she'd been so brazen to a woman with a comatose daughter.

The place was open and airy, an entire section set beneath a skylight. Grill-work stencils lined one wall, and on the other Mardi Gras masks alternated with the gold and black New Orleans fleur-de-lis, city seal, and symbol of the Saints. Cajun fiddle and accordion gushed sweetly from ceiling amps. Dahlia remembered that Tamara had met Colin here. It seemed a kind of place that handsome men would turn up.

Eugenia stood at the cash register, talking quietly to a woman with short brown hair and a port wine stain on her neck. As Dahlia drew closer she wondered whether Eugenia would recognize her from the *bris* last spring or whether she'd have to announce herself. She stood by awkwardly as they concluded their conversation. Flawless, in her tight-fitting jeans and a simple denim shirt, Eugenia seemed as accustomed to admiration as a prism was to light. But unlike a prism, she looked back at Dahlia.

"Hey, you made it. Can I get you anything? Coffee, shot of bourbon?"

Dahlia stood stiffly, aware that her hands were still shaking.

Eugenia tossed her head, saying, "Have a seat. How 'bout our chilled Cream of Crab Soup and melted Roquefort on toast?"

"That sounds really good."

It sounded like a world more innocent than she would ever live in.

"Coffee?"

Dahlia nodded. Eugenia trotted off as fiddle and accordion trilled buoyantly from the sound system. Dahlia became aware that the woman with short brown hair and a port wine stain on her neck had been eyeing them as though she were important—a new kid on the block, conferring with the proprietress.

She looked away to pull out her phone; no reply from Cheryl yet. Dahlia could just imagine Cheryl pounding on Marsha's door to demand that she no longer watch their dogs. "I'd rather they shit all over the living room! Hand over my keys, you hussy!"

Marsha would say, "Huh?"

Eugenia popped back with coffee in a green Fiestaware cup and a small blue creamer. "Soup and sandwich are coming," she said, sitting beside Dahlia at the bar. "So listen, how's your boyfriend's daughter?"

"A little better," said Dahlia, with a reviving sip of coffee. "She's off the respirator."

"Conscious?"

Dahlia shook her head. "Not so far as I've heard."

"Sounds like she's got a cerebral contusion."

"What's that?"

"It's like a bruise in your brain. Nasty."

"They're worried she may become paralyzed."

"She could, if the impact's severe. But my mother, who's a retired RN, says that most contusion patients recover—sometimes with only mild memory loss."

Dahlia sipped coffee again. The merry Cajun music ceded to Billie Holiday smothered in horn: *Some other spring I'll try to love…*

"She's so *young*. She and her twin sister turned fifteen in June."

"Molly says she's very smart."

"Let's hope she continues to be," said Dahlia.

Eugenia speculated, as though she knew something about it: "Can't be easy for the twin sister who survived."

Then a tall man with lively eyes ambled in, saying, "Good afternoon."

"Hey you," said Eugenia, turning around to greet him. They traded a few words, and then Eugenia introduced him as Ed, one of the bartenders. The woman with short brown hair and a port wine stain on her neck presented Dahlia with a bowl of crimson soup garnished with parsley and cayenne pepper, flanked by the melted cheese sandwich. Eugenia introduced her as "Marty. Little Ms. Party." Dahlia took a ravenous bite of melted cheese and Billie Holiday sang how *these foolish things remind me of you*. She glanced at her cell phone. It was too quiet.

"Before I forget…" Eugenia arose and sauntered to a shelf behind the bar. She returned with a lumpy envelope. Three key shapes were traced on it in pen, labeled *Downstairs*, *Medco*, and *Lower*. Arrows showed which way to turn the lock.

"Brilliant," Dahlia commented.

"Molly thinks of everything."

Eugenia smiled warmly and handed the envelope to Dahlia.

"I so appreciate being able to stay at your place. Tamara's is kind of…"

"Crowded?" offered Eugenia, and Dahlia smiled.

"Listen, I have a favor to ask." She slid her phone across the bar. "Would you just—please keep my phone here for a while?"

"Won't you need it?"

"I, uh—I actually need a break from it."

Eugenia's vivid blue eyes glowed and the corners of her lips puckered with amusement.

"Time for a little cold turkey," Dahlia continued.

"I've never understood why they call it that. Cold turkey can be quite tasty."

Dahlia took a long afternoon nap in Eugenia's apartment, a delightfully bohemian lair with blown glass bottles on the windowsills, vintage lamps and sofas, and a mirror so oxidized that the glass looked peppered. Then she headed uptown to visit Tamara. Dahlia loved how Manhattan was delineated neatly into east and west as though it were a grand fish, like sea bass or branzino. The spine would be Broadway, and the little bones would be side streets.

She and Tamara would have private time together before Matt came home and neighbors showed up for Shabbat dinner. ("I can tolerate lighting candles," Tamara had assured. "We do that at the shrine.")

After Shabbat, Dahlia planned to meet Molly and Eugenia and shoot billiards.

Tamara's living room, where the *bris* had been held four months ago, was now a sea of toys, dolls, books, and stained blankets. "We don't even try to keep it neat," Tamara explained unapologetically, Oren propped on her arm. "Just try not to trip, and toss those Mr. Potato Heads and Nerf balls to the floor so you'll have room on the couch."

Big windows kept the room from feeling claustrophobic. Outside on Broadway, sun lingered in the afternoon sky and puffy, Fragonard clouds the color of buttermilk drifted in from the Hudson River.

Tamara had just fed Oren before Dahlia arrived. Now she stroked his silky dark hair and pink cheeks, covering his little head with kisses. "I could nibble and nibble and nibble you!" The baby smiled back at her. Tamara rubbed noses with him, then grinned at Dahlia. "Doesn't his name sound important? Oren Douglas, justice of the peace; Oren Douglas, chairman of the board. After all, he is Molly's nephew."

"Mine too," said Dahlia, leaning back on the sofa. A sharp object poked her back, and Dahlia grabbed a plastic wagon that was wedged into the pillow. "Tam, why don't you talk about your daughters this way?"

"I do. Mira will be our first female Jewish president."

Mira was on a playdate with Olivia, the daughter of neighbors who would join them for Shabbat. Kayla ran boisterously from room to room, bearing rag dolls and narrating an elaborate story about them. They had to get somewhere, they flew, they crashed into a wall. Call me Icarus! Brain contusion! Luckily, a head stuffed with cotton didn't bruise.

"So tell me again," Tamara was saying, as she snuggled Oren in her arms. "He wants you to leave Chicago now?"

"That's right," said Dahlia. "Take the money and run."

"I don't understand. What does he think his wife will do to you?"

It had not struck Dahlia as the most thoughtful proposition, and now, of course, there was a new wrinkle. Not that she'd tell Tamara about the texts between herself and Cheryl. She might confide in Molly later on. Or she might just try to forget about everything.

"Maybe you *should* take the cash and skedaddle. You live there only because of him. You're not crazy about the weather, your job, or anything else."

"I can't just skip out on my rent, or the gallery. I need at least a year."

Tamara shook her head. "Excuses. You'll never give up this guy. And you'll never attain him. You'll live in Chicago twilight forever."

"You're wrong," protested Dahlia.

"He'll never be able to love one woman. It's not his nature. Look, even his own daughters are double."

"That is so—" Dahlia shook her head. "What an absurd interpretation."

"So you're going to tell me it's different now? Remember when it was 'different' on Monday, when he was going to leave his wife and take you to the Michigan highlands?" She looked down at Oren and sang softly, "*Brigadoon, Brigadoon...*"

"You know why that couldn't happen."

"So now, of course, you're over him! You've left your phone with Eugenia and you're washing that man right out of your hair."

"You know why I didn't answer my phone all week, Tam? You know why? To avoid conversations like this. Don't you think I'm upset enough without having you Gilbert-and-Sullivan my life? Don't you think I'm harsh enough on myself?"

Tamara looked vaguely remorseful.

"And don't say you're trying to be funny. If you're trying it's not funny."

"Well, if I told you straight out 'it kills me to see you waste your prime on this self-centered, married guy,' you wouldn't listen."

Dahlia got up to pace, almost tripping on a pile of wooden blocks. She found herself by the window and remembered doing the same thing in the empty apartment that she and Saul had viewed. The real estate agent had left them alone and they'd sat on the floor and talked about Wendy's anorexia. When he'd upset her she went to the window. She always looked out the window to people crossing streets and blinking traffic lights.

"What's worth listening to?" she sighed to the clouds that seemed like masks dangling before a rosy sky. "I'm not 'wasting my prime on this guy.' Love is never a waste. Or a shame."

"You love him?"

Dahlia turned to her sister. "Yes I do. But I need to get away. I need to be a person in a city at six in the afternoon, in a living room cluttered with toys. I need to be a person who gets out of the subway and notices architecture and the color of shadows, not a person always subtly waiting for a phone call." She turned back to the clouds outside. "If that's what you call 'washing that man right out of my hair,' then run Saul and me through your mill. But don't think you're perfect."

"Who implied I think that?"

Dahlia continued looking out the window. There was no way to make a point in this family. There was always a counterclaim—generally, an irrefutable one.

Exasperated, she shot back at her sister. "I know about Phil!"

"About *what*?"

"Have you forgotten him so quickly?"

Dahlia turned again to watch the reference strike her sister. Tamara stopped stroking Oren's back. Kayla ran through the room and out again with her entourage of rag dolls.

"You've been reading my diaries!" Tamara charged, almost smiling at Dahlia and clutching Oren as though to shield herself. "Haven't you?"

"You wish," said Dahlia. "I actually heard it from Molly."

"Molly doesn't know him."

"He traced her from some credit card that you told her I used."

"You're kidding me." Tamara looked horrified and all sarcasm left her voice.

"Why would I kid you? Good thing I figured all that out when she was sitting with me in Chicago, chatting over sushi, Tamara. Good thing I know your wily ways."

"My wily ways? Pardon me, but—"

"Don't. Say. It. Just don't."

Tamara arose carefully, Oren now nestling his sleepy head on her shoulder, pointing to the doorway through which Kayla had disappeared. She glared at Dahlia, hissing "*shhh.*"

"I thought she was autistic," Dahlia reminded her.

"It's more like ADHD."

"Well, she's not listening to us."

"Her ears are magnets," Tamara hissed.

"She's in the other room."

"She's everywhere."

Dahlia swore she wouldn't breathe a word about Phil. But she expressed surprise that Matthew still didn't know—which Tamara dismissed. "He doesn't even know we've paid off our mortgage, because Molly gave me a big chunk of it three years ago."

"How could he not know that?"

"How could Saul's wife not know about you?"

Tamara seemed grateful when the front door squeaked open and Mira showed up with Olivia and her mother. Crestfallen, Dahlia watched Tamara greet them gaily and then pardon herself to shut windows and turn on the air conditioner. Numerous guests were expected, "and the room gets clammy in this weather," she remarked. Dahlia felt a painful distance from her sister, as Saul had warned last spring when she'd read the diaries; *It won't be the same.*

And what a terrible mistake to throw Phil in Tamara's face.

Dahlia tried to strike up conversation with Olivia's mother, who taught sociology at Columbia. But the woman seemed far more interested by the six-year-old girls in their flowery dresses—Olivia with a pale blonde braid down her neck, and Mira with her curly black hair and long lashes—like two antique dolls.

"Do you remember Aunt Dahlia?" Tamara asked her daughter as the air conditioner rumbled on. Mira shook her head, but the word *aunt* prompted her to ask, "Is Molly coming?"

"Molly never comes to Shabbat," Tamara replied plaintively.

Ten minutes later, Dahlia learned why. Matthew entered with the Altmans and their three whimpering toddlers who all had to go potty, and then Olivia's dad showed up with a noisy baby called Schyller. It gradually dawned on Dahlia that the loud little creature was female and that half the girls there were named Ryder or Schyller—such classical, Hebraic names! The boys didn't fare much better, Dahlia thought, as Taylor and Haven Goldstein joined the fray. At that rate, you might just as well name a kid Heathcliff Finerman. Dahlia had to give Marsha credit for naming her son simply Joel.

She was then introduced to Mark Schmulowitz and his fat daughter who picked her nose, and whose name she promptly forgot. By now the place was wretched with mewling kids and babies, though thankfully Oren was asleep. Against Taylor Goldstein's cries of "boo-boo, boo-boo!" as he rubbed his ear, an undertone of feckless parental *shhh*-ing and Schyller's unrelenting squalls, Matthew's voice rang out in perfect pitch: "*Baruch atah Adonai eloheinu melech haolam, asher kidishanu bimitzvotav…*"

After kiddush came the delivery of Chinese food. A wiry, grinning guy with a vinyl sack appeared at the door, occasioning a skirmish over how to tip him. These grown-ups should be pros by now. But many aspects of this new Shabbat seemed tenuous to everyone. Dahlia reflected that their own childhood with jolly relatives toasting "*l'chaim*" did not begin to rank with this turmoil of plastic plates of General Tso's chicken, (or "Generally So-So chicken," as Tamara called it), Broccoli in Garlic Sauce and slices of Challah, sugar cookies and rugelach, halvah, disgustingly sweet wine, and grape juice for the kids, who spilled it everywhere imaginable, including on their parent's clothes and shoes.

Such mayhem would never be permitted at 27 Maribel Lane. Sabbath would be conducted at a formal dinner table with a white cloth and runner beneath it. Cheryl would serve a respectable brisket with potato kugel and *tzsimmes*, and the neighbors would bring Entenmann's cakes with organic Kosher wine. In the kitchen, a Caribbean woman would serve the kids kugel at their own table. No chance in hell would they spill grape juice on their parent's shoes. The only grape juice on Cheryl's taupe pumps was Marsha Traubner.

There were few chairs at Tamara's, and one was broken, so most everyone ate standing up, trying to slice their children's food and to carry on some semblance of conversation. Dahlia found herself squashed by the window of the dining area, parking her fanny on the radiator cover, grateful for window guards behind her. To her dismay, Mark Schmulowitz, the one single dad in the room—who was chubby, had a rash on one cheek, and a yarmulke bobby-pinned to his head—waddled over and asked, "Mind if I join you?" Dahlia realized this was a low-grade setup, and almost reconsidered her vows to keep Phil under wraps.

"Are you aware," Mark Schmulowitz asked, assuming that he was indeed welcome to join Dahlia, "that your brother-in-law won't allow us to discuss the war in Lebanon? He feels that Sabbath is a time of peace, and that New York Jews won't be civilized about Israeli foreign policy."

"I'm sure he's right," said Dahlia, trying to cut her chicken on the plastic plate.

"I was shocked to learn that Matthew's not actually Jewish."

To her, Matthew looked more Irish than Saint Patrick. What was this idiot's problem? He was getting more broccoli between his teeth than down his throat.

Little fists drummed on her legs, and Dahlia looked down into Kayla's beaming face. "Aunt Daya!" sang the girl, before running away in a fit of giggles.

Then the phone rang, and Matthew said to Tamara: "Private number."

"Oh, well we know who that is," Tamara said to Olivia's mother. "Our downstairs neighbor, the Lone Renter. She's got a whole place this size to herself, but she can't stand if my daughters run around, and always calls to mouth off. The beauty of it is that she has no clout with management, 'cause she rents and we own." She then turned to her husband. "Don't answer, Mattie."

"Shabbat Shalom," he said into the phone. Tamara shut her eyes as though she had a headache.

Startled by whoever was on the line, Matthew said, "As a matter of fact, she is." He passed the receiver to Dahlia. Gratefully, she excused herself from Mark Schmulowitz before he sucked even more broccoli between his teeth.

At first no one on the other line said anything, but then she heard a forlorn little whisper of, "Daya?"

"Sasha!"

"Oh, it's good to hear your voice. You've been hard to reach."

The last time they'd spoken was five days ago, when he told her he was unnerved by his empty house, and dreaming of her. Dahlia scuttled off, leaving Schmulowitz by himself on the radiator, past the toilet where a fraught mom was shepherding kids to go potty, to shut herself into Mira and Kayla's messy little bedroom. "First," she said—gasping, throwing herself onto one of their beds, pushing an open picture book out of the way—"you tell me not to answer my phone. Now you tell me I've been truant."

"So good to hear your voice," he repeated.

"You can't pull me in two directions, do you understand? You'll break me."

"Honey, Cheryl got hold of my phone only this morning. She found our texts while I was still sleeping."

"Texts only? Did she find…photos?"

"I trashed those when you forced me to do so after Molly's visit," he said sheepishly. "I do sometimes listen to you. Look, I've been trying to call you for days and you never pick up, not once. So I called Molly to make sure you're okay, and she mentioned you might be at the *oneg…*"

"Why did you call her Tuesday and leave me in limbo for hours? Do you have any idea how freaked I was?…And on my birthday?" Tears pinched her face.

"Don't be mad at me, Daya."

She started sniffling. "I know I have no right to be, but I am."

"Please don't be mad at me. Cheryl's so mad."

"I don't want to be mad at you."

And she didn't want to admit how good his voice sounded, live—not recorded.

"Well, some happy news. Wendy's back. She's groggy and nauseous, and her back hurts like hell. She may have to wear a brace for a while. But she knows who we are, and who she is. We're not out of the woods by any means, but we didn't lose her mind."

"I'm so glad." Dahlia's words formed choppily through her tears.

"She was even grumbling that Jared was there. She'll be transferred to U of Chicago Medical tomorrow afternoon for more tests. Cheryl and Lauren stayed with her, and Lisa and Jared drove home with me."

"So you're home now?" Dahlia asked, still weepy.

"I had to get a new shirt. I couldn't stand myself in the one I had for another day. Honey, I've been through more circles of hell than Dante could conjure after a vat of sixteenth century Chianti…I am so, so tired, so tired. I said to God, 'How about nicknaming me Job? You got anything else in store?'"

"Does He?"

"God said, 'Saul, shut the fuck up. You just netted twenty percent interest from investing in tax liens. Do you know how grateful most people would be? And you have a dear, tender, sexy, intelligent girlfriend who's even Jewish. So you have a teenager in crisis and a bitter spouse—you think that makes you special?'"

"I'm your 'lovely girlfriend?' Thought you were sending me out of town."

"Oh, sweetheart. Please don't misunderstand."

"Start a gallery in Key West? Go to the Sorbonne? What do I misunderstand?"

"Dally, will you excuse me for a second? I'm getting another call."

The phone clicked off, and Dahlia glanced around at the cheerfully jumbled room that her nieces shared, with its dollhouses, bookshelves, and a closet bursting with clothes and neat little shoes from Aunt Molly.

Before she knew it, Saul was back and emphatic. "She's gone haywire. Now that Wendy's conscious, my wife is breaking down. Listen to this, Daya: she's absolutely convinced I've been fooling around with one of our neighbors whose marriage is on the rocks. She just called the woman and gave her hell…"

"Cheryl didn't—text her? Or knock on her door. She called the lady?"

"She's not really a texter. Oy, what a mess."

"Well, didn't your neighbor deny it?"

"Cheryl was so irrational that I couldn't make heads or tail—I've never heard her like this. It's—it's frightening. Can I tell you? It's frightening. I told her I was on the phone with our broker and had to go."

"Who is this 'other woman,' Sasha?"

"No one I'd look at through a kaleidoscope, but Cheryl won't give it a rest. At first I protested vehemently. Then I started playing along, because—I thought— this decoy may just work for us. For you and me, going forward."

"Going forward? Can we go backward to you telling me to leave town?"

"I never meant to imply that you should leave me."

"It sure sounded that way."

"Oh, no, no, sweetie. Now Cheryl is talking about divorce. She feels I've humiliated her, she can't bear to look at me, she wonders if any of our other neighbors know..."

"You really think Cheryl would split up the family with Wendy in a neck brace?"

He was quiet for a moment.

"It all depends on what she thinks other people think. If she feels we can keep our dirty laundry to ourselves she'll stick with this full hamper of a marriage. If she thinks other people know I've been prowling, she might toss me out. Admittedly, both of us are exhausted and crazed. Nothing's going to be decided today. My life seems to reconfigure every hour. Remember how stable I used to be? And bored? Call that Paradise Lost."

"The most important thing is that Wendy's compos mentis."

"Agreed," he said with a sigh. "But there's something I've never told anyone, that only Wendy might remember...which I will tell you now. When I said good-bye to her last Sunday at the camp, she was talking and I tuned her out...I was looking at the lake and hillside, which were so vivid it was like I could see new colors. I imagined you and me around water and land like that, on our trip. She said, 'Daddy, did you hear me?' I said, 'Sure.' But I was fibbing and she knew it. She knew I was somewhere else that had nothing to do with her, and she wasn't used to it. It killed her, I mean—it almost killed her."

"Aren't you overestimating your importance?" Dahlia wanted to cry. But she said only, "I don't know what to make of this, Saul."

"Please bear with me," he begged. "Have patience. I know it doesn't make sense, but you're my friend. When a woman and a man part ways, a woman loses her boyfriend—but the man loses his girlfriend, his best friend, his only friend."

She lay blinking tears down her cheeks. After a while she sat up on the bed and began to wipe her eyes. The door slightly opened, with a breeze, she thought. But Kayla stood there, looking so much like Dahlia's own girlhood photos with chubby cheeks and black bangs falling over her large brown eyes.

"Come here, darling," said Dahlia.

At first the little girl didn't budge. Then she ran in, grabbed Dahlia's legs, and snuggled her head on Dahlia's thigh. She smelled slightly sour, like grape juice and sugar cookies. Dahlia ran a hand over her smooth hair, and Kayla gazed up at her, as if to ask, *Were you crying?* Dahlia tried to smile but felt too shaken. The little girl furrowed her brow in a consoling way and tore out of the room.

Clearly, Mira belonged to Molly. But that night, Dahlia found her niece.

Sub Rosa

"Shit!" Molly's scrambling billiard balls came to a halt on the table. She spun around to Eugenia and groaned, "Why do you bother having me on your team?"

"You make it up in Scrabble," Eugenia said offhandedly. The young rednecks playing against them seemed surprisingly at ease with Molly and Eugenia's affection. That was a difference, Dahlia noted as she sipped her Rolling Rock, between urban and rural rednecks.

As one of the boys in a visor hat chalked his cue stick, Dahlia wondered if that actually accomplished anything or was mere showmanship, like swirling wine in a glass before drinking it. He certainly fared no better than Molly on the table, though he took his defeat more stoically.

Then a more refined-looking man settled on a stool across the room. He wore glasses and seemed to be around Dahlia's age, with a sweep of dark hair, broad shoulders, and sensually rounded lips. When Eugenia moved in for the kill, he lifted his bottle of ale to salute her. Dahlia realized with a tingle that he must be David. Molly had mentioned that he might join them.

Eugenia leaned over to nudge the cue stick between her fingers, a strand of blonde hair curling over her forehead. Sipping her beer again, Dahlia decided that Eugenia had been one of those girls who'd actually known how to play field hockey in high school—unlike Dahlia herself, who was cast as a wing to stand obliviously to the side through many games.

Eugenia tapped the white ball with gentle control, delivering the green into several others. The purple ball lingered by a pocket, as though deliberating before it tumbled down. Eugenia raised her arm in triumph.

"That, in fact, was sexy," Molly declared.

The room noticeably quieted as the pro pocketed her second solid—which led to the call shot. Eugenia paced around the table like a panther, her strong, toned body seeming to protect the girlish innocence of her face in concentration.

Dahlia became aware of David's gaze. When she glanced back at him, he looked away. Eugenia angled in, the balls clacked, and a screech arose from table.

"We won!" Molly cried, slapping Eugenia's open hand. "Not that I did a damn thing," she stage-whispered to everyone else.

"David!" Eugenia called across the room. "David Chakmakian! Molly's bailing on me for next game…"

David shook his head no, holding up both of his hands.

"Oh, come on!" Eugenia urged.

"Buyer beware," he warned in that pleasant, manly voice Dahlia remembered from the call she'd overheard. "I'm far worse than Molly."

"Not possible!" Molly protested. "It kills my Protestant work ethic to be such a liability." Eugenia threw back her honey-blonde head and laughed.

"Dahlia!" Molly then cried. "Why don't *you* take over for me?"

As Molly pointed at her, the young rednecks swayed around to appraise Dahlia with dull, horny interest. She shook her head no, as David had.

"Get up here!" commanded Eugenia. "Why's everyone so chicken?"

"Sorry, I don't play on your team," Dahlia parried.

Molly caught the double entendre, slipping her arm around Eugenia's slim waist. "Jump over your own shadow," she defied, with an Irish accent. "As they say in Dublin."

At that moment Eugenia's young waitress with short brown hair and the port wine stain on her neck—Marty, "Little Ms. Party," who'd served Dahlia chilled crab soup that afternoon—flew into the pub with a scraggy, slouching woman at her heels. They both descended upon Eugenia, who pardoned herself to go speak with them.

Molly bee-lined for Dahlia and beckoned to David.

"Can't help you here," he apologized when he arrived from across the room. Behind his glasses David had intense dark eyes, like a Roman philosopher. Dahlia noted the slight belly that Molly had described—he was by no means chubby but not trim as her Saul.

"By the way," said Molly, "this is Dahlia—Tamara's sister—my 'fellow aunt,' if such a thing can be said. And David."

He extended an arm that was bare of any hair and took her hand for a moment.

"Not a player?" he asked.

"Complete klutz," admitted Dahlia, her face warming as they dropped hands.

"Look," said Molly, "you two duke it out. I'm not doing this again."

"Such ego investment." David turned away from Dahlia and shook his head tenderly at Molly.

"Well, it gets to me. Both Gene and I were trained to perceive objects in space—she through tennis, me through drawing. And when we played *pétanque* in Southern France, we were neck and neck," she said. "But just insert a racket or a cue stick, and I go dopey."

"Oh, you love the challenge," David charged. "It's in your blood."

Molly blanched as he broke into a grin. Then he turned to Dahlia. "Molly's always in control—except when Eugenia brings her to her knees occasionally."

Ready to rebuke him, Molly took a deep breath, her sea-green eyes wide.

"Back in the day—the John Wayne Day—men liked a challenge," he continued. "Now it seems the appetite has grown more in women."

"In those of us worth knowing," Dahlia suggested.

"Hey, Molly!" Eugenia called, from her huddle with the two waitresses.

"Draw straws, toss a coin…" Molly bid them as she skipped away, leaving Dahlia awkwardly alone with David.

"Where are you from?" she asked. "Your accent is familiar, somehow."

"Do I have an accent?"

"I mean…" She shrugged. "Your inflection, maybe."

"Well, my cat and I share a spacious prewar in Astoria, though I doubt I've picked up the local drawl. I went to school in Providence, lived in Woonsocket, Rhode Island, for a while. But I hail from Pasadena."

"That's it," said Dahlia. "I went to Montebello High."

"Ah, we played soccer against your team. You still out there?"

"I live in Chicago now."

He took a slug of beer. "Funny," he said. "Molly had me call Chicago this week. You weren't, by any chance, waiting for a missing man?"

Dahlia raised her brow, and David squinted. She noticed the two young rednecks at the table—practicing, no doubt, to outplay Eugenia.

"Did you ever find him?" David asked, and Dahlia could tell he was trying not to sound involved. She nodded, but a certain frost sank her heart. Yes she'd found him, but it had gotten her no further than colored balls knocking around on the pool table.

"Where was he?" David asked.

"Not...where I thought."

She flipped her head, hoping to shake the mood.

And then they all advanced toward her: Eugenia, Molly, and the two younger women. To Dahlia's horror Marty, "Little Ms. Party," marched right up to her, bearing her cell phone.

"Is this yours?"

Dahlia swallowed some beer and nodded. A circle of onlookers was forming around her. It seemed so significant that the rednecks stopped their game to assemble on the periphery.

"Then I know more about your life than you do," announced Marty.

Dahlia was too shocked to say a word, so David interjected: "Would you care to clue her in?"

"Oh, I can clue you in all right..." the girl stared into Dahlia's eyes so intently that Dahlia felt like crossing her own.

"Tell the whole story," prompted Eugenia. She turned to nod at Dahlia.

"She'll hear it," said Marty, backing away to address the curious bystanders. "But first, some background. Two years ago my girlfriend dumped me to get mar-

221 of Dara Lebrun

ried and live in Hetero Heaven. We were together since college. I'm just getting human again, you understand?"

"All too well," said Dahlia.

"When this phone…" she shook Dahlia's cell in her hand, "rang tonight in the register, Ed answered, thinking it was for Eugenia. But someone asked for me. Even before I got on, I had the feeling it was my ex. So when a woman started screaming that I was 'a homewrecker,' the first words out of my mouth were: 'Fuck you.'" Dahlia's jaw dropped.

"The room was loud," continued Marty. "People talking, live band playing zydeco…I couldn't hear her words, just the screaming. I totally thought it was Robin, my ex. I was like, why the fuck is she calling me here? Figured there was trouble in paradise. Let's just say, Robin was never the type to marry some guy, move to Levittown, and have a baby. So I screamed back to her, 'You've been living a lie, and guess what? Now it's coming apart!' She started to cry, like, how dare I speak to her that way—do I have no heart, no conscience? Then I said, 'When it comes to you, ya know—I don't.'"

Dahlia felt herself turn as purple as Eugenia's billiard ball, hovering on the lip of its pocket. She'd handled Cheryl so elegantly by text that afternoon.

"So then I asked her, 'Why are you calling me here? How did you even get this number?' She goes, 'It's not rocket science.' At that point, I looked at the return number—some weird area code. So I got really defensive. Figured Robin had run off with another woman, so I said, 'You've got balls to the floor, don't you?'"

Dahlia felt everyone stare at her.

Molly smiled and murmured, "Who'da thunkit?"

"We were just screaming at each other," Marty continued, "and I told her I had to go—I mean, I was at work—I said, 'If you ever call me again, so help me, I'll get a restraining order,' and I hung up and threw the phone back to Ed. I had tables to serve. It was a real call to professional discipline."

"Restraining order…" Dahlia lifted her head and imagined what Cheryl must now think of Marsha—and how Saul would be showered by fallout. He thought he had "a lovely girlfriend." Little did he know what dynamite she'd tossed his way.

But she couldn't crucify herself over this fateful mixup. Those were the risks he'd gambled upon.

"Later on, toward the end of my shift, when things were quieting down, Ed asked me why the call had upset me so much." Marty's lip trembled, as though she might start to weep. "I haven't talked to Robin in like, two years. Ed and I were trying to figure out how she knew I worked at Eugenia's, because I only started three months ago. And Eugenia's cell number wouldn't be listed. So then we thought, this bitch must have asked for Molly, not Marty…"

Try Marsha, thought Dahlia.

"And we figured we'd just stepped into some domestic mess between Molly and Eugenia…though everyone knows that Molly wasn't the homewrecker." The girl turned to Eugenia and said, "We all knew that you'd cut in on Molly's sweet little straight life."

"Well, not exactly," objected Molly. "I wasn't dating anyone when we got together."

"But you weren't *not* dating him," said Eugenia.

"We were finished." Molly made a slashing gesture at her own throat. Dahlia found lungs with which to breathe again as everyone's attention shifted to Molly and Eugenia.

"If you asked Jordan, you'd hear another take," Eugenia insisted.

"I sat down with him and itemized my feelings—I couldn't have been more scathingly clear."

"And now you feel so guilty that you give him money all the time."

Molly stared at her lover with concern. "We give lots of people money, Gene." And, pointedly: "We've given to friends of your crazy Colombian ex."

"And to my crazy nephew," Eugenia acknowledged.

Their voices faded as they stepped away for privacy, and attention began to reconfigure around Dahlia. Across the room on a flat TV screen, Derek Jeter hit a foul.

"So who is she?" Marty asked Dahlia. "And did you destroy her home?"

"Do I look like a wrecking ball?"

"You could pass."

"It's not as interesting as you think—or as you made it. How could you have spoken to her that way?" she scolded Marty. "Didn't anyone ever teach you manners?"

"Didn't anyone ever break your heart?" Marty asked.

"Regularly."

Molly and Eugenia joined them again, walking hand in hand over to Dahlia. Now the rednecks, the two young women, David, Molly, and Eugenia all looked at her for an explanation.

But Dahlia said nothing.

"Will we ever know the story behind this story?" David asked, helping to make the moment rhetorical.

"I hope not," said Dahlia. "It's like a rose—with too many petals to trace where it ever began."

"*Be quiet, clumps of roses, don't whisper her name to me.*"

"What name?"

"Oh, that's not me," he said. "I'm quoting some old Czech poet. He seemed to know that some things are said best by a delirium of petals."

Perhaps feeling like intruders, the rednecks returned to the pool table. Molly and Eugenia took turns consoling Marty as the scraggy, slouching friend looked on, and they all migrated imperceptibly away from Dahlia and David.

"You can't reduce beginnings to a single leaf," David added, once they were alone, "any more than Orpheus can look back at Eurydice."

But he was looking at her.

And when she raised her beer bottle, he raised his.

Then they clinked as gently as Eugenia's purple billiard ball had slipped into the pocket.

Acknowledgements

Thanks to novelist mentors Richard Bausch and Sonia Pilcer, and many fellow writers with whom I've studied.

Thanks to Heliotrope Books for editing, feedback, design, promotion, and other forms of support. Thanks to Goodfoot Editorial, and to my select team of advance readers: Dan, Julia, and Jaime.

Thanks to Jeremy for inviting me to blog on *Pale Ghosts*.

Thanks to Leah for banjo and "The Hot Flashes."

Thanks to Kate, who's been so great.

Thanks to P. for uplifting my soul and for your sweet patience with my "writing trances."

Thanks, as always, to my beautiful family.

About the Author

Sub Rosa is Dara Lebrun's second novel in a series called *Children Who Aren't Ours* that began with *The Bunny Hop*.

A native and longtime New Yorker, Dara now makes her home on the West Coast.

www.ingramcontent.com/pod-product-compliance
Lightning Source LLC
Chambersburg PA
CBHW050522260626
47157CB00004B/1432